I0593193

To dreams. They do come true.

RULE BREAKER

SONIA STANIZZO

Rule Breaker

Copyright © 2022 Sonia Stanizzo

Published by JRL Publishing

ISBN: 978-0-6450908-7-1

Cover: Outlined with Love Designs

Chapter 1

Nursing a whopper of a hangover, Aiden Doyle slumped into a leather seat in his boss's office. Apparently being the star of the show, *Family First* didn't stop him from getting dragged out of bed and summoned to a meeting. His irritation wasn't helped by the jackhammering coming from somewhere nearby, escalating his headache to a brain-piercing migraine. He forced his eyes open and searched for the noise. But instead of a construction worker demolishing the walls, the source turned out to be the rain smashing unsympathetically against the floor-to-ceiling windows of Houston Studio's Sydney office. The repetitive *tak-tak-tak-tak* of raindrops on glass fired through his brain like bullets. The bottle of Jack Daniels he'd consumed last night churned like acid in his gut. Over the last two years since the "incident" as he liked to call it, "the more you drink, the more you forget" had become his mantra. Despite the brutal hangovers, alcohol numbed the anger and feelings of pain, guilt, and betrayal for a little while, and the temporary relief was worth it. It was the only way he could get through the day, let alone a shoot. He tipped his head back on the chair, closed his eyes, and prayed for oblivion.

It didn't come.

Instead, Aiden jumped as a door slammed shut behind him. Bright, penetrating light seared his retinas as the person flicked on the lamp on the desk. "Fuck me," he groaned, clapping a hand over his eyes. "Turn that bloody thing off."

The other man didn't. Settling into his plush chair, Lionel Masters said, "I see my driver managed to drag you here." The executive producer's eyes flicked over Aiden from head to toe, his lips pressed together in a disapproving slash.

Shifting uncomfortably in his chair, Aiden tried not to let the other man's censure get to him. Sure, Aiden's clothes were creased, stained, and smelled of cheap perfume, not to mention that his hair hadn't been brushed in a couple of days, and he could do with a shave, but at least he wasn't trying to make a dyed comb-over work. There were some lines he wouldn't cross. Or at least he didn't think he'd cross them, he hadn't started going gray or losing his hair yet.

Pulling his thoughts back on track, Aiden took a few deep breaths through his nose to stop himself from heaving his guts onto the plush carpet. Carefully he lifted his head and tried focusing on Lionel, but he couldn't manage a clear view of his executive producer. Closing his eyes, he dropped his head back and groaned.

"Mya, get Aiden a glass of water and Panadol please." Through the hangover haze, it sounded like Lionel screamed the words through the walls, but when Aiden cracked an eye, Lionel was taking his hand away from the phone.

A few moments later, someone walked into the office and stood next to him.

"I should get Mya to dump the water over your head," Lionel grumbled. "Maybe it would help sober you up."

Aiden shrugged. She wouldn't be the first woman to throw her drink in his face. Hell, it might even feel good.

Sitting as straight as possible, he took the glass from one outstretched hand and two white pills from the other. Before he could thank her, she'd spun on her heel and left the room, leaving only the faint smell of jasmine behind.

Taking the painkillers with the full glass of water, he set the glass down and scrubbed his hands through his unkempt hair and tried again to focus on Lionel. "Can we get this meeting over with? I want to go to bed." He hadn't slept for over twenty-four hours. His party had taken on a life of its own, and by the time he'd ended up in bed, there definitely hadn't been any sleeping going on.

"We can't keep cleaning up your messes any longer," Lionel said. "*Family First* is a family-friendly show, Aiden. Mum and Dad and the kiddies gather on the couch every week for an hour of wholesome entertainment. The father in that show—you, if you need the reminder—is a loving husband, a devoted father, and a hardworking man. He's the definition of 'good family values.' We both know you're not that man, but the audience wants you to be. The studio has done everything they can to keep your drinking and womanizing out of the press, but they're at the limits of what they'll tolerate. Especially after last night." He turned his laptop around to face Aiden. "We've warned you time and again to clean up your act, but you never listened. Now, it's all over the internet. There's no sweeping this under the rug."

Aiden squinted against the harsh glow of the computer. The images were blurry, but not so much so that Aiden wasn't immediately recognizable. The pictures had been taken in his bedroom at the party the night before and showed why he hadn't gotten any sleep. How had he missed someone else in his room?

He had to admit the women and the booze had been a distraction. Had someone from the media sneaked in, or had it been some random opportunist looking to make a few bucks?

In a gentler tone, Lionel said, "We know you've had a rough couple of years. After your wife and daught—"

Aiden cut him off with a hard stare. If Lionel brought up Madeline and the baby's deaths, he was gone. Just the sound of his wife's name brought back the memories he drank to forget.

Lionel cleared his throat. "You should have taken time to grieve instead of jumping straight back into work. Turning up to film drunk or not even coming in at all has cost the studio a lot of time and money, not to mention your costars—and their parents—are starting to complain about your behavior. We sympathized with your loss. We took a four-month break from filming so you could recharge, get back on track, then come back to focus on the job and smash the role like you used to. You promised us you'd come back better than ever. We—no—I believed you. We even had you set to direct the first episode." With a sigh, Lionel sagged into his leather chair. "But nothing's changed, unless it's for the worse. I've been getting regular reports of your bad behavior. You're still drinking, you can't keep it in your pants, and the show—the ratings—are suffering because of it."

"So I drank at a party and had fun with a couple of women. It's my life, I can live it the way I want. I'm *not* the patriarch in a holier-than-thou TV drama. Does the studio expect me to live like a fucking saint?" Anger simmered in his gut. "I'll show up to work and do my job, and you can keep your nose out of my damn business. Happy?" Without waiting for an answer, Aiden heaved himself from the chair and turned to leave, his legs unsteady beneath him.

"Sit down!" Lionel demanded. "I'm not done here."

Aiden turned but didn't sit. He crossed his arms over his chest, and they stared each other down, each waiting for the other to crack first.

Lionel blinked and said, "I'm the executive producer on this show, and I won't let you drag the other actors, the crew, and the writers down with you. I will not allow your selfish behavior to ruin *Family First* for everyone else. So I will stick my nose wherever the hell I want, including into your personal life whether you like it or not."

Blowing out a breath, Aiden ran jerky fingers through his hair. He didn't have to put up with this shit. "Are you done? Because I haven't been to bed yet. Not to sleep, at least," he said with a smirk.

Lionel sputtered before slapping his palm on the desk. "Damn it, this isn't a joke! Your personal problems are affecting *Family First* and everyone involved with it. You have one last chance to pull yourself together, and this is it."

Aiden lifted an eyebrow and scoffed. "Or what? You'll replace me? You can't have a family show without the loving father and husband. Face it, Lionel, you need me. I am *Family First*."

Fixing Aiden with a level gaze, Lionel reached into his desk drawer and pulled out a sheaf of papers: a script for *Family First*. "We don't need to replace you. With a body double and some shots we already have, your character dies, and the next season becomes about how the family pulls together and lifts each other up in the aftermath of a terrible tragedy in a wholesome and heartwarming fashion."

Sobriety hit like a physical blow. "You can't do that," Aiden said.

Lionel tapped the script. "It's done."

"The show will fall apart without me!"

"And right now it's falling apart with you." With a sigh, Lionel said, "This is your last chance. Your last *last* chance. The new season of *Family First* begins shooting in three months—that's the most time I can spare. You need to stay sober and out of sight before shooting starts. One more picture on the gossip sites of you with a bottle in one hand and a woman in the other, and it's over. No more show."

"What are you going to do? Babysit me to make sure my nose stays squeaky clean?"

"I hadn't considered it," Lionel said, stroking his chin. "But that's not a bad idea. Someone needs to watch your arse and keep you out of trouble."

Aiden shoved his hands in his pockets. "You're not serious. What are you going to do, follow me around like a puppy dog, making sure I behave? We both know you don't have the time for that." He felt a surge of satisfaction at getting one over on Lionel.

Lionel picked up the phone on his desk and pressed the intercom. "Mya, come in here, please."

The woman who'd brought him the painkillers—Mya, clearly—returned and walked to Lionel's desk, leaving a little jasmine-scented cloud around Aiden, which he greatly preferred to his own sweat-and-cheap-perfume stink. Her perfume was exotic and somehow sultry, though the woman herself was neither. Mya's golden-blonde hair was pulled up into a severe bun. Thick black-rimmed glasses perched on her upturned nose. Her white blouse was buttoned to her neck and tucked into a knee-length gray skirt that hid her figure.

She gave Aiden a brief glance before turning to Lionel. "What can I do for you, Mr. Masters?"

"I have a proposition for you," he said.

Aiden tipped his head to the side warily. What was Lionel up to?

Mya held up a notepad and pen, ready for instructions.

"For the next three months, you follow Aiden around and keep him out of trouble until we shoot the new season of *Family First,*" Lionel said.

"Ex… Excuse me?" Mya stuttered. Behind her glasses, her expression was horrified.

Aiden crossed his arms over his chest. "You can't be serious."

"I'm an admin, not a sober companion!" Mya clutched her notebook to her chest protectively.

"Aiden's been getting bad press, and if he wants to keep his job, he needs some outside help to keep him honest." Lionel narrowed his eyes.

Blinking in surprise, Mya said, "How could I possibly keep him out of trouble?" She glanced over at Aiden, her brown eyes looking him over. Her nose crinkled in dismay.

Aiden frowned. Who was she to judge him? At least he was clearly getting out and enjoying life. He bet her idea of excitement was Earl Grey instead of chamomile tea. Her wardrobe certainly gave off an uptight-nun aura.

"I can't," Mya said quietly.

"Double pay," Lionel said, ignoring her objection. "For that, he doesn't leave your sight. Twenty-four seven. You live, breathe, eat, sleep together. No drinking, no women. For interviews, you make sure he's sober, showered, and shaved. And I don't see a single word about Aiden Doyle in the press unless he's volunteering to read books to orphaned puppies."

"I'm not reading books to orphaned puppies," Aiden growled.

"I wouldn't even know where to start," Mya said. "And I can't be your assistant and mind anyone else at the same time."

"He'd be your only job for the next three months."

"This is ridiculous! I don't need a fucking babysitter!" Aiden began, but snapped his jaws shut when Lionel tapped the script on his desk.

"I'm sorry, Mr. Masters, but I can't," Mya said.

With a shrewd look, Lionel said, "Double pay and an extra fifty thousand dollars when he shows up on set in three months' time ready to work."

Mya's jaw dropped.

Lionel had him by the short hairs, and they both knew it.

If looks could kill, Aiden would be dead. Mya had gone from uptight nun to murderous-horror-movie nun in just a few seconds. He took a prudent step to the side, out of her reach.

Aiden groaned. "Lionel, it's not her fault. Don't put her on the spot like this. I'll be ready to shoot in three months, I promise."

"Your promises aren't good currency around here any longer." Lionel turned back to Mya. "Well? I won't say it'll be easy money, but there's a lot of it."

"I…" Mya's eyes flicked from Aiden to Lionel and back again. She chewed her lower lip as she considered her options. "I'll do it." Looking at Aiden out of the corner of her eye, she asked, "When do I start?"

"Right now," Lionel answered.

"But I need to organize a few things first!"

Lionel shrugged, ignoring Mya's protests. "You'll have Aiden to help you."

"What if I refuse to go along with this absurd plan?" Aiden asked through gritted teeth.

After a brief hesitation, Lionel said, "I didn't want to tell you this, but word has spread that you're difficult to work with. Unreliable. This isn't just your last chance on *Family First*, Aiden. This is your last chance in the industry." Regret tinged the producer's voice. "If you screw this up, there won't be any more starring roles, no more chances to direct. You'll be finished. Finito. Done. Heck, you'd be lucky to get a part as an extra in one of your brother's movies."

His brother, Ethan, had made quite the name for himself in the film industry, working every shit job he could to pull his family from a life of poverty before making it big with a few blockbusters that had launched his directorial career. He'd taken care of the family when no one else could, and if Aiden refused Lionel's terms and threw his career away, it would be like slapping Ethan in the face.

"Do you accept?" Lionel pressed.

Aiden clenched his jaw so tight he was surprised his teeth didn't crack. Unable to see another way forward and unwilling to let his brother down, he nodded.

"Great." Lionel clapped and smiled like he hadn't thrown Aiden and Mya's lives into a spin. "I'll see you both back here in three months." With that, he rose from the chair and marched from the room.

Mya Saunders took a deep breath to try to control her racing heart. What the hell did she just agree to? A *lot* of money, that's what. Enough to pay her grandmother's nursing home expenses as well as set money aside for Noah's future and hopefully keep Noah's paternal grandparents from suing for custody. How could she refuse?

"Your place or mine?" Aiden Doyle's slurred voice broke through her internal monologue.

She swung her head toward him. "Excuse me?" This close, his bloodshot sea-green eyes were obvious as was the cloud of stale sweat and perfume that clung to his clothes. The crinkled T-shirt and faded jeans looked like he'd either slept in them or picked them up from the floor. His dark-brown hair stuck up in messy spikes around his head like he'd been dragging his fingers over his scalp.

"Your place or mine," he repeated with a salacious wink, "to *babysit* me." His tone suggested something other than *babysitting* as his gaze traveled from her head to her toes. She held her notebook against her chest. She'd only begun working at Houston Studios five months ago and had seen Aiden stumble into Mr. Masters's office once before. His drinking and on-set behavior were common knowledge. Now, she had to fix him.

"Let's be clear, Mr. Masters is paying me to *watch* you. Nothing more." She put on the stern face she used on her son, Noah, when he didn't want to eat his greens. It never worked on her son, and from the wide smirk on Aiden's face, it wasn't working on him either.

"For someone dressed so prim and proper, you have a dirty mind. I'm not suggesting anything untoward." He made a cross over his heart with a finger. "I only wanted to know where we'll be spending the next three months." His tone was teasing, but Mya wasn't amused. After a few moments of silence, his mocking expression melted away, replaced by something harder. "My place it is. If I'm going to have a babysitter, I might as well be comfortable while doing it. Let's go." He stormed out of the room.

Mr. Masters had made it clear that she and Aiden were to live together, but how was she supposed to stay at Aiden's house with Noah? She didn't want her son around someone like Aiden Doyle.

She dropped her notebook and pen on the desk and ran after him. At the open elevator, Mya caught his arm before he stepped inside. Muscles tightened under her hand, and she snatched it away. As he looked down at her, their eyes connected and for a moment, she lost herself in the deep green of his eyes.

The rattle of the door closing broke the spell, and she shook her head. *What the hell was that?* She punched the button for the lift to come back.

"I need to go home first and organize a few things, pack some clothes. It's not like I'm prepared for a three-month stay at your house," she said to ease the irritation she sensed rippling underneath Aiden's exterior. "You know, I was as blindsided by this as you were." She stared at the numbers above the lift to avoid looking at him.

He let out a small sigh. "Okay. I'll text you my address, and I'll meet you there."

They stood so close, waiting for the doors to reopen, that she could feel the heat—and an unpleasant smell—radiate from his body. She shuffled a few steps away.

Once they entered the lift, they exchanged phone numbers, and when they reached the ground level, they parted ways. Mya watched his retreating back with her stomach in knots. Why had she reacted so strongly to an innocent touch? She put it down to being out of practice around men. And she'd never been around a man as hot as Aiden Doyle, even if he was also a hot mess. She'd have to control herself if she was going to make it through the next three months.

What was she going to do about Noah? She couldn't leave him with her sister for three months or bring him to Aiden's house to be surrounded by who-knows-what debauchery? Aiden's behavior was attracting the wrong kind of attention, and she didn't want to be caught up in it. All it would take was one photo of her with Aiden to make the rounds online, and it would ruin her life. She had to stop that from happening for her sake as well as Noah's.

Mya hated the thought of babysitting a grown man, but the money was too good to pass up. She told herself that Mr. Masters had bought her time, not her soul, but she wasn't so sure that was true.

Chapter 2

*M*ya entered the modest clapboard house she shared with her twin sister, Amelia. Giggling and squealing echoed from the lounge, and Mya followed the sound. She found her sister on her back, legs and arms stretched out toward the ceiling, with Noah balancing on her hands and feet.

"I'm flying!" her son shouted when he saw her.

Amelia swayed him from side to side. "Noah flies toward danger to save the day!"

"And then his mother swoops in, snatches her little superhero, and whisks him into her arms." Lifting him from her sister's feet, she pulled Noah to her chest and spun him twice around the room.

She planted kisses on his neck, and he giggled. When the wiggling and squirming got too much, she put him down. He was five and getting bigger by the day. He wasn't the curious infant she'd cuddled what felt like days ago. A pang of longing for his tiny baby years rippled through her.

"What are you doing home so early?" Amelia pulled herself up from the floor.

Amelia, younger by three minutes, had her long hair tied in a messy bun secured with a paintbrush. Her brown eyes sparkled behind red-framed glasses. They looked so much alike that even their mother had a hard time telling them apart. Gran claimed she knew who was who, but sometimes Mya liked to trick her by wearing Amelia's paint-splattered clothes.

"Hey, sweetie." Mya bent and kissed the top of Noah's shaggy dark-blond hair. "I have to show something to Aunty Amelia in the kitchen. How about you do that new puzzle I bought you?"

The grin that never failed to melt her heart was currently missing the two top front teeth. "Okay," he said as he retrieved the puzzle.

With that taken care of, Mya motioned for her twin to follow her. Amelia raised an eyebrow but trailed her to the kitchen, saying nothing until they were alone. "What's going on? Is everything okay at work?"

"Not exactly." Mya massaged her temples.

"Don't tell me you lost your job!"

"I haven't lost my job. More like I got a new one that comes with a fat bonus."

Confusion crossed Amelia's features. "You're home early to tell me that?"

"No, I'm home because I'm going to need your help. I've got one whopper of a new job description."

"Ohhh, sounds interesting. I need wine to hear this." Amelia stood, grabbing a bottle from the fridge and two glasses from a cupboard. She sat at the table, opened the bottle, and poured a generous amount of wine in each glass, taking one for herself and sliding the other to Mya.

Pushing her glasses up her nose, Mya glanced at her watch. "It's only three in the afternoon."

Amelia shrugged and grinned. "Like they say, it's five o'clock somewhere."

Joining her sister at the table, Mya left her glass untouched. "Mr. Masters wants me to babysit Aiden Doyle twenty-four seven for three months." Aiden was the one who used the *babysit* term, but it's exactly what she'd been told to do.

Amelia coughed into her glass. "What?"

"I'm not supposed to leave his side. Somehow I have to stop him drinking, partying, and screwing around. If any debauched behavior gets into the media, I'll be held responsible, he'll lose his job, and I certainly won't get that bonus. Heck, if the debauchery is salacious enough, I might end up out of a job. And wouldn't that just be reason enough for Bob and Julie to take Noah away from me?" Mya placed her elbows on the table and dropped her chin on her fists.

"We won't let that happen," Amelia said firmly. She tapped her finger against her lips. "But you will have your work cut out for you. I've seen stories of the wild parties he's thrown splashed over the tabloids. The last one with the threesome was rather kinky. How are you supposed to stop a grown man from having the adult fun of his choosing?"

"Great question. Wish I knew the answer," Mya said, her tone rueful. "He'll lose his job if he can't rehabilitate his image into the wholesome, caring, loving man he plays on his show. I'm hoping this is a wake-up call for him and he'll behave."

"And do you think he will?" Amelia asked.

Mya dropped her head in her hands and groaned, "I doubt it."

"That's rough. This must be important to the production company if they're paying you to do this. How much is the bonus?" she asked before sipping her wine.

"Mr. Masters is doubling my pay, and at the end of the three months, if I keep Aiden out of trouble, I'll get a fifty-thousand-dollar bonus. I've sold my soul to the devil," she sighed.

For the second time, Amelia choked on her drink. In between coughs, she gasped, "Fifty thousand dollars!"

"With that money, we can get Gran into a better nursing home."

"You don't have to do that! It's your money, and it sounds like you'll earn every last cent. You could use it for you and Noah." Amelia helped with finances whenever she could, but artists didn't always have a regular income, so Mya's salary paid most of their bills. She never begrudged her sister for spending hours in her studio instead of a nine-to-five job, though. Amelia's paintings filled their hearts and home with joy.

"We have everything we need. And even if I can't keep Aiden completely out of trouble, I'll still make double pay for as long as I've watched him. Besides, barring a disaster of epic proportions, I'll still keep my admin job."

Amelia slid her palm along the table and held Mya's hand. "Thank you." She smiled with misty eyes. "I know Gran would thank you too."

Words stuck in her throat. Mya nodded and smiled back.

"You said you need my help?"

Mya's shoulders sagged, and she slumped in her chair. "I do. I need help with Noah. I have to move in with Aiden, but I don't want my son around *who* or *what* he has in the house. Before Noah can move in, I'll need a few days to straighten out Aiden's life. Can you watch him for that time?"

"You know I'd do anything for you. And I'm here for whatever you need. I can't believe your boss asked you to do this! I wish you could tell him to stick this job up his arse."

"I've thought about going back to the office and telling him just that. But the money is too good to refuse. It will help so much." The thought of leaving Noah tore a hole in her heart.

As if reading her mind, Amelia said, "Don't worry about Noah. I already watch him twice a week while you're working. He's happy with me, and I'll keep him so busy he won't have time to miss you." She smiled. "And you'll have him back with you in no time."

Amelia was like a second mother to Noah, and Mya trusted her with his life. She knew he would be safe and happy in her care, but it still hurt to leave him.

"When you say you can't leave his side... How will this affect your decision to date again?" Amelia refilled her glass.

"Oh no! I forgot all about that. I'll have to delete my dating profile." She started to get out her phone to do just that.

Amelia shook her head and pointed a finger at her sister. "It's taken me years to convince you to jump back into the dating pool. You can't back out now."

But Mya didn't have a choice. Dating was definitely off the menu for the next three months. "It's for the best. Besides, my date last month with Jim was a disaster. This might be a blessing in disguise." She was being a little unfair to poor Jim, who'd been kind and funny and hadn't deserved Mya's awkwardness around strange men. Particularly one she was trying to date.

"Consider that a practice round."

Mya laughed. "Then I'm going to need a *lot* more practice and I don't have the time now."

"It's taken you years to finally put yourself out there. You've concentrated on raising Noah and putting him first. But you've said it yourself—Noah is at an impressionable age where a good father figure is important. You won't find Noah a daddy by sitting at home and literally watching paint dry," Amelia said with an outrageous wink.

Mya knew firsthand what growing up without a father was like—tough. It had been the main reason she'd let Amelia convince her to join a dating site. She wanted so much to provide Noah with a happy, stable home with two parents who loved him. "I've waited over five years to date again—three more months won't make a difference."

Amelia emptied her glass in one more swallow, then said with a grin, "There is a plus side to living with Aiden."

"Really? Because I can't think of one," Mya grumbled.

"You'll be spending every moment with Aiden Doyle. He's freaking hot! Do you really think all those housewives tune in every week for an hour of squeaky-clean family-friendly entertainment? Please." She snorted. "That man is the definition of sexy. Use *him* to practice on." She waggled her eyebrows suggestively.

Mya's mouth dropped open. "I'm not practicing on Aiden."

"Why not? If you can charm the likes of Aiden Doyle, the next dad candidate that comes along won't stand a chance! You'll be a smooth-talking sex goddess, and he'll fall madly in love with you."

Sighing, Mya said, "I'm hoping when a man falls in love with me, it's because we're compatible in other ways. Not just sex."

"Pfft." Amelia rolled her eyes. "Great sex is key, the rest you can build on."

Honestly it felt like dodgy advice from her perennially single sister. Still despite her doubts, Mya kept quiet so Amelia wouldn't keep nagging her about Aiden, sex, and dating. "You wouldn't be calling him the sexiest man who ever lived if you'd seen him in the office today. Bloodshot eyes, disheveled clothes… a drunken mess. He stank of— of I don't even know what! There's nothing appealing about him at all." Even as she said the words, she remembered the thrill that had zipped through her body when she and Aiden had touched at the elevator. And the way she hadn't wanted to look away when they'd made eye contact. She shifted self-consciously in her seat, hoping Amelia wouldn't notice.

She did.

"Oh my God!" Amelia's eyes grew round. "You're attracted to him."

"Didn't you just hear me say he's a drunken mess? Why would I be attracted to that?"

"Even if we didn't have a twin bond, it's written all over your face." She laughed. "Finally, a man who has sparked your interest! Maybe you can finally lose your virginity."

"Um, I have a five-year-old son. That's proof the deed's done."

Amelia waved her hand in dismissal. "After five years without sex, you're considered a born-again virgin."

Mya rolled her eyes. "That's not how it works. Look, I'm not interested in Aiden Doyle. He can't even take care of himself!"

"Who can't take care of himself?" Noah asked as he bounded into the room.

Amelia made the universal zip-lip motion across her mouth.

Mya picked up Noah under the arms and slid him onto her lap. He squirmed until he found a comfortable position. "There's a man at the studio who needs someone to watch over him for a few months."

"Is he sick? Will he stay with Gran?" Noah tilted back his head to look at her. When she and Amelia had put their grandmother in a nursing home, they'd told Noah it was because she was sick and needed constant care, more than they could do. Now every time someone came down with the sniffles, he wanted to know if they were going to stay with Gran.

"No, sweetie. He's not staying with Gran, but he needs some care and my boss, Mr. Masters, asked me to do it. So, you're going to stay with Aunty Amelia for a few days while I watch him."

"You're not coming home?" His bottom lip trembled. "You read my bedtime stories."

Amelia rose from the chair and squatted next to him. "I'm going to read them to you. I do much better voices than your mum, anyway." She tickled his side, teasing a giggle from him. "And we're going to have so much fun. I'll take you to the zoo tomorrow."

"The zoo! Can we see the lions?" He wiggled with excitement.

"Sure, we can see whatever you want."

"Yes." He pumped the air with a small fist, slid off his mother's lap, and ran out of the room.

"See? He'll be fine," Amelia reassured her.

As Mya packed a bag of her clothes and toiletries, she tried to tell herself it was normal for parents to get a few days away from their kids now and then. She could definitely cope with being away from Noah for a night or three.

Maybe Aiden wouldn't miss her if she sneaked away for an hour or so at night so she could read to Noah while he fell asleep. He was a grown man! He could surely be left to his own devices for a little while.

Feeling good about that plan, she said her goodbyes, tossed her bag in the car, and drove to the address Aiden had provided in Bellevue Hill. She could still see Noah at bedtime, and Aiden could keep himself out of trouble for an hour.

But when she pulled into the driveway, she could barely think over the raucous music blaring from Aiden's house.

Heart sinking, she revised her already revised plan. As it turned out, Aiden Doyle could not keep himself out of trouble for an hour.

Chapter 3

"He can't be serious!" Mya fumed. Given the music and the luxury cars lining the driveway, Aiden was throwing a party. What part of 'stay out of trouble' did Aiden not understand? Apparently all of it because throwing parties would definitely fall under Mr. Masters's idea of *trouble*. What a way to start the first day of her new job by utterly failing to control her charge. She might as well bid that bonus goodbye. Dropping her head on the steering wheel, Mya sucked in two deep breaths to calm the anxiety clutching her chest.

She hadn't meant to stay at home for as long as she had, but she'd gotten sidetracked talking to Amelia. Now she had to pay the piper for her lack of attention.

"Well, I better start earning my money," she mumbled, getting out of the car. She pulled her luggage from the boot and made her way to the front door. Now that she'd be living here, did she just walk in? Or should she press the buzzer? Nibbling her bottom lip, she decided politeness might be the way to go and hit the button, although she doubted anyone inside would hear it over the blaring music.

When no one answered after a second press of the buzzer, she threw manners out the window and let herself in. After a brief hesitation at the threshold, she crossed the marble-tiled foyer and propped her bags in a corner. She wiped her sweaty palms on her thighs and took a breath to steady herself. Time to find Aiden and shut this party down—good practice for Noah's teenage years.

Mya slipped into a room crowded with men and women laughing, drinking, and dancing. No one noticed her standing at the outskirts of the room, or if they did, they didn't acknowledge her. An underdressed assistant was as good as invisible in the midst of mostly B-list celebrities.

She searched for Aiden in the mass of people but didn't see him anywhere. She'd have to ask and hope she got lucky.

Mya tapped on the shoulder of the nearest woman— an actress from a popular crime show—who turned and raised a perfectly manicured eyebrow. The unspoken questions were clear: Who are you and what do you want?

Skipping the first unasked question, Mya jumped straight to the second. "Have you seen Aiden Doyle?" she asked, raising her voice to be heard over the music.

The actress shook her head and returned to her conversation. Crap!

The next person she tried to ask—a news anchor— looked her up and down and dismissed her with a wave before she could even open her mouth. Gritting her teeth, she stormed from the room and into another even more densely packed with celebrities. Did Aiden know them all?

On the far side of the room, Mya spied someone tall and dark haired. Aiden? She began weaving her way across the makeshift dance floor as the man disappeared from sight. Double crap!

As she hurried to follow, a comedian she'd never let Noah watch in a million years tripped over his own feet, and the glass in his hand collided with her chest. Cool red wine immediately soaked her white shirt, which became translucent and clung to her skin. She gasped at the temperature and the shock. Anger quickened her pulse.

With a lascivious grin, the comedian said, "Oh shit, let me clean that up," as he reached for her breasts.

Mya slapped his hands away. "No need," she gritted through clenched teeth. *When I find Aiden, I'm going to wring his neck!*

Backing away from the comedian's groping hands, Mya saw a former scream queen sipping from a crystal champagne flute and decided to try her luck. "Have you seen Aiden Doyle?"

"I last saw him leaving with a woman. They were getting friendly, if you know what I mean." She gestured with her glass. As Mya started to move off, the woman added, "Hydrogen peroxide and dish soap."

"What?"

"For the stain."

Mya nodded. At least not all of Aiden's friends were awful. "Thanks!" She headed in the indicated direction. If she did find Aiden, what should she do? She'd rather pull her teeth out than catch him doing who-knows-what with a woman. She chewed on her cuticle. Could she pretend this wasn't happening? Let him have this party to get it out of his system and start fresh tomorrow?

Unfortunately, no. Mr. Masters had given her a job to do. If he found out about the party and that she'd done nothing to stop it, she could say bye-bye to getting Gran into a better nursing home.

"Dammit," she spat before taking a deep breath and continuing her search.

The last room downstairs had huge timber double doors. Hoping to find Aiden here instead of one of the bedrooms upstairs, she pushed open the door and walked into a library. Her jaw dropped. Floor-to-ceiling shelves covered with books lined three walls. Any other time, Mya would have loved to use the sliding ladder to search for hidden gems on the top shelves, but she had another mission now and her target was in her sights.

Aiden sat slumped in a leather wingback chair with a woman wearing only a black lace thong gyrating in front of him. Between the dim light in the room and the deafening music, neither had registered Mya's entrance.

Mya's face flushed nearly as red as her stained blouse. The door was unlocked. Anyone could just walk in! Including someone with a mobile who could have photos uploaded on the internet in an instant. This was beyond reckless. She'd laugh at Aiden's brazen behavior if her job wasn't on the line.

Mya took in the scene. The woman was doing all she could to grab Aiden's attention, but even though his eyes followed her movements, he seemed bored. One hand held a glass of amber liquid that he never raised to his mouth. His eyes drooped, and Mya thought if he blinked one more time, he'd fall asleep.

Not wanting to appear voyeuristic by lingering any longer, Mya drew herself to her full height and stepped out from the shadows near the door. Aiden's eyes widened with shock before the indifferent expression settled back onto his face.

After another beat, the dancing woman noticed Mya. With a gasp, she straightened.

Mya found a small black dress on the floor and tossed it

to her. "I'm sorry to break up your fun, but it's time you leave."

The woman put her hands on her hips, her too-perfect-to-be-real breasts on full display, and snapped, "Who are you, his *wife*?"

"Worse," said Mya. "I'm his babysitter. This party is over. And you can forget about coming back here for another three months."

The woman rolled her eyes. "So he's, like, grounded?"

"Yep." Aiden's companion seemed to be waiting for more of an explanation, but Mya was in no mood to elaborate.

The two women stared at each other and when Mya didn't back down, the other woman huffed, "Whatever," and sashayed out of the room without even getting dressed first.

Thank God Noah was safe at home with Amelia. She'd hoped it wouldn't take long to get things sorted out enough to bring him here, but now she couldn't imagine why she'd ever thought Aiden would behave himself.

Aiden unfolded from the chair and downed the remainder of his drink before dropping it on the desk. "You know how to suck the life out of a party," he grumbled.

"From my vantage point, it didn't look like you were having much fun. I thought you'd fall asleep at any second and I'd have to roll you to bed."

"You get near my bed and there'll definitely be no sleeping." His gaze dropped to the stain on her top. "I can help you get cleaned up."

Mya tossed her head back and laughed. "Do those lines work often?" Did this man really think she wanted to go anywhere near his bed when he'd just had a woman giving him a lap dance? Yes, he was drop-dead gorgeous.

And yes, he'd caused a buzz in her stomach when their eyes had met earlier, but looking around and seeing the man behind the sex symbol was enough to stop any attraction from getting out of hand.

"I don't need a line to get a woman in my bed." He ambled closer, eyes boring into her hungrily.

For a second her heart fluttered against her ribs. She forced herself to remain calm. He was trying to push her buttons and get her to react. Nothing more. And she wouldn't give him the satisfaction of a response. "Good for you. Now I—we—have to shut this party down before Mr. Masters finds out about it."

She turned to leave, but he grasped her wrist and pulled her back around. They stood as close as they'd been earlier at the elevator, and once again, she could feel the heat from his body. One more step and she could press herself against him, basking in his warmth. Instead, she slipped her wrist free and backed away, glaring at him.

"Come on, Mya, the night's still young. We can have some fun of our own and no one, especially Mr. Masters, needs to find out about it."

The gleam in Aiden's eye told Mya exactly what kind of *fun* he had in mind. Even if her skin hummed with electricity when he was close, she didn't want his idea of fun. "The night's over, and I'm sending everyone home." She was the mother of one five-year-old and had to act like the mother of a grown man with the self-control of a toddler. Why had her life gone so off the rails?

"Good luck trying to get everyone out," he chuckled as he poured himself another drink. "If you change your mind about having some fun, you know where I am."

"Don't you care what acting like this could cost the both of us?" Not waiting for an answer, she stormed over and snatched the glass from his hand. Glancing around the room, she spotted a houseplant and poured the liquid into the pot, hoping she didn't kill the peace lily. Then she snatched the almost empty bottle from the table before Aiden got the chance. "No more alcohol. No more parties. And no more women. Those are the conditions. I personally don't care how you live your life, but that's what Mr. Masters wants."

"Have you ever tried breaking the rules? You might like it," he said with a crooked grin.

"Fun doesn't pay the bills. I need this bonus. Don't ruin it for me." She turned on her heel and marched out. It was easier to ignore the fire in her belly when his sexy smile was out of sight.

She needed to get her emotions under control. If she couldn't last three minutes alone in a room before needing a cold shower, how was she going to last three months? She'd have to come up with a plan for keeping away from Aiden, but first, she had to figure out how to empty the house before any compromising photos made it to the internet.

Aiden pulled another bottle from his stash in the desk drawer. Little Miss Follow The Rules couldn't take everything away from him. He poured a glass of Jack and knocked it back in one gulp. The whiskey left a trail of fire down his throat and into his chest, chasing away the dull ache that normally lived there.

Fuck Lionel and his conditions, and fuck Mya for her obedience. Couldn't she see he was a lost cause?

Maybe she did see. She'd said she needed the money, and even though she'd never get that promised bonus, double her pay for as long as she could stick it out was a pretty penny.

He knew he was on thin ice. He was very publicly spiraling out of control, and if he lost *Family First*, he'd be box office poison. Sure, his family would stick by him, but he couldn't ask Ethan to pull his arse out of the fire again. Thinking about his family and what would happen if they knew the studio would fire him was too much to process. A low, dull pain blossomed in the center of his skull, and his eyelids grew heavy. Time to hit the sack. Bringing the bottle with him, he took another swig of whiskey and stumbled up the stairs to his room. Alone.

He left a trail of clothing from the door to his bed. As he flopped down onto the bed, relief rippled through him. Mya had been right. He hadn't been having fun with Lily. Lola? Laura? Lacey? Whatever she'd said her name was. If he'd taken her to bed, he'd have had to perform for her, and even though he craved the distraction, having sex would have felt like a chore.

Downstairs, the music cut off, and he was left with the throbbing inside his head, causing the room to spin faintly around him. He ignored it all. For the first time in months, Aiden dropped into a deep, dreamless sleep.

Chapter 4

"Can I get everyone's attention, please." Mya shouted, attempting to make herself heard over the pounding music and the hum of conversation.

One man glanced her way but quickly dismissed her as unimportant.

She tried again. "Okay, this party is over!"

Again, no one seemed to hear her. Frustrated, she searched the room until her eyes landed on Aiden's state-of-the-art stereo system. The thing was sleek and appeared to need a remote control to operate it. A remote control that was nowhere to be seen. She tried pressing what few buttons she could find on the system, but the blaring beat only got louder. She pressed her lips together, reached behind the stereo, and tugged the cord—hard.

The music cut off midbeat, and every eye in the room turned to her. Silence reigned.

Screwing up her courage, Mya straightened and said in her best mum voice, "Party's over. The bar is closed. I don't care where you go or what you do, but you're not doing it here."

"Who are you to give us orders?" the same comedian who'd stained her shirt and tried to grope her earlier asked.

"The woman who'll be sending you the cleaning bill for the wine you spilled," she replied quickly, glaring at the man over the rim of her glasses in her best stern mum pose.

The man glanced at her shirt and then at the large red wine stain on Aiden's silk rug and blanched. Mumbling about annoying women, the man scurried off.

Emboldened by her success, she turned to the rest of the crowd. "Anyone else have any objections?"

The crowd scattered.

"Are you going to be okay?" a woman's voice asked from her left side.

She turned to see the scream queen from earlier. "What do you mean?"

"This place is a mess. Are you going to be okay?"

"Are you offering to help?"

The woman laughed. "And chip these nails? No way. But I do know a great cleaning service."

Considering the woman's profession, that made sense. Still, there was no way she was going to call someone who might let it slip that Aiden had thrown one hell of a party. "Thanks, but no. I got this."

"Suit yourself. And if hydrogen peroxide and dish soap don't work, try club soda and vinegar."

"Thanks, I will."

Mya watched as celebrities and hangers-on filed out of the door. A few of them called her names, but she didn't care. She'd done it! She'd won this first battle.

The house finally empty, she found garbage bags in a kitchen drawer and cleared up the rubbish. Being a housekeeper was not in her job description, but there was no way she could live in a pigsty. She was sure Mr. Masters had known that she was far tidier than Aiden and had fully intended to make her work for her money.

Next, she went in search of alcohol, dumping the glasses from the partygoers into the nearest loo. An assortment of liquor was stashed in the kitchen cupboards. God, she could do with more than a few sips of wine with Amelia after the day she'd had, but unlike Aiden, she had self-control. Instead of pouring a glass, she dumped the booze down the drain. She'd bet her bonus from Lionel that Aiden had more bottles hidden away somewhere, but exhaustion weighed her down too much to look for more. She'd search again tomorrow.

With nothing more to do for the night, she grabbed her bags from the foyer and hauled them upstairs in search of a guest room. The first room she found a bed in she'd claim as hers for the next three months. Unless Aiden occupied it, of course.

Then again, the house was so big, he probably had his own separate wing.

She opened the first door. The room was too dark to see if Aiden was inside. She avoided turning the light on, just in case. After pausing briefly in the doorway and not hearing any signs of life, she declared it safe to enter.

Stepping inside, she rolled her luggage behind her. When the wheels snagged on the carpet, she yanked the handle of the bag with such force that she stumbled. Before she could right herself, her feet caught on something on the floor and she hit the back of her legs on the bed, falling on the mattress. With the light from the hallway spilling inside the room, she glanced down to see jeans twisted around her feet and a T-shirt lodged in the wheels of her bag. The clothes looked very much like the ones Aiden had been wearing.

Turning with a mixture of excitement and dread, her gaze landed on Aiden sprawled on the bed.

Mya sprung off the mattress like she'd been shocked. "Oh crap!" Realizing she'd gasped out loud, she clapped a hand over her mouth, hoping he hadn't heard the commotion. One heartbeat. Two. And no response. Aiden hadn't stirred, his deep breathing confirming he was out cold. Mya relaxed. Now she could slink out without him knowing she'd ever been there.

She untangled the jeans from her feet, dropping them approximately where they'd fallen when Aiden had stepped out of them. Curious, she looked at him. He lay on his back, naked from the waist up. The soft light did nothing to hide the contours of his body. What would it feel like to run her fingers down his chest and stomach? Did he sleep commando? One quick twitch of the sheet would reveal the truth. A warm flush spread across her body.

Oh God! What was she doing? What was she thinking? It wasn't appropriate for her to stare, but she couldn't tear her eyes away.

She'd have to be blind not to notice his amazing body. Too bad the man inside it wasn't nearly as spectacular. She didn't need to get involved with someone who couldn't get his life together—someone who seemed hell-bent on self-destructing.

What she needed was stability for herself and for Noah. And she'd done damn well providing that for them. Her small family, which included Amelia and Gran, was all she needed—most days.

Amelia was a great sister, but when Mya didn't need her help with Noah, she locked herself in the studio, creating her next masterpiece. Sometimes, Mya wouldn't see her for days. And, of course, Gran didn't live there any longer.

When it got a little lonely, she imagined sharing her life with someone. Someone she could rely on to stick around and be there for her and her family. It's the reason she let Amelia convince her to join a dating website. She needed companionship, and Noah needed a father figure.

As she stood lost in thought, Aiden made a snuffling sound and stirred. Guilty of daydreaming and ogling, Mya spun on her heels and crashed into her luggage. A startled yelp escaped her lips as she hit the floor.

"Whoozit?" Aiden asked, his voice husky from whiskey and sleep. He sat up, the sheet falling away, revealing boxer briefs.

Crap! She'd woken him. Maybe if she rolled, she could hide under the bed before he spotted her.

"Mya?" Aiden scrubbed at his face. "What are you doing on the floor?"

Too late.

Busted. "Sorry," Mya said. "I didn't know which room was yours. I didn't mean to bother you, but I tripped." She was thankful that she was backlit by light in the hall because it meant he couldn't see her staring at his crotch. What was wrong with her? She'd seen half-naked men before. No big deal.

Although… from what she could tell given the dimness of the room? No. *Big* deal.

"Have you changed your mind about joining me in bed?" His voice dripped with a sexuality that made her insides quiver against her best judgment.

He began to get out of bed.

The thought of a nearly naked Aiden Doyle touching her—even nonsexually—spiked her heart rate, and she clambered to her feet in a panic. "No! No, it's fine. I'm fine. This is your room; I'll find another." When she reached down to pull her bag back onto its wheels, pain zinged through her wrist. "Ow!"

"You've hurt yourself." The bed creaked as Aiden got to his feet and walked over to Mya.

"It's nothing." She waved away his helping hand, causing her wrist to throb with the sudden movement. Her knee decided to join the chorus of pain, and she knew she'd have a bruise in the morning.

Ignoring her dismissal, Aiden put one hand under her elbow and one around her back and lifted her to her feet.

Once standing, he left the hand around her back for support. Their bodies pressed against each other. Mya stepped away, Aiden's fingers skimming along her back.

Taking her hand, he slid his hand from elbow to wrist, leaving a fiery trail along the way. She hissed. From the ache in her wrist or his smoldering touch, she wasn't sure.

"You *are* hurt," he said, oblivious to the fire he was spreading from his gentle caress. Between his seminudity, the whisper of his fingers on her skin, and his proximity, the bedroom felt like a sauna—and Mya was overdressed.

"It's nothing." She pulled free and shook her arm to prove her point, smiling through the discomfort, then grabbed the handle of her bag. "See? All good."

"I'll take it," Aiden said, clearly not taken in by her stoicism. As he took the bag from her, he added, "I'll show you to a room you can use. Unless you want to stay here?" He raised an eyebrow and grinned like the devil ready to play.

"Another room will be fine. And don't you want to"— she waved a hand up and down the length of him—"you know, put pajamas on?"

Glancing down at himself with not an ounce of modesty, he spread his arms to the side and shrugged. "Don't own any."

"Then put some clothes on, please." She turned her

head to give him privacy, but she couldn't resist sneaking a peek out of the corner of her eye. His dark, rumpled bed hair made him look sexier than ever.

"You have a problem with sleeping nearly naked?" Through her peripheral vision, she could see him bend down to pick up the rumpled jeans from the floor and shove his legs into them.

"Not at all. I've heard it can help you sleep better, reduce stress and anxiety and can lead to more se—"—she covered the word *sex* with a cough—"uh, more sleep."

"You already mentioned sleep, but I'd like to know what you were really going to say. It sounded *interesting*." He chuckled, and she knew her cough hadn't fooled him for a second.

Aiden pulled her bag to the door. The light from the hallway illuminated his bare chest and the hollows of his hip bones just above the waistband of his jeans. It had been years since she'd seen a man this gorgeous in the flesh.

Noah's dad, Daniel, had been attractive, and she'd fallen for his good looks. Not long after, he'd shown his true colors. The only good thing that had come from their relationship had been Noah. Daniel had taught her a huge lesson, though: she should think less with her lady parts and more with her head. And for years now, she'd been doing just that.

Until now.

Looking at Aiden awakened certain parts of her body from hibernation. Why was she reacting this way? She wasn't a silly schoolgirl who drooled over any guy with a nice body and a big… house. She was a responsible adult!

It had been a stressful day. A good night's sleep would make her feel better.

Maybe she should sleep naked. She'd heard it helped with se... uh, sleep.

"If you're going to just stand there, I'm going back to bed," Aiden said from the doorway. "The offer's still open if you change your mind." His gaze slid over her body, lingering on the wet stain that caused her shirt to cling to her chest.

The leer snapped her back to reality. Hands on hips, she said, "Let me make myself clear. While we're forced to live together, I will not join you on that bed." When he opened his mouth to say something, she cut him off. "Nor on any other bed or piece of furniture." She raised her eyebrows. "Understood?"

With a casual shrug, he said, "Understood." He walked away, leaving Mya surprised at how easily he'd agreed after making so many innuendos. Maybe there was more to him than she'd thought.

When she stepped into the hall, she saw a light shining from a doorway a few rooms down. She entered and found Aiden staring out the window, his back to her, his broad shoulders tapering to a narrow waist. At first, she wondered what he was looking at, but when she glanced around the room, she realized he was looking away rather than at.

They stood in a nursery. The white walls were decorated with a mural of cute baby animals romping in a field. A huge pale-pink sheepskin rug softened the floor. A mobile of clouds and rainbows hung over a white timber cot, a soft pink baby blanket draped over the rail. A rocking chair loaded with pillows sat in one corner. In the middle of the room stood a queen-sized bed with a floral coverlet, perhaps intended for a nanny. She remembered seeing the headlines in the trashy magazines at the supermarket checkouts. *Family First* Star Loses Daughter and Wife in Twin Tragedies. Aiden Doyle Spirals Following Loss of Family. *Family First* on Hiatus Due to Star's Grief.

She couldn't imagine the hell he'd been through. Heart softening, she asked, "Is there another bedroom I can use?" Even if he never came in to see her while she was here, he'd still know someone was in his baby's room.

"All the others are unfurnished. Sorry about the decor." Aiden faced her. Anger was written largely in the lines on his face, so different from his usual flirtatious grin.

Unsure of what to say, she floundered. "I'm so sorry about your wife and baby. I can sleep on the couch if you'd rather. I can't imagine what you've gone through."

"I don't care where you sleep." His lips twisted into a crooked grin that didn't touch his eyes. "Unless you want to sleep with me."

It was a touchy subject, so she ignored the come-on. "I'll pass, thank you."

He shrugged and walked to the door. "The couch is uncomfortable. I wouldn't recommend it." His gaze flicked around the room. "Redecorate, if you want."

"But I'm only here for three months!"

He left the room, not bothering to respond.

Mya blew out a long breath, dropped onto the mattress, and gazed around the room. The space had the disquieting air of a museum after all the guests had gone home for the night. She would have expected sadness from Aiden seeing this room, but he'd been angry instead. Was it just the memory of everything he'd lost? Everyone grieved differently; she knew that. But his reaction didn't make any sense.

If anything ever happened to Noah, she didn't know how she'd cope. She already had to deal with the threat of him being taken from her. If she so much as sneezed the wrong way and Daniel's parents heard about it, she'd be facing their army of Armani-suited lawyers petitioning for custody.

She'd have to make sure not to give them any reason to pursue custody of Noah. That meant leaving Mr. Masters's money on the table if it looked like Aiden might drag her down with him. She needed the money for Gran, but keeping custody of Noah was the most important thing. Ultimately, Aiden's job was his problem, and if it came down to him or Noah, she'd choose her son every time.

This job was going to be harder than she'd expected. And when Noah moved in, juggling the two of them would be difficult.

Exhausted, she didn't have the energy to think about how she'd manage them both. Hopefully, with a few hours of sleep, things would look clearer in the morning.

In desperate need of a shower before bed, she opened a door she hoped led to an en suite. The doors opened into a huge walk-in wardrobe filled with clothes. On one side, tiny outfits decorated with pink flowers, butterflies, and hearts hung from the racks, flanked by shelves of small shoes: a wardrobe their precious daughter would never wear.

A lump formed in Mya's throat, and she brushed away a tear.

She quickly turned her head away from the reminder of a life lost far too soon. Her eyes landed on the other contents of the closet. Women's clothes. Lots and lots of women's clothes. Everything from evening gowns to T-shirts, stiletto heels to sneakers. Were these Aiden's wife's clothes? If so, then why were they in the same room as the baby's things? Was it too hard for him to part with them but too painful to keep them in the room they'd shared? Nothing about him made any sense.

Closing the wardrobe, she opened the door on the opposite wall, which proved to be the bathroom. Just like the wardrobe, the bathroom contained the items necessary for a baby: soft towels, creams, talcum powder, nappies. On the vanity, makeup and perfume were scattered around like the person getting ready had stepped away for a moment. When Mya took a second look, she saw medication bottles, bandages, and latex gloves sitting amongst the foundation and Chanel No. 5. She searched her memory but couldn't recall if Aiden's wife had been ill.

She had no doubt now that this room had belonged to Aiden's wife. Why would he keep all this stuff? The pain of seeing it must be like a knife to the heart. She ran a finger along the smooth stone of the vanity, and dust gathered on her fingertip. No one had cleaned in a long time. Her first assessment of the nursery as a museum hadn't been so far off.

She couldn't stay in the room, not like this, and she clearly couldn't redecorate. Even if he refused to admit it, she knew why the room hadn't changed in the years since his loss. And the drinking and self-destructive behavior made sense too.

It looked like she'd be sleeping on the uncomfortable couch. Better that than spending a night with the ghosts of Aiden's lost family.

Chapter 5

*a*iden woke with a dry mouth and pounding in his
head. Swinging his legs off the bed, he held his
head in his hands, trying to stop the room from spinning.
When the walls stopped moving, he lurched to his feet and
staggered into the bathroom for a long, hot shower.

Feeling moderately more human, he headed downstairs
for coffee to find Mya bustling around the kitchen. He'd
forgotten all about her. Damn Lionel! Surely, yesterday had
only been a scare tactic.

Without saying a word to Mya, he opened a cabinet,
pulled out a box of Panadol, and swallowed two without
water. Pouring a cup of coffee, he slid onto a stool at the
breakfast bar, watching as she stacked glasses in the
dishwasher and cleaned counters.

"Did Lionel also hire you to be my maid?" he said,
breaking the silence.

She paused for a beat, then threw the sponge into the
sink. "No, and don't get any ideas either. I'm only doing
this because your party guests made a mess and I hate
living like a pig. By the way, we have Rachel Fraser from

Sydney Buzz coming over for an interview." She glanced at her watch. "In forty-five minutes."

"Who the hell organized that?"

"I got a call nice and early this morning from Mr. Masters's *new* assistant," she said with a clipped tone. Whether she was more annoyed about watching him or being replaced, he wasn't sure. "Additionally, I was also reminded of the terms of the deal." Her eyes slid to his damp hair. "At least you've already showered, and you're as sober as you're likely to get. You'll need to shave before she arrives."

"I'm not doing it. If I'm not filming, I'm not doing interviews." He sipped his coffee, black and bitter.

"Mr. Masters isn't taking 'no' for an answer. This interview is your chance to explain your absence. He wants your audience to know you're taking a break because of scheduling conflicts, *not* because you need to get your life on track."

"Nothing wrong with the way my life is going." It was a lie, and they both knew it. A hazy memory of the night before emerged from the fog: looking out the window in the unused nursery. His chest tightened, and the little voice in the back of his head that he drank to silence began whispering the truths he didn't want to hear.

Mya opened her mouth to speak, then apparently changed her mind. Sighing, she said, "Anyway, we need to get you ready to dazzle Rachel Fraser."

"I don't dazzle," he grumbled.

"Then fake it! Are you an actor or not?" Mya asked with an edge to her voice. "Do whatever you need to do to fix your reputation so I can get back to my life and you can get back to yours."

Back to his life.

What life? Madeline had torn his life away along with

his heart. In the years that followed, he'd realized that loving—and living—wasn't worth the risk.

Finishing his coffee, he got up and spread his arms out to the sides. "I'm ready."

Her gaze traveled over him again, and she wrinkled her nose. "Those are the same clothes that were tossed on your bedroom floor last night. Change into something clean and professional. Jeans if you must, but a button-down shirt with them. Shave and comb your hair. While you're doing that, I'll double-check the living room to make sure there isn't any evidence of last night's party." With that, she spun on her heels as he watched her leave the kitchen.

Even though she wore a baggy pink T-shirt and loose jeans, his eyes were drawn to the sway of her hips, the curve of her behind. Heat surged through his body. There was nothing alluring about her under those shapeless clothes, so why was he imagining what she looked like beneath them?

Habit, maybe. The lingering buzz of last night's whiskey. Once the coffee kicked in, he'd see things more clearly.

Pouring another cup of coffee, he returned to his room. There was probably no way he could get out of this interview. He'd bet Mya would tie him to the chair to get it done. Why did she need the money badly enough to put up with his shit? He scrubbed his hands through his hair. Not his business.

Better to do what she said before she came looking for him with that rope. An image of her bound to his bed, wearing nothing but a satisfied grin, entered his mind. Now that could be fun. He shook away the fantasy. No way anything like that would happen with Little Miss Follow The Rules. She looked like a movie librarian with her black glasses and neatly coiffed hair, and he didn't figure she was the type to mix business with pleasure. Besides, he knew plenty of women willing to let their hair down and have fun with no strings attached, just like he wanted. He bet straitlaced Mya was nothing but strings—way less fun than ropes. Definitely not his type.

Freshly shaven, dressed in clean jeans and a navy shirt, he found Mya directing the media crew to set up in the living room. When she saw him, she walked over to him and smiled approvingly. The gesture lit up her face and caused an unexpected thrum of satisfaction in his chest.

"Much better," she said, unaware of his reaction.

When was the last time someone had aimed a genuine smile in his direction? He couldn't remember. People scowled or looked disappointed or concerned or embarrassed for him, or they'd given up on him too and merely pretended to be happy. Mya's smile reminded him that some people cared.

"Your hair is still a mess. Can I?" At his nod, she reached up to run her fingers through it, taming the unruly brown locks. It gave him the opportunity to study her face up close. Behind her heavy-framed glasses, her brown eyes were flecked with gold. Her skin was flawless except for a small freckle on the side of her pink mouth, one that practically begged to be kissed.

Their eyes connected, and her fingers stilled in his hair. When his gaze fell to the freckle, she dropped her hands and stepped away, a pink flush staining her cheeks.

"Umm… I think… they're ready for you," she said, flustered. She turned her back and walked away.

He'd seen that look on her face on women dozens of times before. He doubted it would take much to get her willpower to crumble. Even though he'd invited her to bed the night before, he'd known she'd refuse. It'd been a test. An act. He'd wanted to take her measure, and Mya had passed with flying colors. Besides, he'd be stupid to complicate their living arrangements with sex. No one-night stands with his babysitter, after all. They had to weather three damn months together. He hadn't had sex with the same woman for that long since… The thought of Madeline caused his stomach to clench. He needed a drink.

When he opened the bar in the corner of the room, it was empty of everything except for glasses and a jar of cocktail onions. A quick check of the rest of the cupboards revealed that there was no alcohol to be found. "What the hell? Where's my stuff?" he called out to no one in particular.

Mya rushed over with a bottle of water. She twisted off the cap and shoved it at his chest. "Here's your *water*." The intensity of her gaze made him think she was trying to tell him something telepathically. "I'll get more stocked this afternoon. I just know how much you love *water* to stay hydrated," she said, nodding her head slightly to the side.

Over her shoulder, the magazine crew were staring at them with feigned disinterest.

Through a tight smile, she whispered, "We have to convince these people you're squeaky clean. Mr. Masters made it clear that you can't stuff this up. Your job and my bonus are on the chopping block, and I won't let you ruin this for me. Do you understand?" Her eyes flashed again, but it was less of an *I want to tear your clothes off* look and more of an *If you make a mess of this, they'll never find the body* look.

Without waiting for his response, she continued, "He's left me here to handle this." She waved her hand to indicate the room. "I don't know what I'm supposed to do. I answer phones and pick up Mr. Masters's dry cleaning. I don't know anything about any of this. Don't make it harder than it needs to be."

Her panic was clear, at least to him, but all he'd wanted was to be left alone, and now he had to put on an act for the journalist conducting the interview if he wanted to keep his job. Between him and Mya, he'd save his sympathy for himself.

"I'll be on my best behavior," he said through gritted teeth. Forcing a cheerful grin, Aiden took his seat in front of a camera. A woman with a makeup brush hurried over and dusted his face with powder and stepped away when Rachel Fraser took a seat in front of him.

He answered all the questions with a smile. Anything too personal got laughed off with noncommittal banalities. Mya crossed his eyeline every few seconds as she paced across the room, no doubt terrified that he'd fuck up both the interview and her bonus.

He couldn't say he blamed her.

To Mya's untrained eyes, the interview was going well. Aiden didn't want to be there, but it didn't show. He looked comfortable in front of the camera, and Rachel Fraser soaked up his every word, giggling like a schoolgirl one minute and flashing sultry smiles the next. Who wouldn't be attracted to Aiden Doyle? Showered, shaved, and in clean clothes, he was a gorgeous man. For a second, Mya got trapped in his sea-green eyes. Thank God she had the strength to not fall in. Aiden Doyle was not the man for her, even if her insides quivered when they were close.

As the interview ended, the crew began packing up their equipment. Rachel Fraser slid from her chair in front of Aiden to the seat next to him on the couch, so close their thighs pressed together. With a hand on his knee, it was plain to see what she had in mind.

No, no, no. Mr. Masters said *no women*. Especially not a reporter. She had to put a stop to this!

Before she could take a step, her mobile phone buzzed in her pocket. When she pulled it out, Amelia's name glowed on the screen. Looking at Aiden and Rachel and back to her phone, she sighed. She couldn't ignore the call. It might be about Noah. Giving the couple one last glance, she left the room.

"Hi, Amelia. Is Noah okay?" she asked as she entered the kitchen.

"Yes, he's fine, but we have a problem."

Her stomach clenched. "What is it?"

"Daniel's parents are here."

"What?" Mya's heart pounded hard against her ribs. "They don't have their monthly visitation for a couple of weeks." She ran jerky fingers through her hair. "If they find out I've left Noah with you to stay with Aiden, they're going to… to…"

"No. They will not take Noah." Amelia's voice was quiet but determined.

"They can and they will if they think I'm reckless and irresponsible."

"I've told them you've just popped out to run some errands and will be back soon."

"What if Noah tells them where I am?"

"I told him to play a game of pretend and say you're at the shops. If he gives you away, he won't win a bag of lollies, and we both know what he'd do for sweets. I know it's a shitty thing for me to ask him to lie, but he won't say anything."

Mya wasn't a fan of sugary rewards, particularly for

SONIA STANIZZO

bad behavior like telling lies, but this was an emergency, and Amelia had had to think fast.

"How soon can you get here?"

Mya glanced at her watch. "I can be there in twenty minutes."

"What about Aiden?" Amelia asked.

Crap. She couldn't leave him alone with Rachel. Who knows what they'd get up to? But Noah was more important. Hopefully no one would find out about Aiden's latest tryst.

"I'm going to leave him." She dropped her elbow on the counter, and her head fell into her palm. What if Mr. Masters found out?

"There is something else we can do," Amelia said thoughtfully.

Hope surged through every cell in Mya's body. "What?"

"Noah's with them at the moment. I can tell them I'll be in my studio to give them some alone time with their grandson. Then I'll change into your clothes, sneak out of the house, walk through the front door, and pretend to be you."

They hadn't done the twin swap in years. The stakes had been lower when they'd played tricks on Gran or the teachers at school. Now, though… "Do you think it will work?" At least Amelia's hair wasn't a pink-and-purple pixie cut anymore. "They might know you're not me."

"Leave them to me. It will be a miracle if they can tell the difference."

"Noah will." What if he gave away the game?

"He wants lollies. He'll play along."

Mya blew out a long, relieved breath. "You're amazing."

"Yes, I am." Mya could hear Amelia's smile through the phone. "This is gonna be fun."

Mya ended the call and scrubbed her hands over her face. God, she prayed Amelia pulled this off.

Now, it was time to check on Aiden. She walked back into the living room, only to find that Aiden and Rachel had disappeared.

ive minutes! He'd been out of her sight for five freaking minutes, and already he was up to no good! Not even Noah needed as much supervision. The crew's van was gone from the driveway, but Rachel's shoes and jacket scattered on the floor told Mya she was still in the house. Most likely in Aiden's room.

Oh God, did she have to go in there and tell her to leave? Following the trail of clothes, she trudged up the stairs. *I'm not getting paid enough for this.* At Aiden's bedroom, she paused. There was no way she could just walk inside; who knew what she'd see? Taking a deep breath, she pressed her ear against the door.

"Hear anything interesting?"

Mya spun around with a squeak and came face-to-face with Aiden. His eyebrow rose in a silent question, and a small smirk played at his lips.

"I didn't... I wasn't..." She pulled her shoulders back and dropped her hands to her hips. "You need to ask Rachel Fraser to leave."

"Why would I do that? The fun's just getting started." He lifted a champagne bottle to his lips.

"You're not allowed to drink." Where the hell had he found that?

"I'm not allowed to do a lot of things and yet…" His gaze flicked toward the door, and he shrugged.

"You need to give me that bottle and tell your new *friend* to leave." He was shirtless, and his jeans sat low on his hips. She struggled to keep her eyes on his face.

"And if I don't, what are you going to do? Tell Lionel?" She tilted her chin up. "Yes."

"If you do, you'll lose all that extra money." He gave a sly grin as if he'd won the argument.

"Maybe. Maybe not. But I'm not the one who will be out of a job." She hoped. She couldn't let him know that her threat didn't have any teeth.

"Fine. Go ahead, call Lionel. I don't care." He tried to nudge past her.

Bluff called, Mya changed tactics. She flung out her arms, blocking the entrance to his room. "I'm not going to let you throw your career away."

"You think sleeping with Rachel is going to do that?" She lifted her chin. "I know it."

He shook his head. "And you think you can stop me from getting in there?" He put the bottle on the floor, dropped his hands on her waist, and lifted her out of the way like she weighed no more than a toddler. Picking up the champagne and opening the door, he said, "See you later." And went to close it behind him.

But Mya was too quick and she slid through the gap.

Blowing out a frustrated breath, Aiden ran his fingers through his tousled hair.

"What the hell are you doing?" Aiden said, not hiding the frustration in his voice.

"What is she doing in here?" Rachel squealed, sitting in Aiden's bed with the sheet yanked up to her chin.

"I'm sorry, Ms. Fraser, you have to leave," Mya said firmly.

"Aiden, what's going on?" Rachel asked.

He placed the champagne on a dresser and folded his arms across his chest. "Mya, get out."

Mya mimicked his stance. "No."

"Aiden, should I leave?" Rachel asked.

Aiden answered "No," at the same time Mya said, "Yes."

He pinned Mya with a hard stare, and she arched a brow. She wasn't intimidated, and she wouldn't back down.

"You know what?" Rachel slid off the bed with the sheet wrapped around her body. "I'm leaving. There's obviously something going on here."

"Don't go anywhere, Rachel," Aiden said while glaring at Mya.

Rachel hesitated at the foot of the bed, looking uncertainly from Aiden to Mya.

"Actually, you can stay if you'd like," Mya said. At Aiden's smug, satisfied grin, she added, "But there might be… repercussions."

That stopped Rachel in her tracks. "Repercussions? What kind of repercussions?"

"There are no repercussions!" Aiden barked.

Mya's gaze flicked down to Aiden's crotch and back to the reporter. "Off the record, you might need to see a doctor after your 'visit.' But I'd recommend you stay away from him for a few months until he has the situation cleared up. I'm sure you understand."

Rachel looked from Mya to Aiden one last time, then made up her mind. A blank professional smile settled onto her face. "Thank you for your time, Mr. Doyle." She slipped out the door and made her way down the stairs, collecting her clothes as she went.

"Rachel. Rachel! She's lying! There are no repercussions!" Aiden followed her out, trying and failing to talk her back into bed.

Mya used the distraction to pour the rest of the champagne down his bathroom sink.

Aiden flew back into the room, nostrils flaring. "Are you going to cockblock me for the next three months?"

"Yes." And she wasn't sorry. She couldn't bring Noah into a house with a revolving door of women, booze, and parties. For a second, she worried how Amelia was handling Noah's grandparents. Were they buying the twin-swap act?

One crisis at a time. Keeping Aiden out of trouble was her job. And if she had to keep throwing naked women out of his bed and draining bottles of alcohol down the sink, then that's what she'd do.

One of his eyelids twitched several times, and his lips were a harsh line.

"I understand how frustrating this is for you. It is for me, too. Do you think I enjoy babysitting a grown man?"

"Looked like you enjoyed it to me," he grumbled.

"Well, I didn't." With her mum voice, she added, "Stop being difficult." With that, she spun on her heels and stormed from the room.

———

Aiden had seen pissed-off women before, but Mya beat them all. She didn't have to yell and scream to make her point. The subtle movements in her body and the edge in her voice told him she'd reached her limit. What if he kept

SONIA STANIZZO

pushing her buttons? Would she quit and let him go back
to living his life?

No, she had fire behind those black-framed glasses. She
wouldn't give up without a fight.

Maybe he could coax out just the right amount of
anger to get her chest heaving again. The movement had
been a pleasant distraction.

He reminded himself that Mya wasn't his type.

But then, if Little Miss Follow The Rules was throwing
out all the women who were his type, he'd just have to find
new ways to break them.

Chapter 7

Sitting at Aiden's kitchen counter, Mya chewed on her fingernail as she waited for Amelia to finish telling her how the twin swap had gone with Noah's grandparents. "Do you think you convinced Bob and Julie that you were me?"

"They didn't suspect a thing. In fact, I think they like you a little more now. You were very charming," Amelia snickered.

"If you were too sweet, they'd know for sure we switched places," Mya replied wryly. "They rub me the wrong way, and I can't hide my feelings well. What about Noah?"

"Oh, Noah recognized me straight away."

"And he didn't let on?"

Amelia hummed a negative before saying, "The boy's amazing. You need to put him in drama classes."

Groaning, Mya said, "And have to deal with another actor? I'll pass." Her heart rate slowed to normal. "Thank God you pulled it off. I can only imagine what they'd do if they found out."

"They are not taking Noah away from you. Even if they tried, they'd lose. You're a great mother. You make a good living now. They don't have a leg to stand on."

"They'd love to drag up my sordid past to get what they want. All they need is one slipup." To keep herself from nibbling her nails down to the cuticles, Mya rose, grabbed a sponge, and began wiping the kitchen counters.

"That all stopped the minute you found out you were pregnant with Noah. They can't do anything—you've been pure as the driven snow for five years!"

"But now I'm stuck with a man who's doing all sorts of… of *stuff*. If Noah's grandparents find out I'm staying with Aiden Doyle, they'll giggle like kids on Christmas and run to their lawyer with the news that I've shacked up with a lowlife who's putting their grandson in danger. You know they will."

Amelia didn't try to argue; they both knew how Bob and Julie were. "And if they do, we'll fight it. Make that boss of yours testify that it's a job, not a hookup. By the way, have you had a chance to work on your next book for Noah?" her sister asked, changing the subject. "He asked about it after seeing his grandparents."

A flash of guilt lanced through her, she'd been writing stories for Noah for years. When Noah was born, she'd wanted to make something that was personal and sentimental for him. Something he could keep and pass on to his children someday. She'd written twelve of them so far and was working on the thirteenth. "I haven't had time. First all the stuff at work with Mr. Masters and now…"

"And now you have to babysit Aiden Doyle," Amelia finished for her.

"Yeah."

"No worries. Noah's a good kid; I'll just tell him you're still working on it."

"Which I am!"

"Of course you are! Now on to the real reason why you haven't been able to work on the book lately. So, how is that hunky, tortured actor of yours?"

"He's not *my* actor." But he was the reason she hadn't had time to write, and he was tortured, Mya wouldn't deny that. It had been two years, but Aiden's pain still ran deep. The man needed healing, not more booze or another one-night stand.

Unaware of her twin's wandering thoughts, Amelia asked playfully, "Are you going to do what I suggested and practice sexy time with him?" Knowing her sister, she was probably wiggling her eyebrows suggestively.

"No," Mya answered flatly.

"Why not? You have the perfect opportunity to clean the cobwebs out of your vajayjay for when the love of your life shows up."

"If the love of my life shows up, he won't mind the cobwebs."

Amelia laughed. "Trust me, my way will be a lot more fun!" She paused. "Actually, we should go shopping for some cute lingerie because you're not seducing anyone in those floral knickers."

"I'm not seducing anyone, full stop," said Mya. The front doorbell rang. "Sorry, gotta go. Someone's at the door. Love you." Saved by the bell! She would not be shamed for her perfectly sensible choice in undergarments.

She didn't hear Aiden heading toward the foyer. The house was his; he should be the one to get the door. But when the doorbell rang again and there was still no sound coming from upstairs, she walked to the entryway. She was going to live there for three months. Didn't that make it her house now, too?

A pretty woman with dark-brown hair that fell in waves

behind her shoulders, sea-green eyes, and a petite body dressed in a white tank top and floral wraparound skirt stood on the veranda.

How many women was Aiden involved with?

"I'm sorry, Aiden is unavailable," Mya said with a polite smile, not bothering to ask the woman's name or why she was there. It didn't matter anyway; her job was to keep Aiden on the straight and narrow, and that meant no women. "Come back in three months."

As she started to close the door, the woman slapped her hand on the frame. "Wait! Why three months? Is he sick?" she asked.

"No, not sick. Just preoccupied."

The woman raised her eyebrow. "I'm Chloe Doyle. Aiden's sister. I know how my brother likes to *occupy* himself, and I think it's *you* who should be leaving." For a small person, she squared up like she was ready to go a few rounds with a prizefighter.

Instantly contrite, Mya cursed inwardly at her assumptions. "I'm so sorry. I had no idea Aiden had a sister. Please, come in." She held the door wide.

The woman narrowed her eyes and stared at Mya for a beat before entering the house. She walked directly to the living room like she'd been there before. Which if what she said was true, she probably had been. "Who are you, and where's Aiden?" Chloe crossed her arms over her chest, a stubborn set to her jaw.

"I'm Mya Saunders. I work for Houston Studio. Last time I saw Aiden he was… in his room." Mya's face grew warm.

Mistaking Mya's flushed cheeks, Chloe said, "Don't worry, it's not the first time I've busted Aiden with a woman."

"Oh, no. It's not like that," Mya said, waving her

hands. "I work for Mr. Masters, the showrunner for *Family First*."

Chloe's gaze traveled the length of Mya's body. "I should have guessed. You're not his type."

No, not when she dressed in baggy shirts and jeans with her hair pulled back in a low ponytail and glasses perched on her nose. Judging from the women she'd seen him with, his type was drop-dead gorgeous and wearing tight clothes. Mya didn't fit into either of those categories.

Pushing down the twinge of hurt at Chloe's words, Mya said, "You're not the first person to jump to conclusions. I jumped to one myself earlier. I'm sorry."

"No worries. Why don't we start over from the beginning?" The woman stuck out her hand with a gleam of happiness Mya didn't understand in her eye. "I'm Chloe."

Mya shook the proffered hand and flashed Chloe a polite smile. "Nice to meet you."

"What's the story between you and my brother?" Chloe dropped onto the couch, kicked off her heels, and tucked her feet under her, getting comfortable as she waited for Mya to fill the silence.

"Well… ummm… Maybe Aiden should tell you." Mya shuffled her feet. She didn't know how close he was with his family. Chloe appeared comfortable in his house, but that didn't always translate to fondness. She didn't know how much Aiden had told his family, or how much he'd want them to know. And while Chloe seemed to know her way around, it didn't guarantee that the woman was really Aiden's sister. It was better to be safe than sorry.

Stiffening, the woman shifted, leaning forward. "I'd like to hear it from you. Aiden doesn't provide details. I think you'd tell me the truth." The happy sparkle in Chloe's eyes had vanished, replaced by concern.

A second passed.

Followed by another.

Silence stretched between Chloe and Mya, becoming uncomfortable.

"Stop hassling my babysitter."

Both women swung their heads toward Aiden, who stood with his shoulder propped against the doorframe. He hadn't bothered putting on a shirt from his aborted tryst with Rachel Fraser, and Mya's stomach did a little flip-flop at the sight of his bare chest.

Aiden pushed away from the doorframe and sauntered over to Chloe. "I see you've met my nosy sister," he said to Mya as he leaned over and planted a kiss on Chloe's cheek. Well, that answered one question—Chloe was who she said she was.

She threw Aiden a dirty look. "I'm not nosy."

He snorted. "You're always sticking your nose into my business."

"You're family. There's no such thing as nosy when it comes to family." She crossed her arms over her chest. And for a moment, Mya thought she might stick her tongue out at Aiden like a child. "And did I hear you call Mya your babysitter?" She glanced from Aiden to Mya, her brow furrowed with confusion.

"Babysitter… Jailhouse warden. Either is accurate." He threw Mya a dirty look, and she rolled her eyes.

Chloe gave the sigh of a long-suffering sibling and pinched the bridge of her nose. "Someone needs to explain what's going on." She aimed her next comment at Mya. "I'm hoping you can give me some answers because this lump is not making any sense."

Mya sat on the couch next to Chloe and took a deep breath. "Starting yesterday, Mr. Masters, the executive producer at Houston Studio, instructed me to stay with

Aiden for three months and help him…" She looked at Aiden, hoping he'd fill in the blanks, but his lips remained firmly closed. She sighed. There was no way to sugarcoat why she was here. "Aiden's a mess at work. He has a squeaky-clean *Family First* image to uphold, and he's failing miserably. Mr. Masters is giving me a frankly obscene amount of money to watch Aiden twenty-four seven and stop the parties, drinking, and women—hence the cold shoulder earlier. If I can't, *Family First* continues without him." The words poured out in a rush, and Mya slumped back on the couch.

Chloe's eyes grew round, and her mouth opened and closed like she wanted to say something but couldn't find the words. Then she burst out laughing. "That's the best thing I've heard in days!" Tears rolled down her face as she chortled with glee.

"You think it's funny I'm being threatened to clean up my act?" Aiden snapped.

"No, not that part—that might do you good. What's funny is you have a twenty-four-hour babysitter!" Chloe said through her laughter.

"Yeah, it's freaking hilarious," Aiden grumbled.

Not wanting to get in the middle of a minor family reunion, Mya said, "Well, I've delivered the bad news, so now I'll leave you two alone to catch up." Mya rose from the couch. "It was nice meeting you, Chloe."

Chloe wiped away the tears and grinned at Mya. "I'm so happy to have met you. I may be in touch to get updates on my brother's progress with sober living."

Mya didn't know what to say to that, so she just nodded and left the room. What the hell had she gotten herself into?

"I like her." Chloe grinned at Aiden.

"You don't even know her." If he couldn't have a proper drink, a coffee was the next best thing, and he went to the kitchen, hoping his sister would take the hint and leave. No such luck. She followed him and sat at the counter.

He turned on the coffee machine. "Do you want one?"

Chloe propped her chin on her fists. "Yes, please. I'd appreciate it if you could inject it straight into my veins."

Aiden chuckled. That was Chloe: caffeine addict and all-around pain in the arse.

Chloe gasped with shock, and it took him a moment to realize why.

It had been a long time since anything like a laugh had bubbled out of his throat. As gravelly and harsh as it had been, something had loosened in his chest.

One step toward lifting the tightness there. A million more to go.

As Aiden pulled out mugs, he asked, "Shouldn't you be asleep?" He knew that as an agent to some actors working overseas, she didn't keep regular hours.

Chloe waved off his question. "Had an early night. So, tell me about Mya."

He waited for the coffee to brew before answering. Aiden poured each of them a cup and slid one to Chloe, resting a hip against the counter. He shrugged nonchalantly. "Nothing more to say, really. She explained it as well as I could."

"Is what she said true?"

He nodded before taking a sip of coffee.

She set her cup down with a clink. "Wow. All humor aside, I think this might be the best thing for you."

He saw the concern in her eyes, and he focused his attention on the dark liquid in his mug. He'd seen that look so many times from his family. Wanting to help him through his grief. Watching him spiral out of control. Expecting that he'd work his way through the pain to the light at the other side.

But none of them knew what had really happened. They'd all loved Madeline. Thought the sun shone from her arse. The truth would devastate them as it had devastated him. He still couldn't bring himself to process what had happened. Hell, he couldn't really even think about it, just linger near the edges like a bystander outside of the police tape. And even that hurt. He'd dealt with that pain and devastation with booze and women, but all of that had ended when Mya had moved in.

Anger burbled in his chest, and he emptied his coffee in one gulp. "The best thing for me is to be left alone to live my life the way I choose." Whatever happiness he'd felt earlier had been buried beneath the memory of Madeline.

"You haven't been doing a great job of it."

He poured himself another cup of coffee. "That's your opinion. I was quite happy."

"Were you really? Because you haven't cracked a smile in two years. And today, not only did you smile, but you laughed because Mya has taken away all the bullshit you've buried yourself under. I can't wait to see how you'll change after three months."

Aiden threw back his second coffee and placed the mug in the sink. "Nothing's going to change after three months."

Chloe raised an eyebrow like she didn't believe him.

"You can stop with your weekly check-ups on me now. You've been replaced."

"I visit because I want to see you, not because I'm checking up on you."

He chuckled, then stopped himself. He didn't need Chloe making a big deal of it again.

Too late. Chloe beamed at him. "There it is. God, I've missed that beautiful face of yours."

Aiden rolled his eyes. "As you can see, I'm good. You can leave now."

"Fine," she huffed as she slid off the stool. "Ethan and Holly are coming home from their honeymoon tonight, and I'm having a dinner party for them at my place. Mum's bringing dessert. You can bring Mya."

"No." He didn't bother to elaborate.

She grinned. "Well, you have to, don't you?"

"You misunderstood what I said. I'm not coming to dinner tonight." He paused, struggling to come up with a viable excuse. When none appeared, he said, "I'm busy."

She narrowed her eyes at him. "You are not 'busy' because you're on house arrest. Dinner starts at six. Don't be late." Before he could protest further, she walked out of the kitchen. As he chased after her, he heard the click of the front door closing and knew his presence at dinner was mandatory.

That didn't mean he had to bring Mya, though. Surely she couldn't object to him having a quiet evening with his family without her there.

And if, once he'd said his goodbyes, there was the opportunity to blow off a little steam, well, these things happened, didn't they?

Chapter 8

*M*ya spent the next hour exploring Aiden's home, poking into each and every nook and cranny in her search for caches of alcohol. Each room was largely the same, empty of furniture and personal effects with packing boxes piled in the corners.

The kitchen had minimal cooking appliances and utensils. A coffee machine sitting on the counter looked like it was the only thing regularly used. The living room had a lounge suite and stereo system. The only rooms fully furnished were Aiden's bedroom, the nursery, and the library.

After Aiden's sister left, he'd gone into his bedroom. When he didn't come out after a while, Mya thought about checking on him. What if he'd snuck a bottle of alcohol in there? Or worse, she found him naked with an offer to join him in bed again? Deciding to trust him, she left him alone.

Having disposed of the contents of all the bottles she'd found on her second search, she went into the library, hoping to find something to read to pass the time. She ran her fingers gently along the spines of *The Great Gatsby*, *To Kill a Mockingbird*, and *Lord of the Flies*. She didn't understand why he had such an extensive library. It was difficult to imagine him poring over Dostoyevsky. Reading a *Playboy* in bed seemed more his style.

Noticing a box in a corner, she opened it and found it filled with books on a variety of subjects: self-help, mystery, romance, and even a few book club staples like *Eat, Pray, Love* and *Big Little Lies*. At the bottom, she found Jane Austen's *Pride and Prejudice*, *Sense and Sensibility*, and *Emma*. She pulled one out and leafed through the pages.

"You can have them if you like."

Mya jumped, clutched the book to her chest, and spun around. She hadn't heard Aiden come in, and he was standing close enough that her heart skipped a beat. She took a step back. "You shouldn't creep up on people like that!"

"I didn't creep. Anyway, it's my house."

Last time she'd seen him, he'd been only wearing jeans. He'd covered up with a gray T-shirt. She tried to tell herself she was happy about it, what a lie. He should never cover up his body. God, she needed to stop fantasizing about his abs.

"Why are these in a box and not on the shelves? Are they not to your taste?" She put the book away.

"Madeline enjoyed reading those. I'm donating them." His tone was so nonchalant that she immediately suspected that it was false.

"I've noticed the empty rooms and boxes around the house. Are you moving?" She knew she probably shouldn't pry, but she couldn't help herself.

"That's the plan," he said in that same tone. "Most of the stuff in boxes belonged to Madeline."

"It must be hard letting go of your wife's things." Mya thought about the nursery filled with his baby's and Madeline's clothes. The room that was also a memorial.

He shrugged like it meant nothing, though the stiffness in his body told another story. "Never got around to throwing it out. That's all."

Mya didn't buy his dismissive response for a minute, and while it really wasn't any of her business, curiosity won out and she said, "I think you've held on to your wife's things because you still love her."

His expression darkened. If he'd looked tense before, now he was as hard as stone. "Her things mean nothing to me, and my love for her died the moment she did. Actually, months before."

Mya sucked in a startled breath at his harsh words. "That can't be true." Anger was one of the stages of grief, wasn't it? Is that why he was so angry with Madeline? It wasn't her fault she got sick and died.

"I wouldn't be fucking other women if I still loved Madeline," he said bitterly.

"It's your way of masking the pain. The drinking is too."

He shook his head and closed the distance between them. "There's no pain to mask. Would you like me to prove it?"

He ran his hand up her arm to cup her chin in his palm. When his gaze dropped to her mouth, she knew where his intentions lay. She knew he didn't mean it—he was just proving a point—but her body still tingled with the anticipation of the kiss. As he bent his head, the pad of his thumb slid across her lip. She froze like a deer who'd just heard the crack of a twig beneath a hunter's boot, and the book she held slipped from her hand and thudded to the floor.

The sound broke Mya from her trance, and she shoved Aiden away. "I'm not one of those women parading through your house, desperate for your attention. And I'm not a Band-Aid for the open wound your wife left behind." Irritated with what her body had almost allowed her to do, she brushed past him and slammed the library door behind her.

She tried to calm her breathing as she hurried up the stairs and into the nursery. The couch had been as uncomfortable as Aiden had warned, and she'd confirmed that this was the only other room with a bed in the house. Ghosts or not, this was going to be her home for the next three months. She sat on the edge of the bed and scrubbed her hands over her face.

It was all Amelia's fault. She'd encouraged Mya to clear out the cobwebs and practice on Aiden before she began dating again. That's why she'd forgotten herself and let him get too close. She flopped onto her back and stared at the ceiling. She'd been here just over a day, and she'd almost let him kiss her! What would she let him do in three months?

She needed to control herself around him. He was bad news. Not relationship material at all and obviously still in love with his wife, no matter what he said. Why else would he keep this room as a shrine? Then his words came back to her. *My love for her died when she did. Actually, months before.*

What if he'd been telling the truth?

No. Whatever had happened between Aiden and his wife was none of her business. She had bigger things to worry about, like helping Gran or keeping Bob and Julie at bay. Her job was to keep Aiden celibate and sober. And to do that, she needed to make sure her libido didn't overrule her brain every time he got close.

Or every time he walked into the room.
Or every time she thought about him.
She could handle three months of this.
Right?

Chapter 9

*A*iden spent the rest of the afternoon locked in his room, avoiding Mya while replaying the near kiss in the library in his mind. What had he been thinking? He didn't mess around with women like Mya. Aiden preferred a woman who wasn't spitting fire at him for every little thing he did. A woman who didn't need any convincing to take off her clothes. She probably had sex with the light off and her bra on. *Definitely* not his type.

Damn, the urge to taste her full, captivating lips was strong. He hadn't really meant to kiss her, just rattle her cage. However the closer he got to her, the more he wanted to touch her, and all thoughts of why he shouldn't flew out the window. Thank God she'd put a stop to it. Who knows what they might have done if she hadn't?

When it was time to leave for dinner at Chloe's house, he quietly opened his bedroom door, glanced up the hallway toward the nursery where Mya was staying, and paused at the threshold, holding his breath. His ears strained for any sounds indicating Mya was around. When he heard nothing, he let out his breath and headed toward the staircase. This was his house! He shouldn't have to sneak around like a teenager coming home past curfew!

"Just where do you think you're going?" Mya's voice shot out from the top of the stairs as he reached for the front door handle.

Busted!

Aiden's head slumped. Fuck, he'd almost made it. Slowly, he turned around to face Mya. "I'm going to Chloe's for dinner."

She narrowed her eyes. "I don't believe you."

As well she shouldn't, but he wasn't about to tell her that. "Why would I lie?"

"Maybe because you'd rather be drinking and womanizing." Her face flushed pink, and she averted her gaze. He'd bet his right arm that she was thinking of their near kiss.

"Well, you'd be wrong. I'm going to have dinner with my family." It was the truth… mostly. He *was* going to dinner at Chloe's. He just wasn't telling her about the rest of his plan. So it wasn't a lie, per se, just an omission. "You can call her if you'd like." He pulled out his phone and held it out to her.

But she stayed at the top of the stairs. "I'm not supposed to let you out of my sight." She nibbled at her plump bottom lip, and he couldn't look away.

"Unless you can tie me down—as fun as that sounds— I'm going to dinner. Chloe will be pissed if I don't show."

Mya pushed her glasses up the bridge of her nose. "I'm coming with you. Give me a second to change."

"No." If she tagged along, not only would he have to explain her to the rest of the family, but he wouldn't be able to go out and break Lionel's rules once dinner was over.

"You won't let me change?"

"You're not coming with me." He folded his arms across his chest. There was no way he was going to let her spoil his plans. He'd just have to out stubborn her.

She mirrored his stance. "Yes, I am. You know the rules."

He waved her words off. "And rules are meant to be broken. Haven't you ever wanted to live life without restriction?"

Something dark flickered across her features before she managed to stamp it down. What had caused such a somber expression? "That only gets you into trouble."

The way she said it implied that she was speaking from experience. Interesting. "I like trouble."

"That's the problem." She shook her head. "I'm coming with you. Will you wait while I change?"

"No."

Her shoulders sagged, and she sighed. Trotting down the stairs, she caught his wrist and pulled him upstairs.

"Honey, I don't have time for a quickie. Chloe's waiting for me."

She threw him a dirty look over her shoulder. At the entrance of her room, she stopped and turned around. "Stay right here while I change."

Still hoping he'd be able to encourage her to let him out of her sights, he said, "A strip show and a quickie. You've convinced me to stay home." He leaned a shoulder against the doorjamb.

She rolled her eyes at his act. "I'll get changed behind the door. And I'll be talking to you the whole time to make sure you haven't sneaked away," she instructed. Mya pulled what she needed from her suitcase, closed the door halfway, and ducked behind it.

The temptation to peer around the door to see what she was hiding underneath her baggy clothes was strong, but he wasn't that much of an asshole. Sure, he wasn't above a quick peek if the goods were on offer, but Mya had made it clear that they weren't. So as hard as it was, he stayed rooted to the spot.

"So… what's your favorite color?" she asked over the rustle of fabric. He tracked her jeans and T-shirt with his eyes as they sailed to the bed.

She must be standing in her bra and undies. He groaned inwardly, imagining the sight. Did they match? Were they lacy and sexy, or practical and plain? He didn't even care which, he just wanted to see her in them.

"Aiden. Are you still there?" Her head popped out from around the door. Except for an exposed shoulder, the rest of her body was hidden. The pale-pink bra strap entranced him. "Oh good, you're still here. When you didn't answer, I thought you left. So, what's your favorite color?"

"Pink," he answered. "No… blue."

She glanced down at her shoulder, and he knew he'd been caught. She shook her head. Ducking behind the door again, she asked, "What's your favorite meal?"

"Pizza." Although he hadn't had much of an appetite in a while, he was suddenly starving—and he didn't think it was for food. More slithering fabric sounds came from behind the door, and he was glad that his jeans were loose in the front. How long was this torture going to last?

"Favorite movie?"

"*Die Hard*." And that's what would happen to him if he couldn't get the image of her naked from his mind.

She laughed. "Typical guy film."

"Hey! It's got everything! It's even a Christmas movie."

"It is not," she countered, stepping out from behind the door.

Aiden's jaw about hit the floor, and he couldn't think of

a coherent counter to her statement. Mya had changed into a pale-yellow dress with a tiny white flower print. Spaghetti-like straps exposed most of her shoulders, a thin white belt cinched in her waist, and the skirt fell just below her knees. Mya could have worn the dress to church and no one would have said a thing, but Aiden couldn't help but notice the way it clung to her curves and swirled around her legs as she walked to the dressing table. Taking down her ponytail, she fluffed her long blonde hair with her fingers, the waves tumbling past her bare arms.

A flash of heat rushed straight between his legs, and he smothered a moan with a cough.

She glanced over. "Are you okay?"

"Yep. I'm fine." He shifted so that his erection was obscured better. "Are you done? Chloe's waiting." He shoved his hands into his pockets to stop from reaching out and combing his fingers through her hair.

"Just need to put on shoes." She sat on the edge of the mattress and slipped her feet into sandals. "Okay," she said as she hopped to her feet and grabbed a denim jacket. "I'm ready. I swear, minding you is more exhausting than minding Noah. I don't know how I'm going to manage the both of you."

Aiden frowned. What did she mean by 'manage the both of them'? But he didn't ask that, instead he feigned nonchalance and asked, "Who's Noah?"

"My son."

A rush of icy dread flooded through him, extinguishing the burgeoning burning lust he'd been experiencing. Was she married? He didn't see a ring, and she hadn't mentioned a husband. He didn't think Mya was the cheating type. "You never told me you had a son."

She shrugged. "With everything happening, I haven't had the chance."

"Where is he now?" Please say the boy was with his father. Please.

"He's staying with my sister, Amelia, while I get settled. You'll meet him in a couple of days when he comes to stay."

"You want him to stay here?" He could barely get the words out. "That's out of the question."

Her eyes grew round. "He can't stay with Amelia for three months."

"Arrange something else." He crossed his arms over his chest.

"No. I'm not leaving my son for that long. You can't expect me to abandon my child like that."

No, he couldn't, but he didn't have to like it. Through gritted teeth, Aiden said, "I don't like kids. Make sure he stays out of my way."

With a sound of exasperation, she waved her arms to take in the room. "How can you say you don't like kids? You'd planned a family." Realization dawned, and she sucked in a sharp breath, slapping a hand over her mouth. "I'm sorry, I didn't mean… I wasn't thinking…"

Shoving down the riot of emotion, he ran one hand through his hair and said, "Let's go. We're running late." He spun on his heels and headed for the car, not caring if Mya was following him or not.

———

Mya wanted a sinkhole to open up under her feet and swallow her whole. She couldn't leave Noah with Amelia for three months! Bob and Julie would catch on to Amelia's ruse eventually, and besides, Noah wasn't a dog she could drop off at a kennel when he became inconvenient! She'd been so angry that she hadn't considered how insensitive her words were.

But how could he say he didn't like kids when he had a roomful of baby things to suggest otherwise? She might be biased, but who couldn't love a beautiful boy like Noah? Aiden hadn't met him, but once he did, he'd see what a great kid he was.

They sat in stony silence on the drive to Chloe's house. When Mya couldn't take it any longer, she began, "I'm sorry for—"

"It's fine," he snapped, cutting her off. The tendons on the backs of his hands stood out as he tightened his grip on the steering wheel.

"Losing your baby… I can't imagine what you're going through."

His glance was icy cold. "I said it's fine."

Even though it obviously wasn't fine, she let the matter drop. Tears pricked the back of her eyes for his loss. She could see his pain even if he didn't want to acknowledge it. Changing the subject, she asked, "Are we really going to Chloe's house for dinner?"

"Yes. Why?"

"I thought you were going to some strip club or dingy bar."

"Maybe next time." He flicked her a glance—warmer this time—and a small smirk played at the corner of his lips. "Unless *you* want to go to a strip club or dingy bar?"

Her answer was a no-way-in-hell glare.

Aiden shrugged. "You're missing out on a lot of fun. Oh, wait, you're the have-no-fun police."

Mya rolled her eyes.

They pulled up to a charming sandstone terrace in Balmain with a black wrought iron railing and pots of colorful flowers on the small porch.

Getting out of the car, Mya smoothed out the skirt of her dress and turned toward Aiden. When his gaze traveled the length of her, his eyes sparked with something that looked very much like desire. While her summer dress was simple, when he looked at her that way, it felt like she was wearing something sexy.

A light on the terrace's veranda flicked on, and Chloe came bounding from the house. "You're late." She scowled at Aiden, then gave Mya a hug. "I'm so happy to see you again, Mya."

A little taken aback by the warm gesture, Mya stiffened in Chloe's arms. "Lovely to see you too," she said into Chloe's shoulder.

Chloe held Aiden's hand and pulled him toward the house while Mya followed. "Mum, Ethan, and Holly are already here," Chloe said.

Mya paused on the top step. "It's not just us?" Aiden hadn't mentioned his family were joining them. If looks could kill, he'd be dead. His brother, Ethan, had won an Oscar and a BAFTA for goodness' sake! She should have worn something fancier or at least done her hair. Oh God, she'd have to keep her inner fangirl under tight rein.

"No worries, Mya. I've told them all about you, and they're excited to meet you," Chloe said.

Aiden snorted. "No doubt you've exaggerated everything."

Chloe's head tilted to the side, and she playfully shrugged her shoulders. "Just told them what I saw."

Aiden narrowed his eyes at his sister, which only made her laugh.

Mya was confused. What could she have seen? Their meeting that morning had been brief. There couldn't be much to tell.

Noticing Mya's hesitation, Chloe linked her arm

through Mya's and pulled her and Aiden inside into the living room where Aiden's family had gathered.

"Everyone, this is Mya. Aiden's *babysitter*." She gave the Doyles an exaggerated wink, and Mya blushed. "Mya, this is my brother, Ethan; his wife, Holly; and my mother, Nancy," she said as she pointed to each family member in turn.

As Chloe introduced Mya to her family, she couldn't help being starstruck. Sure, famous people passed through her office at work every day, but Ethan had won an Oscar for one of her favorite movies. She had to stamp down her inner fangirl as she shook his hand. He was slightly taller than Aiden, with darker hair. His eyes weren't as green, nor did they have shadows dimming the sparkle as he smiled. All three Doyle siblings bore a strong resemblance to each other, and they'd all hit the good-looks jackpot. Observing their mother, Nancy, it wasn't hard to see who they got their looks from.

"You were amazing in *The Last Man*. Your performance was absolutely brilliant. It's the best movie I've ever seen!" The words tumbled free, gushing out of her like water out of a burst dam. To her ears, her voice was high pitched, breathless.

So much for controlling her inner fangirl.

"I'm glad you enjoyed it." Ethan glanced past her at Aiden and chuckled. "I like her."

Well, at least Ethan didn't think she was a complete nutter.

"It's so lovely to meet you." Aiden's mother glided forward with a friendly smile. She gave Mya a warm hug, gold and silver bracelets chiming on her arm. Nancy whispered, "I'm so grateful you're looking after Aiden. I know he'll be so much better now you're in his life." When Nancy pulled away, Mya noticed a sheen to

Nancy's eyes and a wobble in her chin. Mya knew the look: a mother who loved her son and wanted the best for him.

But surely the Doyles weren't relying on her to pull him out of whatever funk he was in? Mr. Masters had directed her to get Aiden's life on track for work, that was all. His personal life was none of her business. But she couldn't squash Nancy's hope, so she smiled. "I'll try my best."

Next, Holly gave Mya a welcoming embrace. Mya was quickly learning that the Doyles were big huggers. Belatedly, she realized that Holly and Nancy had also won Oscars for Ethan's movie—they'd worked behind the scenes. "Congratulations to you two as well! You're all so talented! I'm afraid you've got me a little starstruck."

They all chuckled except for Aiden, who slouched, brooding, in a chair in the corner of the room, looking like he had better places to be than at a family gathering.

"I need to check on dinner," Nancy said, distracting Mya from Aiden's moodiness.

Holly and Chloe stood too. "Mya, will you come keep us company?" Holly said.

"I promise we're much more fun than Aiden," Chloe said, sticking her tongue out at him when he glowered at her.

Mya nodded and followed them to the kitchen.

"Thank you again for taking care of Aiden," Nancy said as she put on oven mitts and pulled a roasting pan from the oven. "We've tried helping him through the loss of his family for two years now, but he just pushes us away." The smell of roasted pork and potatoes drifted through the room.

Chloe sat at the breakfast counter and watched her mother- and sister-in-law bustling around the kitchen preparing dinner. "I don't cook," Chloe said, catching

Mya's curious expression. "I provide the house and clean up at the end, and they provide the culinary skills."

"I swear Chloe could burn water!" Holly giggled.

Mya chuckled at that, then turned serious. "Nancy, I don't want to get your hopes up. My job is to get Aiden ready for the new season of *Family First*. I'm supposed to keep him out of the tabloids and try to salvage his reputation in the entertainment business. Anything personal he's going through is beyond the scope of my responsibilities. And, frankly, my abilities."

Nancy paused in slicing the roast and put the knife down. "From what Chloe told us, you're already helping him personally."

Mya looked at Chloe, brows furrowed. "But I barely spent any time with you this morning."

"It was what happened after you left."

"I don't understand," Mya said, confused.

"Aiden smiled. He even chuckled! Do you know how long it's been since I've heard him laugh?" Chloe continued without waiting for Mya to answer. "Two years. He hasn't laughed since Madeline and their baby passed away." Chloe frowned, her eyes growing distant. "Maybe even before that."

"Are you saying I had something to do with that?" It seemed outrageous.

"Yes, I am. Whatever it is you're doing, please keep it up."

"We've mostly been getting on each other's nerves. I can almost guarantee that'll continue to happen." Mya didn't think the few instances of smoldering heat between her and Aiden were worth mentioning. Especially not to Aiden's family.

As Holly wiped her hands on a tea towel, she said, "I don't know if you're aware, but he hasn't taken his eyes off you since you both arrived. He doesn't look annoyed. More… interested."

Mya wrinkled her nose. "You've read his expression wrong. I am definitely not his type. He's told me that enough times," she said with a self-deprecating chuckle. "He's throwing daggers at me because of the news I dropped before we left the house."

"What news?" Nancy asked. "Nothing bad, I hope."

"I suppose it depends on your point of view. I told him my son Noah is coming to live with us. I'm hoping to bring him over in a few days."

All movement in the kitchen stopped, and the Doyles stared at Mya with wide eyes. She felt like a specimen under a microscope.

Nancy was the first to speak. Clearing her throat, she said, "You have a son? How old is he?"

"He's five."

"And Aiden agreed he could stay?" Nancy fussed with the meat on the serving platter.

"I have to live with Aiden for three months until the show starts shooting again. He doesn't have a choice. There's no way I'd leave my son for that long." By their solemn faces, Mya worried there was something seriously wrong with Aiden beyond the drinking and the women. "Should I be concerned about having Noah around Aiden?" If he posed a threat to her son's safety, she'd leave. The money meant nothing compared to Noah.

Nancy gasped, rushed to Mya, and grabbed her hands. "Oh no, nothing like that, I promise! It's just that after Madeline lost the baby, Aiden hasn't been himself. He can't even look at another child. It must drag up too many painful memories. Maybe being around Noah, he'll see things differently and it will help him heal."

Mya doubted that. Aiden had made it clear he didn't

want Noah around him. And she planned to keep them apart as much as possible.

Thankfully, Mya didn't have to respond to Nancy's wishful thinking because Ethan sauntered into the kitchen, wrapped his arms around his wife's waist, and nuzzled her neck. "How's my favorite dish?"

"Get a room, you two. The honeymoon's over." Chloe's tone was wry, but she had a smile on her face.

Watching the pair, it appeared that the honeymoon glow was going to last a long time. Mya held back a sigh. She didn't like her chances of finding a man who looked at her like Ethan looked at Holly. It was hard enough finding men interested in dating a single mum. When they learned about Noah, they dropped from the face of the earth. Now that she was stuck babysitting Aiden, her search had been put on hold for longer.

Oh well. She'd been single this long—what's a few more months?

Chapter 10

*D*inner took longer than Aiden had expected. Ethan and Holly gave a day-by-day description of their honeymoon in Africa, so the meal dragged on.

Mya genuinely seemed to enjoy their stories, laughing and asking questions and cooing happily over the photos on their mobiles. The rest of his family had already welcomed her like she'd been in his life for years. They'd better not get too comfortable having her around—once *Family First* started shooting again, she was out of his house and out of his hair. Her and her kid.

On second thought, maybe having the kid around would be a good thing. If she was distracted by the boy, maybe Aiden could break a few rules while her back was turned.

When they returned to Aiden's house, Mya headed for the kitchen. "Coffee?" she asked. Plain Janes weren't his type, but the way Mya's hips swayed beneath her skirt made her seem anything but *plain*.

She paused at the door and turned to him with a raised eyebrow. What did she want? He racked his brain. *Oh!*

She'd asked if he wanted coffee. He cleared his throat. "I'd love a cup."

She nodded and disappeared through the doorway. He blew out a long breath, ran his hands through his hair, and followed. Christ, he needed to get out of here. One cup, and he'd wait for her to go to bed. Then he was out of here. He needed alcohol and a woman. And it didn't need to be in that order.

Pulling two mugs from the cupboard, she put them on the counter and waited for the coffee to brew. "Your family is great. You're very lucky."

He snorted. "You wouldn't say that if it was your life they were interfering in."

Mya shrugged. "Maybe. You've still got a good family."

"If you say so." He motioned to the coffee. "You gonna pour that?"

"I'm not your maid," she said as she filled two mugs, adding milk and sugar to hers and passing the other to Aiden. "And I do say so. Your family is great. They love you and want to know you're okay. Having a family who cares for you like that is wonderful."

He took a seat at the breakfast bar, and Mya sat next to him. Their thighs brushed together, and Mya twitched away like she'd been shocked. Even so, her movement wasn't fast enough to stop the flame of desire from shooting through his veins. What the hell was wrong with him? Why did he have such an overreaction from a simple touch?

The pink in her cheeks suggested she'd felt something too. Interesting.

To get his mind off wanting to strip Mya naked and bend her over the kitchen counter, he asked, "Do you have any other family apart from your sister and your..." He forced himself to say the word. "... your son?"

She stared into her mug, swirling it idly. "My mother died when we were young. I never knew my father. Gran raised us, but she's been ill, and we had to put her in a nursing home a few months ago. Mum was an only child, so there're no aunties, uncles, or cousins. At least, none that I know of." The corners of her mouth dropped.

"I'm sorry to hear that," Aiden said. And he genuinely meant it. "I lost my dad at ten. It was the worst time of my life. But we were lucky to have Mum; she was our champion. Things got tough when she was grieving, but she held us together so we all came out the other side."

She slid her palm across the counter and gave his hand a comforting squeeze before realizing what she'd done and snatching her hand away. "Nancy is awesome. I love her even though I've just met her."

Aiden smiled. "She has that effect on everyone." After everything she'd done for him, it had been hard to see the worry etched into her face over the last two years. Tonight, though, there had been something else. Hope? What did she have to be hopeful about?

"Your whole family is great! How did you all end up in the entertainment business?"

"Ethan started the ball rolling. A clip of his school play went viral, and an agent scouted him. He was in a few commercials, and then he got some small roles in TV shows and movies. When he started starring in blockbusters, he scored jobs for Mum and me. Mum was the glue that held the family together, but Ethan's paychecks put food on the table until we were all independent. I even owe him my career." A career he was pissing up the wall.

She nodded. She wouldn't be here if he weren't killing his golden goose.

Lightning flashed outside the window, a crash of

thunder soon rattling the plates in the cupboard. Mya nearly jumped out of her skin.

Aided eyed her with amusement. "You scared of storms?"

"No, it just startled me." She jumped off of her stool. "I actually love them! I'm going outside to watch it."

He stared at her like she'd sprouted another head. "Are you crazy? It's dangerous."

She waved his protestations away. "I won't stand out in the open with a metal rod. I'm not that silly. I'll stay under the awning."

As she headed for the French doors, Aiden realized that this was his chance to give her the slip and go wherever the hell he wanted to. He could say good night and be in his car and out of sight before the distraction of the storm passed.

But that would mean he would have to tear himself away from the endlessly fascinating Mya. A woman who seemed to be everything and nothing like she seemed. Intrigued, he followed her outside.

As he stepped out onto the veranda, she tossed him a smile over her shoulder, and it hit him like a bolt of lightning to the chest. Dammit! He wasn't supposed to be feeling things like this. Not about her. Never about her.

He turned his attention to the sky, where lightning lit up the night. Again, when the thunder smashed, Mya jumped.

"Are you sure you're not scared of the storm?" he asked, amused. "You jump every time there's thunder."

"I know it's coming, but it still catches me off guard. It's just a reflex reaction," she said without taking her eyes off the sky. A blast of cold air hit them, and she shivered.

"Are you cold?"

She rubbed her bare arms. "A little. I left my jacket inside."

"Here," he said as he pulled off his coat. "Put this on." He placed it on her shoulders, letting his hands linger.

Her long blonde hair caught under the collar, so he slid his hands to her neck and slowly pulled her hair free. The soft strands slid through his fingers like silk. Goose bumps pebbled her skin.

"Is that better?" His voice came out as a husky whisper.

She turned toward him, as if to speak, and brushed her cheek against his hand. Her eyes were heavy lidded, sensual and inviting. His hand moved to cup her chin, and he ghosted his thumb across her full lips. He was dying to taste them. Would they be as soft as he imagined? Would she even let him kiss her? Aiden hoped the answer would be yes.

Mya shifted ever so slightly, their bodies touched. Her breath quivered as she inhaled. As if making up her mind, she put her hands on his waist and guided him closer. He gasped when her breasts pressed against his chest. They felt fuller than he'd suspected, and he longed to touch them, to suck them, to see them bobbing as she moved beneath him.

"Mya?" It was a question, a request for permission.

She nodded. "Please…" The word came out as a whisper filled with need. A need that echoed deep inside.

He lowered his head, hovering above her mouth, and she bit her lower lip with… with what? Anticipation? Uncertainty? Hunger? Then her tongue darted out and all doubts flew from his mind. He crushed his lips against hers as the storm rolled ever closer. For a second, she didn't move, didn't react, and regretfully, he pulled away. Mya let out a soft moan and melted against him, wrapping her arms around his neck and surrendering herself to the kiss.

It was a surrender he was quick to take advantage of. Deepening the kiss, he slanted his mouth over hers, tongue slipping out to taste her lips. Trace the seam of her mouth. Coax her tongue out to play. She tasted like caramel and coffee, a heady combination. Aiden couldn't tell if the pounding in his ears was thunder or his own racing heart. If lightning still flashed, it paled in comparison to the electricity between the two of them.

Breaking away from her lips, he trailed kisses over her jaw, down to her neck, his tongue lingering over her beating pulse. "God, you taste sweet," he mumbled against her smooth skin. He could spend a lifetime kissing her like this.

He stumbled away from her. Where the fuck had that thought come from? Sure, he'd take her to bed in a heartbeat, but that was all. One good fuck, then call you never. No lifetime commitment, no endless kissing, no emotional connection. He didn't do forever. Not anymore.

The desire he'd seen on Mya's face only moments before morphed into surprise. She touched her lips, then shrugged out of his jacket and handed it to him; Little Miss Follow The Rules was back. "It's late. We should go to bed." Even in the dim light, he could see her blush. "I should go to bed. And you should go to bed. Separately. Not together. Definitely not that." She scurried past him back into the house.

Aiden blew out a long breath, put his hands on the railing of the veranda, and hung his head. The mist of the rain dampened his hair, but he didn't move. Why the hell had he kissed Mya? Was he a horny teenage boy who couldn't go two days without getting his rocks off? If she had this effect on him in a matter of days, how could he possibly last three months?

Then he remembered that she wanted her son to move in, and his dick deflated like a popped balloon. There was nothing like a kid to pour cold water on the whole situation. Hopefully a lot of cold water.

He needed to get out of the house. To forget about Mya and wash away the taste of her lingering on his tongue. Alcohol. He needed alcohol. Stat. He marched into the house and grabbed his keys from the kitchen counter. Once inside his car, he cranked up AC/DC so loud he could feel the music vibrating through the seat and took off for the nearest club.

There was nothing like some booze and barhopping to cure what ailed him. Specifically an unwelcome attraction to his boss-appointed babysitter.

———

Mya placed her fingers on her tingling lips and stared at herself in the bathroom mirror. Her mouth looked pinker and a little swollen from Aiden's kiss. Her cheeks were pink too, and her eyes shone with something she couldn't immediately identify. When was the last time she'd been kissed so masterfully? Like every stroke of his tongue rippled through her entire body?

Never. Her drunken hookups had never been interested in her pleasure. Even Daniel, Noah's father, hadn't really understood how to make her feel so alive, like electricity crackled through her veins and warmed her from the inside out.

And it had only been a simple kiss! Clothes on, feet firmly on the ground! But damn, it made her want to explore the next step with Aiden. Maybe even the one after that.

She turned the light off in the bathroom, changed into her pajamas, and slipped into bed.

Thank God he'd had the good sense to stop things before it went further. Because she didn't know if she would have been able to. She wanted him too much.

She shook her head. What was wrong with her? He wasn't the type of man that should make her feel this way. He wasn't her type. Or at least he wasn't the kind of man that she wanted. She wanted someone loyal, hardworking, and sober. Someone who'd love Noah. Someone who would love her. Aiden was none of those things. The look on his face when she'd told him about Noah and that she was bringing him here... Well... it spoke volumes. Noah was a deal breaker. And she wasn't his type. While she'd hoped they'd at least get along, it didn't seem to be in the cards. Because like it or not, Noah was going to live with them for the next three months. Mya and Noah were a package deal, so Aiden would surely keep his distance.

She had to believe that was the case, because she was beginning to think Amelia was right about cleaning out the cobwebs. And that Aiden was just the person she wanted to do it.

Chapter 11

*A*iden's alarm went off way too early the next morning, and he stared blearily at the screen of his phone. It took him a moment to recall that he'd set it with the intention of working out in the gym he'd set up in the garage. Drunk Aiden had thought it was a good idea. Hungover Aiden disagreed.

He needed coffee. Now. Once he'd shuffled to the kitchen, he poured himself a cup in the largest mug he had and gave a happy sigh as the bitter scent filled his nostrils. Coffee truly was a gift from the gods.

"Rough night?"

Aiden turned and found Mya sitting at the counter, a laptop open in front of her. He hadn't noticed before, too impatient for his morning caffeine fix. "Nothing out of the ordinary." Taking a sip of coffee, he leaned his hip against the counter.

"You're right. Last night wasn't anything different from how you've been spending the last two years of your life." Her anger was almost palpable. "I swear I need to hang a cowbell around your neck so I can hear when you're trying to sneak out. Or better yet, we need one of those invisible fence systems for dogs that gives you a shock if you try to go out of bounds. Except I think your average Yorkie has a shorter learning curve."

His laughter died as she spun the laptop to face him.

Some gossip website was pulled up in her browser, and a picture of him at The Factory filled the screen. Empty bottles littered the table in front of him, and he was flanked by two women. Mya clicked to the next picture, and he saw himself nuzzling the neck of the woman on his right, whose hand was perilously close to his crotch.

"It's not what it looks like," he began lamely.

"No one cares about your explanations or your excuses, Aiden!" Mya shouted.

"I needed to blow off steam." But he hadn't. The second photo had caught the moment when he'd told the woman he wasn't interested in what she was offering. He hadn't been able to get the kiss he'd shared with Mya off his mind, and since he couldn't have Mya, he hadn't wanted anyone.

Based on the daggers she was shooting him, he still couldn't have her. Ever.

"Well, I hope your steam was worth it," she snapped. "I had to beg Mr. Masters for a second chance. Mine, not yours. I think he's written you off as a lost cause."

Aiden winced. Mya's cheeks were full of color, and she was breathing hard, her chest heaving. He couldn't help but remember the night before, when she'd been flushed with her chest heaving for a different, much more pleasant reason.

And... he probably shouldn't be turned on right now.

"I'm supposed to visit Gran today. I was hoping I could

leave you for an hour, but obviously, I can't. God"—she slapped a hand on the counter as she rose from the seat —"you're more of a troublemaker than my five-year-old. I'm leaving in ten minutes. Be ready."

Aiden chuckled as she slammed her laptop shut and stalked out of the kitchen. He scrubbed a hand through his hair. He should feel bad for all the trouble he'd caused her, but she was sexy when she was angry. Maybe she'd be just as fiery in bed. He tried to bury the image of her face and the feel of her lips deep down but found he wanted to bury himself deep inside her instead.

God help him during these next three months. He was going to need it.

Mya drummed her fingers on the steering wheel, but what she really wanted to drum was Aiden's head. With sledgehammers. Sure, she was mad that he'd caused her to beg for her job, but she was also mad that after they'd kissed, the first thing he'd done was go out and pick up women. It was humiliating. Soul crushing.

She'd felt something in his arms. But clearly he hadn't. And worse, she'd fallen for it! The husky voice and the bedroom eyes and the lingering kisses... The man was an actor, and she'd fallen for his act hook, line, and sinker. He'd been the one to break off the kiss, and then he'd immediately shown how little it had mattered to him.

Aiden had shown his true colors, and Mya wouldn't be fooled again.

For now, she needed to let last night go and fill him in on Gran's condition. Pulling into a parking spot, she killed the ignition and twisted in her seat to face him. "Gran has

Alzheimer's. She has her good and bad days. Sometimes she recognizes me, other times she thinks I'm my mother or doesn't know me at all."

"I'll stay in the car and wait for you. It might confuse her seeing an unfamiliar face." Normally, she'd agree, but he'd already proven she couldn't trust him. "Pfft, no chance. I'd rather my car be right where I left it, and I have no intention of spending the day going from club to club looking for you."

"They're not open this early," he said with a grin that made her tummy flip.

She was still too angry for any of his attempts at charm to work on her. "You're coming inside with me. I'm not letting you out of my sight."

After signing in, they went in search of Gran. Usually she liked to sit with the other patients in the common room, but a nurse told her she was in her room knitting. Gran had forgotten how to do a lot of things, but knitting wasn't one of them—yet.

"Hi, Gran." Mya smiled, hoping Gran was having one of her better days.

"Hi, my sweet Mya." Gran smiled back, and Mya gave her a kiss on the cheek. Seeing the recognition in Gran's eyes instantly turned her day around. She just hoped Gran's clarity would last.

Mya turned to Aiden. "This is…" What the hell did she call him? Her coworker? Man-child she had to babysit? The man who was doing funny things to her insides? Their relationship was too complicated to easily explain. "My friend, Aiden." Aiden arched an eyebrow, a smile twitching the corners of his mouth. "Aiden, this is my grandmother, Celia."

"Lovely to meet you." He turned on the charm that

had thousands of women tuning in to *Family First* every week.

"Oh my. You are a handsome young man. Mya, I like him already." Gran's knitting sat forgotten on her lap.

Ignoring her grandmother's comment, Mya perched on the edge of the bed. "How are you feeling today?"

"My knee's playing up; that's why I'm not with the others playing cards. Too much of an effort to cart myself out there."

"I can help you if you'd like."

Her grandmother waved her hand. "No need. Margarete's only going to cheat again, anyway. I'd rather stay here and talk to you and your handsome husband. He reminds me so much of my Jonny."

Mya and Aiden both made a choking sound.

"Gran, he's my friend. *Not* my husband."

"Have you seen Jonny? I know he'd like to meet you." Her eyes were pale and watery. Mya's heart sank. Just like that, the day had turned sour again.

"What are you making, Gran?" Mya asked, trying to pull her back to the present.

Gran looked at her lap and picked up her knitting. "It's for my granddaughter Mya, she's having a baby."

Lifting the soft wool, she showed Mya the start of a little white cardigan. When Mya had been pregnant with Noah, Gran made a lot of these with matching booties. Then, the stitches had been tight and even. Now, even to her untrained eye, Mya could see the imperfections.

"It's beautiful," Mya said, her voice unsteady.

"You've always loved my knitting. And when your new baby arrives, she can wear this too. Just like Noah did."

A heaviness sat on Mya's chest. Gran was very confused today. Now she thought that there was a new baby on the way. Where had that come from?

It was best if they left. The longer they stayed, the more confused Gran would become. If she became too confused, she'd get upset, and the nurses would have to give her something to calm her down. Mya didn't want that.

Mya stood and gave Gran a kiss. "I'll be back again soon, Gran. I love you."

"Love you too, honey pie." Her grandmother turned her attention to Aiden. "I'm so glad Mya married you. I hoped my girls would find a good man like my Jonny, and I was so sad when my daughter, Helen, and then Mya didn't. They both made questionable choices in their men." She reached out and patted the back of Aiden's hand. "I know you'll look after her. Give her the love and respect that she deserves."

Mya's chin hit the floor at her grandmother's speech. What was that? For a moment, she was too scared to see Aiden's reaction. Nothing she'd said could have prepared him for this curveball.

Taking a peek at Aiden, she saw a warm smile instead of a look of horror. He leaned over and gave Gran a gentle hug. "Don't you worry. I will take good care of Mya," he said as he straightened. He took Mya by the hand and waved at Gran as they left.

Once outside of the room and out of earshot, he dropped her hand, and his expression of happiness dropped with it.

"I'm sorry about that," said Mya. "She only ever gets visits from family, so she must have assumed you were family too."

"No need to apologize."

"What she said… about us being married and having a baby—"

"It's okay. She's not well."

"But if it upset you—"

"It's fine. I'm fine." He stopped at the passenger side of the car and waited for her to unlock the door with a surly expression on his face.

Something told her he was not *fine* at all.

Chapter 12

"She mistook Aiden for your husband?" Amelia asked through poorly concealed laughter.

"It's not funny. He didn't look happy when we got into the car." Mya sat in the living room with her feet tucked underneath her on the phone with her sister. From the garage came the twin sounds of heavy bass and Aiden working a punching bag. As long as she heard him exercising, she didn't need to check in to see if he'd sneaked out again, risking his job and Gran's chance at a nicer nursing home.

"He'll get over it. Have you given any more thought about blowing out your cobwebs?" Amelia asked. Mya imagined the smirk on her sister's face.

"Umm…" The memory of the kiss with the storm as a backdrop entered her mind, and she bit her bottom lip, trying to stop herself from sighing. "Definitely not going to happen."

There must have been something in her voice because from the other end of the phone she heard Amelia gasp and say, "Oh my God. Something's changed."

"Nothing's changed," she said, lying through her teeth and hoping her sister wouldn't notice. "He's still a man-child needing constant supervision." If she told her sister they'd kissed, she'd go nuts about it. Better to keep it to herself.

"No, not your arrangement. Something has changed between the two of you. I bet you've kissed!"

"Wait… what? Why would you say that?"

"Twin bond. And I can tell by your voice. So, tell me: is he a good kisser?"

They did share a twin bond, often feeling what the other was feeling. Sometimes it came in handy. Right now, it was annoying, because it meant she couldn't lie to Amelia.

"Fine. Yes, we kissed."

"I knew it!" Amelia crowed.

Mya ignored her sister's jubilant outburst and continued, "*I* thought it was amazing. Not so great for him, though." If he'd felt a smidgen of what she had, he wouldn't have gone out looking for women to *blow off steam* with.

All sounds of celebration stopped. "What happened?"

"We were watching last night's storm. When I got a bit cold, he put his jacket on my shoulders, and then it just happened."

"You kissed?"

"We kissed," Mya confirmed. "But as quick as it began, he pulled away. I thought he was going to bed, but instead he went out to a club, and an online tabloid website caught him drunk with women hanging all over him. I almost lost this gig because of his midnight adventure." She blew out a frustrated breath. "This job is more than I bargained for."

"I'd say it's the most excitement you've had in years," Amelia chuckled. "I love it, and it's good for you."

"'It's good for me.' Are you insane? Did you hear what I said?"

"Yes, and this is what I think. From the beginning, we knew Aiden wouldn't be easy to live with. That's why Noah is staying with me for a few days so you can sort him out. We also knew he was a man-slut, although the media likes to blow things out of proportion, so he may not be as bad as we think. And we knew he's not husband material. Even if it's exaggerated, you don't need to be with someone with his reputation. *But* he's the perfect bloke to fool around with. Hot as hell, a ripped body, no strings attached... And I bet he's phenomenal in bed."

"Even if I agreed with everything you said—which I'm not—he pulled away from the kiss. He's not interested."

"Hmmm. He must have had a reason."

"Yes, and the reason is he's not attracted to me!"

"We can fix that. A bit of silk, some lace underwear, something to show off those legs of yours," Amelia said, getting caught up in making over her twin.

"I'm not dressing up for any man." Mya snapped. The time for putting on a miniskirt and a tight top to attract attention was long past. She used to love the power she felt when she'd dressed sexily, but that had all changed. Now, the thought of wearing a push-up bra and high heels brought up memories of a time she'd rather forget.

"Fine, I'll stop pushing," Amelia said with a sigh. "But are you even dressing for you? Hiding underneath baggy clothes can't be making you feel good about yourself. If you like them, that's fine, but I know you."

Amelia did know her. If she had a choice, she'd bin her entire wardrobe and start over from scratch. But that wasn't going to happen. She had to play the part of the respectable matron in order to keep Bob and Julie at bay. Mya picked at a thread on the bottom of her jeans. "I don't want to draw any attention to myself."

Her sister seemed to pick up on what she wasn't saying. "Noah's grandparents won't take him away because you're wearing a short skirt. You can't let them rule your life."

"I'm not taking any chances."

Amelia was silent for a beat, probably sensing Mya wanted to drop the subject, then said, "Who initiated the kiss?"

Mya groaned. Amelia wouldn't stop with the questions unless she gave her something. "Aiden."

"So he's obviously attracted, but we need to know why he pulled away."

Mya thought back to the night before when she'd told him about Noah. He hadn't reacted well, and Nancy said he had a hard time being around children. Maybe that was the problem. "I told him about Noah, and he wasn't happy about him coming to stay here. After losing his newborn baby, he stays away from kids. I guess he remembered I come with a child, and it turned him off."

"That sucks if that's the case. I remember reading about his wife and baby." Amelia sighed, and Mya could almost visualize the expression on her twin's face. "You might be right," she said grudgingly, "he might think you're looking for a new daddy for Noah. But if you make it clear you only want sex, then all is good in your world."

"All is not good. I am looking for a new daddy for Noah. I don't want a man who'll be with me one minute, then run to another woman the next."

"Oh, honey. If you're doing it right, he won't be running from you at all. He'll never let you out of his bed."

Mya had to laugh. Her sister was too much.

The music coming from the garage stopped. Mya got

off the lounge and walked to the front window to see if Aiden was leaving in his car. What could she do if he did? Call the police and tell them a grown man had left the house? She needed to find his keys and keep them on a chain around her neck.

"I'm going for a shower, not running away." Aiden's deep voice rumbled behind her.

Mya spun around, and her mouth fell open. Aiden stood at the bottom of the stairs wearing gray gym shorts with no shirt and a towel draped over his shoulders. Sweat from his workout flowed in rivulets down his chiseled abs. His dark hair was damp and disheveled. Her knees shook. He was the sexiest man she'd ever seen.

"I wasn't… I didn't…" Her tongue tangled in her mouth, leaving her unable to speak.

"You wanna join me?" he asked with a raised brow.

"What's happening? Is Aiden there?" Amelia said in her ear.

"Yes," she answered.

Aiden's eyes widened for a beat. A satisfied smirk settled on his face. Mya realized he must have thought she was speaking to him.

Putting out her hand like a stop sign, she held out the phone and waved it in his general direction. "My sister! I was talking to my sister!"

"Mya, tell me what's going on." Amelia's voice rose with impatience.

Aiden shrugged. "If you change your mind, you know where I'll be." Mya watched him jog up the stairs.

A long sigh escaped her lips as she dropped onto the couch. "Oh God."

"What? Don't leave me in suspense. What. Just. Happened?" Amelia's impatience came through with an edge to each word.

"Aiden finished a workout and… and…" Mya shook her head to banish the half-naked, sweaty man from her mind. It didn't work.

"*And* what? Mya, if you don't spit it out, I will come down there and find out what's going on myself!"

"Calm down. Aiden jokingly asked if I wanted to join him in the shower and thought I'd agreed, but I was really talking to you." Just the thought of the running water coursing down his naked body at this very moment made her shift on her seat.

"Oh, Mya, you're so naive; he wasn't joking. And there's nothing stopping you from taking his offer."

"I'm not getting involved with him, and I'm done talking to you about it. When Noah gets home from day care, tell him I'll FaceTime him."

"Okay, I will. And Mya… was Aiden sweaty?"

Mya sighed with defeat. Amelia wouldn't let this drop. "Yes."

"Was he shirtless?"

"Yes."

"Does he have abs carved from stone?"

"Yes."

"Do you want to join him in the shower?"

"Yes," she said through gritted teeth.

Amelia crowed in triumph, "I knew it! Love you. Gotta go."

Chapter 13

*a*fter Aiden showered, he went into the library and scanned the boxes of Madeline's books. He needed to donate them along with the baby furniture and clothing in the nursery, but he couldn't bring himself to pack them up himself. Every time he tried to go into the room, he broke out in a cold sweat. There was no way he could stomach packing up that room; he needed to arrange someone to do it for him. But the thought of strangers pawing through it all made his heart clench. He couldn't do it. While he'd already had the Salvation Army collect the furniture Madeline had picked for their home when they'd moved in, more of her things needed to go before he could sell the house. A house that once had been filled with laughter and joy had now become a pile of shit.

An old *Family First* script sat discarded on a shelf. When he'd auditioned, he'd known the show would be a hit, but no one, not even Lionel, had anticipated the Australian small-town family drama being a worldwide sensation. The show had a phenomenal crew, and the chemistry between the cast members was unbelievable. *Family First* had a lot more life left in it—if his behavior didn't kill it stone dead.

Lionel's threat wasn't empty. He'd give Aiden the axe if it meant saving the show, and Aiden had no doubt that the rest of the cast would be brilliant in the wake of his character's sudden demise.

How much did he want to continue? He'd once loved every moment of filming. Loved his job. But after Madeline… Things didn't look the same, taste the same, feel the same. All the joy had been sucked out of his life.

Until Mya.

Mya had awakened something dormant inside him. His body buzzed whenever she was near. His hands itched to touch her. There was no mistaking the desire for him flashing in her eyes, even if she tried to fight it. It wouldn't take much to convince her this arrangement should be more than a working relationship. They could spend the next few weeks doing more enjoyable things, like spending time in his bed.

At least, they could do that if she didn't have a kid. A son. Who'd be living here with them. What a curveball!

Kids were the ultimate cold shower. An immediate dick deflator. Maybe it was harsh to assume all single mums were looking for a replacement dad for their kiddies, but he couldn't do it. Not after Madeline and the baby. After that, he'd avoided children like the plague.

He'd been joking when he'd asked Mya to join him in the shower. Until she'd said yes, anyway. Then all his blood had drained to his dick, and he'd imagined her naked, wet, and slippery with his hands sliding all over her body. It had actually been a relief when she'd showed him the phone and told him she was talking to her sister.

As much as he wanted her, he'd keep his hands to

himself. He couldn't risk her wanting to get serious when his commitment was to keeping things casual.

His phone vibrated on the desk for the fourth time today. Women he'd met at the clubs—beautiful women, the sort that walked runways and made the cover of Vogue —just looking for a quick hookup. He let it go to voice mail. Those women leaned into their sex appeal and fucked like porn stars, but what was currently getting his dick hard was the thought of peeling off baggy layers of clothing and revealing Mya's naked, yearning body underneath.

He raked his fingers through his hair, wishing he could reach inside his head and rip all thoughts of Mya out. "She has a son," he told himself through clenched teeth. He waited for the reminder to work its magic and defuse his erection, but it remained as strong as steel.

Time to take another shower. A cold one.

***

Mya didn't see Aiden for the rest of the afternoon. He'd disappeared into the library for hours. A couple of times she'd held her ear up to the door to listen for any signs of life. It wouldn't surprise her if he'd sneaked out a window. Rustling sounds from inside had confirmed he hadn't escaped.

When the hunger pangs made themselves known, she padded down to the kitchen. The cupboards were mostly bare—bachelor pad this most definitely was—but she managed to scrape together a chicken stir fry. As she went, she made a list for her next grocery shop. She had to set the counter in the kitchen as a makeshift table since the adjacent room that was supposed to be the dining room was empty aside from a pair of cardboard boxes.

She couldn't work out what Aiden's situation with the house was. So many of the rooms had boxes in them and nothing else, but the boxes had a layer of dust on top, which meant he wasn't actively moving in or out. What had been interrupted? Unpacking, or selling the house? If it was the latter, why was it taking him so long?

Before she could call Aiden for dinner, he sauntered into the kitchen. "Something smells delicious." He slid onto a stool while she dished their meal onto the plates.

"It's not much. I didn't have a lot to work with."

"Looks good to me." Taking a bite, he said, "Tastes good, too."

"I'm glad you like it." She set a glass next to him. "Water?"

He screwed up his nose like the glass held poison but accepted it anyway.

Mya chuckled. They sat in silence for a few moments, eating their meal.

"After we visited with your grandmother, I'm sorry if you thought the situation upset me," Aiden said.

"Something bothered you about it." She was surprised he'd brought it up at all.

After another long pause, he said, "I overreacted about the baby thing, that's all. Your grandmother didn't know what she was talking about. She wasn't talking about me, and I should have remembered that."

Losing his wife and baby had cut so deep. Could he ever recover from such a tragedy? She slid her hand along the counter and clutched his. She only meant it to be a comforting touch, but a sizzle of electricity flew up her arm. Did he feel it too? He glanced at their joined hands but showed no emotion.

"Maybe she could sense that you were a husband before," Mya said. Would he share his past with her?

Would talking about it ease some of his hurt? "How long were you married?"

He stiffened at her question, pulled his hand away, and scrubbed it over his face. "Three years."

That was more than she'd ever gotten out of him before. "How did you meet?"

"We went to high school together."

"Oh, high school sweethearts! That's so cute! Did you date until you got married?"

"Yep."

She felt like a police officer interrogating a suspect. "I bet she was beautiful." He always had beautiful women around him. She couldn't imagine his wife being plain like Mya herself. The idea of it was a dagger in the chest. She didn't turn heads, especially not the heads of sexy actors. And she was fine with it. Really! She was. She was plain old ordinary Mya. But he'd kissed her like she was far from ordinary. For one glorious minute, she'd been as beautiful and sexy as any starlet on the red carpet.

"From the moment I sat next to her in year eleven math class, I thought she was the most beautiful girl I'd ever seen. Even on the day she died, when the disease left her a hollow shell, she was still beautiful. But what you see on the surface isn't always what's inside."

He blew out a breath, propelled himself off the chair, and marched to the door that led outside. Instead of stepping into the backyard, he stared through the glass into the night.

Mya stood next to him. Tonight, the only storm that raged was the one in Aiden's body. "Was your marriage not a happy one?"

"I thought it was. We had our moments like all relationships. Little ups and downs. But things changed."

He fixed his gaze on something outside, but she doubted he was seeing anything but the memories of his past.

"What changed?" She had to know. She couldn't leave it where it was.

He turned to her, his green eyes darkening like a stormy sea. Angry lines etched his face. "She fucked another man."

Chapter 14

*a*iden's hands clenched into fists as he spoke. No one knew, not even his family. They'd adored her just as much as he had, and he hadn't wanted to take that from them. For most of their relationship, he had been the adoring husband. He'd loved Madeline—idolized her—but her affair had shattered what love he'd felt for her the instant he learned of it.

"She had an affair?" Her eyes widened with surprise.

He gritted his teeth and nodded.

"But you had a baby!"

She reached toward him with sympathy etched on her features, but he jerked away. He hated being pitied. And sympathy was just another form of it. It was just another reason to hide the truth so he'd never have to see that look on the faces of his friends and family.

He gave a mirthless laugh. "*She* had a baby."

She gasped and covered her mouth with her hand when she grasped his meaning.

"When she cheated, I was going to leave. Then she

found out about the pregnancy and begged for me to stay, for us to fix our marriage."

"She wanted you to stay knowing she carried another man's child?" Her voice was incredulous, and Aiden envied her innocence.

Bitterness filled him as he said, "She let me believe the baby was mine, and I thought maybe we could work things out for the baby's sake. I'd loved her since high school; it wasn't easy walking away." What a fool he'd been. He'd never let himself be vulnerable like that again. Never let love cloud his judgment. He'd learned his lesson. "Then she got sick," he continued. "Breast cancer. Stage four. She couldn't get treatment if she was pregnant. The doctors waited as long as they could to give the baby a chance, and then did a cesarean. I don't know why—guilty conscience, maybe—but before she went under, she confessed. Told me it wasn't my baby. The baby was so small…" His voice trailed off. "She was right on the bubble of viability. She only made it a few hours. Madeline got the cancer treatment. Maybe it was too little, too late, or maybe it was a broken heart, but she died four months later. She lived here until the end. I didn't tell my family what had happened. I couldn't. No point in upsetting my family further."

"Oh my God," Mya whispered in shock. Tears glistened in her eyes, and he turned back to the window and stared into the dark yard. "Why would she put you through that?"

"She complained I worked too much, and she got lonely. She met a man, fell in love, and wanted to leave me to move in with him. When she told him she was pregnant, he dropped her like a bad habit and disappeared." For the first time in months, the weight on his chest felt a little less heavy.

He hadn't meant to say so much, but somehow it was easy to spill his darkest secrets to Mya. Even the ones he couldn't tell his family. Especially those.

"You still stayed married until she died."

The words tasted like ash on his tongue. "We lived together, yes, but not as husband and wife. The marriage had ended, but I couldn't leave her. She had no family to look after her and help her through treatment."

"Not many men would have done that, no matter the situation. She was lucky to have you."

He turned from the window to meet Mya's eyes. "I did it for myself, not Madeline."

She raised a questioning eyebrow.

He didn't like the reason that he'd stayed with Madeline. But if he was being honest, he might as well go all the way. "How would it look if I'd left my dying wife? The media would've had a field day! My reputation would have been worse than what it is now."

"I don't think that's why you did it." Mya put a hand on his arm, and this time he let her, her warm touch a soothing balm on his anger. "You did it because you loved her. No matter what she did to you, you still loved her."

He couldn't stand her sympathy a second longer. Shaking her hand away, he brushed a stray lock of hair behind her ear. As his fingers skimmed her temple, he saw her eyes shift from pity to desire.

He knew he should leave her alone, should walk away, but instead he stroked her cheek. She stepped into him, and their lips met, his mouth stifling her soft gasp.

Her hands shifted to his waist, and she tentatively brushed her fingers along his hips. The gesture wasn't erotic, but her touch burned through the fabric of his T-shirt and branded his skin.

He pressed her to the glass, her body melting against his. There was no hiding how much he wanted her.

He placed wet kisses from her jaw to her shoulder and back again to her mouth, and she sighed with pleasure. He cupped a breast in one hand and rubbed the nipple between his thumb and forefinger, drawing forth a moan that somehow made him even harder.

She wrapped her arms around his neck, and their lips locked. God, she tasted sweet. Her hands trailed a hot path to the front of his jeans and fumbled with the fly, finally yanking down the zipper and freeing his dick from its denim prison. He hissed and tossed his head back as she rubbed her hand against his length.

"I want you in my bed. I want to touch and explore every inch of you." His voice was raspy with need.

Mya froze for a second, then put her hands on his chest and shoved him back. "No, no, no. Stop." She ducked past him and hurried to the far side of the kitchen counter, Aiden following dazedly behind. "What are you doing?" she demanded.

A little dazed, Aiden shook his head at Mya's sudden explosion. He'd heard of women running hot and cold, but one minute her body was plastered against his, the next it looked like she wanted to shoot firecrackers up his arse.

She didn't give him time to answer. "You're treating me like all the other women you use to help you forget about your wife!" She narrowed her eyes. "I take that back. You kiss me, and then disappear to pick up random women for one-night stands. I'm just the warm-up, aren't I? Well, I hope you enjoyed it, because I won't be used!"

"What? No—"

"I won't fall for it again even if you are a good—" She slammed her lips together around the end of her sentence.

"Good what?" Aiden asked.

She crossed her arms over her chest and averted her gaze. "Kisser. You're a good kisser, and I can easily get sucked in." She pinned him with a serious stare. "But it won't happen again. Keep your lips and hands to yourself. Just because you can't have someone else doesn't mean I'm available for your pleasure. Or any other reason."

As Mya began walking out of the kitchen, Aiden said, "I didn't screw around last night."

"I saw the photos."

She'd never get attached if she thought he was out womanizing, so why did he want her to know the truth? Attachment was the last thing he wanted. He shouldn't try to set the record straight. Yet he found himself saying, "It wasn't what it looks like. I was asking them to leave."

Mya's eyes grew wide. "Why?"

"Because of you."

"Me?" Her voice rose.

"I kept thinking about our kiss and couldn't get you out of my damn mind. I wanted to fuck *you*, not them."

Mya's mouth dropped open, closed, and opened again.

"Don't worry, I'll keep my hands and lips to myself so we don't break any *rules*," he said, wanting to cut this conversation short so he could take care of his erection in peace.

"Well… good. It better stay that way with me *and* other women. Is that clear?" She pushed her glasses up her nose.

"Crystal."

"Good." She left the room. Aiden enjoyed the view. Did she know how sexy she was? Even when she pushed her glasses up her nose it turned him on. She didn't have to try, and she had him wanting to take her to bed, strip her naked, and make her moan his name.

And he'd nearly got the opportunity.

Was she right? Was he using her to block out the

miserable thoughts plaguing him? He agreed that he used other women for that purpose. But with them, he thought about what he didn't feel: the temporary distraction from the hollowness inside him. Mya was different. With her, he felt her. The taste of her lips, the jasmine scent of her perfume, the smoothness of her skin, the way her body curved into his like they were made for each other… And he'd told her the truth about Madeline and the baby. He hadn't told anyone the truth.

He made his way to his room. Light spilled from the crack under Mya's door. If he walked in and kissed her, she'd be putty in his hands. But he'd literally just promised her he'd keep his hands to himself.

Why couldn't she just admit that she wanted him?

He knew why. He had a reputation for casual flings and a distaste for commitment. Mya wasn't in it for a night or for three months. There would be no casual hookups for her. Especially with a son, she was looking for a long-term serious relationship with someone who wanted to be a father.

Someone Aiden could never be.

He closed the door to his bedroom and stripped out of his clothes. His bed called invitingly from across the room, but memories of Mya's silky skin and full lips pushed him in a different direction.

The shower.

He had urgent business to attend to.

Chapter 15

*T*he next morning, Mya poured herself a strong coffee and willed the liquid to work its magic and breathe life into her. She didn't usually need a pick-me-up in the morning, but after the night she'd had, she'd take any help she could get.

She'd tossed and turned in her sleep, thinking about the bombshell Aiden had dropped. *He didn't sleep with the women in the photos because he was thinking about me?* How should she feel about it? Shocked? Yes. Relieved? Her body wanted to sag onto a chair with the news.

Unless he'd just said that to get her into bed. She wouldn't put it past him. Just like she hadn't put it past him to sneak out again and had spent half the night listening at his door to make sure he was still inside. She'd even gone so far as to peek inside his bedroom to make sure he hadn't pulled a runner.

"Morning." Aiden ambled into the kitchen. "Any more coffee left?" Gray sweatpants rode low on his hips. He was barefoot, shirtless, and sporting serious bed hair.

Mya had trouble dragging her gaze away from his bronzed chest. "Yes."

He reached into a cupboard above the counter, and Mya almost swallowed her tongue watching the skin stretch over the firm muscles of his back. She sighed into her mug.

"Did you say something?" He turned with a cup in his hand.

"Sleep well?" Oh God, she needed to pull herself together before keep your hands to yourself became put your hands all over me.

Hands. Lips. Tongue. Other things.

Was it hot in here, or was it just the coffee?

"I would have if you hadn't made so much noise checking on me last night."

"You heard me?"

"Honey, I think the people living next door heard you."

The word *honey* dripped over her skin, making the room even warmer. "I was quiet," she said, mortified he'd busted her checking on him.

Aiden poured his coffee and took a sip. "You stomped up the hallway like a herd of elephants. The doorknob rattled like someone upturned the silverware drawer, and you breathed like you'd just got done running a four-minute mile."

"Elephant… breathing…" She stuttered. When she could string a sentence together, she said, "I did none of those things. You didn't move a muscle and were fast asleep."

Aiden chuckled. "Trust me, I was not asleep."

Putting her mug on the kitchen counter, she dropped her hands on her hips. "Why didn't you say something?"

"And ruin your fun?" He'd finished his coffee and cleaned up the mess. He propped his hands on the counter, leaning back on his arms. The muscles bunched in his biceps.

Mya, distracted for a moment, forced herself out of her lustful haze. "Getting up at all hours of the night is not *fun*," she grumbled.

"Then don't do it."

"And have you sneak out? No thanks, I don't want to get fired."

"I won't sneak out."

Mya rolled her eyes. "Your track record doesn't give me a lot of reassurance."

"You don't trust me?" He stared at her with a serious expression, and she had the idea that her answer mattered to him.

"I want to trust you," she said carefully. "But your actions so far haven't given me cause to trust you."

"That was before last night. Before we talked." He ran a hand through his hair, which did funny things to her insides. "I wouldn't have told you about Madeline if I didn't trust you. And I want you to trust me. If I tell you from now on I'll stay home, that means I will."

She searched his face for the truth. "Are you acting?"

A flash of hurt flickered behind his eyes. "Not right now."

"Then okay." She hoped he'd keep his word. She wasn't sure if she was making a giant mistake, but something inside of her told her that she could trust him this time. Flashing him a friendly smile to lighten the mood, she said, "Now I can sleep without having to pace the hallway like an elephant—just what every girl likes to be compared to, by the way."

His chuckle vibrated through her body. "Maybe I exaggerated." He grinned. If she wasn't careful, that grin could short-circuit her heart. She needed distance. Too bad they lived together.

It would get easier with Noah here. She could focus on him and not how Aiden looked without a shirt on. He'd be the wall between her and Aiden. "I've decided I'm bringing Noah today." If Aiden was as good as his word, she wouldn't have to hunt him down in the middle of the night. And God, she missed her beautiful boy.

The playful grin dropped from his face. "So soon?"

"It's been three days. I need him with me, and he can't stay with Amelia any longer. She's busy with her own life."

He massaged his temples. "Keep him quiet and out of sight while he's here."

Mya raised her chin. "He's an active five-year-old boy. Unless I chain him up in a room and gag him, he's going to make noise." When Aiden opened his mouth to say something, she pointed a finger at him. "Don't you even suggest I do anything like that!"

Aiden blew out a long breath. "I'm not a monster. I was only going to suggest he use one of the empty rooms as a playroom. That way I don't have to keep running into him if he's left wandering the house."

"I will do my best to keep him away from you."

"Thank you." He pushed away from the counter and left the room.

Watching him leave, she drew a shaky breath and hoped bringing Noah here wouldn't be a big mistake.

When Mya entered her house, Noah shoved his plastic dinosaurs to the side and cried, "Mummy!" Jumping up, he shot toward her like a cannonball, wrapping his arms around her waist.

Tears sprung in her eyes, and she bent to pick him up and propped him on her hip so she could pepper kisses over his face. She'd missed the little boy smell of a fresh bath and Vegemite. She squeezed him tight until he squirmed in her arms, and she had to put him down. "I missed you, my baby boy."

"I'm not a baby, Mummy," he protested.

"You'll always be my baby," she said, tousling his curly blond hair.

He pulled a face, and Mya laughed. "Where's Aunty Amelia?" she asked, looking around.

"Right here," Amelia said as she strolled in from the kitchen.

"Thanks for looking after him. I hope he wasn't too much trouble."

Amelia waved a dismissive hand at the comment. "He was an angel. We had loads of fun. Didn't we, buddy?" She directed her question at Noah, who nodded.

"Are all his things packed?" Mya asked.

"We filled one suitcase with clothes and the other is bulging at the seams with toys and books. I had trouble convincing him one suitcase for toys was enough. He'd pack the entire house if I'd let him." She pointed to the luggage sitting next to the stairs.

Mya laughed.

"So, anything to report? You know…" Amelia tried to convey her meaning with hand signals and eyebrow wiggles.

"No." She'd keep last night's make-out session to herself. Otherwise Amelia would refuse to give up Noah until Mya had a bag packed with sexy lingerie and a box of condoms.

"Pity." Amelia said with a frown.

Mya got Noah settled in the car and placed his luggage

in the boot. "Thanks again for having him," she said and hugged her sister goodbye.

"No problem. Any time. Especially if you need some *privacy*." Amelia gave Mya an exaggerated wink.

Mya laughed and shook her head.

On the drive back to Aiden's, Noah grilled her with one hundred and one questions about where they were going. Who were they living with? What did the house look like? Will he have his own room? The questions didn't stop. When they reached Aiden's house, she pulled onto the driveway and parked the car.

Then he asked a question she'd like the answer to herself.

"Who's that?" Noah pointed to a woman in a skintight fuchsia miniskirt and a black top with a plunging neckline strutting down the front steps. Her long auburn hair was mussed like someone had been running their fingers through it, and she flicked her hair over her shoulder. She gave one last smoldering glance at Aiden, who leaned a shoulder casually against the doorframe, before she slid into a white BMW and pulled out onto the street.

Mya's attention flew to Aiden. He was still dressed the way she'd left him: no shirt, bare feet, and track pants. That didn't mean his visit from Little Miss Miniskirt was innocent. Nothing Aiden did with women was *innocent*. She'd learned that firsthand.

He watched the woman's car drive away. His gaze snapped toward Mya, and he stiffened and disappeared inside the house.

Mya's knuckles were white on the steering wheel. He wanted her to trust him. Made her believe she could. She never would have left him home alone if she'd had any doubt. The moment she'd turned her back, he got up to his old tricks.

The worst part was that he'd kept to the letter of his promise! He hadn't stolen out of the house like a thief in the night, and he hadn't promised not to have any women over, so that's what he'd done.

God, she'd been so naive! Why on earth did she think he'd change his ways after only a few days? Because of what had happened between them? Why would she, plain old Mya, mean more to him than all the beautiful women who came and went? She should have known better.

"Mummy, are we going inside?" Noah's voice broke through the red haze blurring her vision.

"Yes, sweetie." She got out of the car, retrieved his luggage from the boot, and rolled it into the house.

Noah's head tilted so far back to take in the huge house that he almost fell over. He whispered in awe, "Wow. Mummy, this place is awesome! We get to live here?"

"Yes, we do. But only for a short time. Come on, help me get these bags upstairs and into our room. Then I'll show you around."

There was no sign of Aiden. Probably hiding himself in his room to get away from Noah. She was too mad to find him. If she spoke to him right now, she didn't know if she could hold back her temper. Noah didn't need to see his mother lose her cool. As soon as she calmed down and Noah was out of earshot, Aiden would know what she thought about his quickie while she was out.

In the nursery, she unpacked Noah's clothes and put them in drawers. She'd had to remove some of Madeline's things to make room for Noah's, and touching the dead woman's clothes had been disconcerting. The whole room made her uncomfortable. It was a memorial of betrayal and loss. Why had he left this shrine for two years and then told her, a stranger, she could redecorate?

"Why is there baby stuff in here, Mummy?" Noah

asked as he looked inside the cradle, picked up a pink, fluffy bunny, and played with its ears.

"It belonged to a baby. But she's not here anymore."

He nodded and put the soft toy back, happy with the answer. Mya was relieved he didn't ask more questions about it.

After Mya packed away his clothes, they took the bag of toys to the empty room next door. She pulled out cars, trucks, action figures, and Lego bricks. Under all the toys was a stack of picture books. "You brought all these books too? I think you've packed the whole house." She chuckled and kissed his chubby cheek.

"I love your books, Mummy. I missed you reading them to me."

"Aww, that's sweet. I missed reading them to you too."

These books weren't bought from a shop. Mya had written them.

She'd written that first book when she'd been pregnant with Noah, and Amelia had illustrated it. Gran had gotten it printed and bound, and Mya would read it to him every day. After getting sick of telling the same story, she'd written another book and then another. Over the years they had accumulated until now Noah had twelve children's books written by her in his collection. Book thirteen sat in a file on her laptop, waiting.

After placing the books in a neat pile in the room, they made their way to a, thankfully, empty kitchen.

"Are you hungry?" she asked Noah.

"I'm always hungry!" He smiled, flashing her his gap-toothed grin.

Mya laughed. Growing boys ate like a horse. She made him a ham, cheese, and tomato sandwich with a glass of milk.

After he finished eating, she gave him a quick tour of

the house, avoiding Aiden's room and the library because she didn't want to run into him. As soon as Noah saw it through a window, he took Mya's hand and practically dragged her to the backyard.

The only time she'd been out the back had been the night of the storm when she'd watched the lightning flash across the sky and Aiden had pulled her in for a kiss. She mentally shook the image away. She was mad at Aiden. She had every right to be mad! He'd just proven he had no feelings for her. She would not think about the kiss; if she did, she might be less mad when she remembered how it made her weak in the knees.

"The backyard is huge!" Noah darted away, arms outstretched to either side, making airplane noises as he zoomed around the yard. It had plenty of grass to run around and trees and shrubs to explore. A perfect place for Noah to play.

Sitting on the spongy grass, she stretched her legs in front of her, leaned on her hands, lifted her face to the sun, and closed her eyes. The warmth seeped into her skin, and she took a deep breath. The tension in her shoulders and neck eased. She was so happy to have Noah with her.

A shadow blanketed the light, and she opened her eyes. Aiden stood over her with an unreadable expression on his face.

She glanced at Noah, busy poking in the dirt in a flower bed with a stick. All the tension she'd just released once again seized her body. She rose and dusted off her butt.

"What are you doing outside?" she asked.

"It's my house. I can go wherever I want."

"Yes, but you made it clear you wanted to stay away from Noah." She glanced at her son, relieved he was still too preoccupied to notice Aiden.

He dug his hands in the pockets of his jeans. She was glad he'd changed and put on a shirt. The soft fabric clung to every muscle, hiding nothing. But out of sight, very slightly out of mind.

"And I still do. Just want to make it clear you need to keep him away from me as much as possible." With that, he walked back inside.

Mya frowned, watching his retreating back. Why had he come outside where Noah was to tell her to keep Noah away from him? It didn't seem to make any sense at all.

"Who's that, Mummy?" Noah stood beside her with a dirt streak across his cheek.

Mya used her fingers to rub it off. "That's Mr. Doyle. The man I have to look after for a little while."

"I brought a soccer ball. Can I ask him to play with me?" He looked up at her with hope in his eyes.

Her heart broke for him. She'd wished so many times that Noah had a father figure in his life. Someone to do for him what Aiden's character did for his kids on *Family First*. As much as she didn't get along with Daniel's parents, Bob was a male presence in Noah's life. Bob was older, though, and couldn't keep up with Noah's rambunctious five-year-old energy.

And now Noah had seen a man close to her age who was big and strong, and he wanted to make that connection, and now she'd have to disappoint him. "I'm sorry, baby. He's very busy and doesn't have time to play."

His crestfallen look made her curse the day she'd ever laid eyes on Aiden Doyle.

Chapter 16

*a*iden hadn't intended to follow Mya outside. He'd watched her from the library window as she soaked up the sun. Her golden hair shone in the morning light. Her smooth neck stretched out, exposing the skin he'd kissed. And before he'd known it, he'd forgotten her son was outside too. It was like his feet had had a mind of their own. When she'd mentioned her kid, it had felt like a splash of ice water in his face, and he couldn't get back inside fast enough. Now he was sitting like a prisoner shut in a room in his own home.

There was a knock at the door. "Come in," he called.

Mya popped her head into the room. "Can I talk to you for a minute?"

He gestured for her to enter, and she shut the door behind her. "Where's the kid?"

"His name's Noah. He's having an afternoon nap. You've been in this room all day. You can come out. He won't bite."

"I'm not scared of a child."

"You could have fooled me," she said, shaking her head

slightly before continuing, "I'm not Madeline. I have no intention of trying to trick you into daddy duties. So, relax. But I'm not here to talk about Noah. I'm here to discuss your *visitor* this morning. You're lucky I've calmed down because earlier, I was ready to slap you silly."

"Oh?" He quirked an eyebrow.

She perched on the edge of his desk. "I trusted you, and you repaid my trust by having a woman in the house as soon as I was out of sight. I'm wondering if I should phone Mr. Masters and call the whole thing off. You're not serious about pulling your life back together, and I have a life I've put on hold for this. Right now, this is a waste of everyone's time. You're not even trying."

"Not even trying? I've been sitting in my house for days! *My* life's been put on hold too. I'm not working, not drinking, and not fucking. How can you say I'm not *trying*?"

"You had a woman here today! You can't pretend I didn't see her leaving your house."

"Yeah, Francesca was here. Uninvited. And yes, she wanted sex, but I turned her away."

With a snort of derisive laughter, Mya said, "You don't expect me to believe that, do you?"

He shrugged. "I could have had those clothes off her in two seconds flat if I wanted to. But I kept thinking how I wanted to get my hands on a woman with blond hair, black-rimmed glasses, and baggy clothes."

"I might've believed you last night, but I'm not falling for that line again."

There was hurt hidden under her angry tone, a hurt he found himself inexplicably wanting to ease. "It's the truth." He ran a hand through his hair. "I don't know why the fuck I can't get you out of my mind. You're driving me insane."

Her eyes widened, and she bit her bottom lip. That

small gesture flooded his gut with heat. Heat, and also desire. Never tearing his eyes from hers, Aiden placed a hand on her knee, watching for any hint of refusal. When she didn't swat his hand away, he slid it higher.

"You're not looking for a daddy for your son? Good, because I'm not volunteering for the job. But why keep denying the attraction between us? If we're going to spend the next few weeks together, let's make the most of it."

His hand reached her hip. She reached out and touched his arm, sending goose bumps rippling across his skin. He put his other hand on her other hip and slid her so she sat securely on the desk. Her legs parted in an invitation. He stepped between them and pulled her to him ever so slightly. Mya's eyes fluttered closed for a beat as she gripped the edge of the desk. He hissed as she tipped her hips into him. Lowering his head, he placed kisses along her jaw below her ear, skimming his tongue down her smooth neck to the spot where the curve of her neck met her shoulder. She tilted her head to the side. An invitation for more.

And, oh God, how he wanted more! Proof of his desire was hard to miss, but she made no move to end the encounter.

When his lips left her neck, she groaned her displeasure. He kissed her mouth instead, and she sighed, let go of the desk, and clung to his shoulders, her body slowly rocking against him.

Aiden's hands found their way under the hem of her T-shirt, the heat of her skin burning his fingertips as they trailed to her chest. One finger brushed below her breast, and she arched her back. He cupped her breast and swiped a finger over the peaked nipple straining through the fabric of her bra.

Wanting less clothes and more skin, he whipped her T-shirt off over her head and threw it across the room. He stared down at her body. Full breasts heaved, threatening to spill over the white cotton bra she wore. It was plain and practical, and he'd never seen anything so beautiful—or been so turned on—in his life.

Reaching behind her, he unclipped the bra. The straps fell off her shoulders, and he launched her bra across the room to join the T-shirt. He placed a hand on the center of her chest and gently pushed her back onto the desk.

She sprawled out on the desk and he followed her down, his chest brushing her nipples while she hooked her legs around his waist.

"You're beautiful." Why had he ever thought she was plain? Forget the starlets in red-carpet makeup and the club girls in their skimpy dresses—Mya was the sexiest woman he'd ever seen.

The shy smile she gave him made him harder than he thought he'd ever been before. He planted his hands on either side of her head and kissed her. Her hands tightened on his body, urging him closer. Any closer and he'd be inside her, which was exactly where he wanted to be. Mya must have been thinking the same thing because her hands went to the fly of his jeans, unbuttoned them, and slid under the waistband of his underwear.

"Oh God." His moan echoed through the room, and he dropped his head onto her left shoulder as she stroked him.

His blood pounded so hard it was a buzzing in his ears. That had never happened before. Was his brain about to explode from the torture of her touch? The only thing he wanted exploding was in her hand, and if she continued, that's what would happen.

The buzzing came again, and they both paused.

"Did you hear that?" she whispered, her voice low and husky.

The fact that she'd heard it too probably meant he wasn't on the verge of a stroke. Even if he was, at least he'd go out with a bang. "It's probably nothing."

She frowned, looking around. "I think it's the doorbell."

"Let's hope they go away." He bent down to kiss her, but she placed her hand on his chest.

"Maybe it's one of your women callers," she said when the doorbell buzzed again. And just like that, harsh lines replaced the lust that had softened her features moments ago.

He blew out a long, frustrated breath and straightened.

Scrambling off the desk, she covered her breasts with her hands. He tilted his head in confusion. Why would she bother hiding them? He'd already gotten an eyeful.

The buzzer went off again as she went in search of her clothes. "Whoever it is, they're persistent. You better answer it."

Buttoning the fly of his jeans, he wanted to groan with frustration at the interruption. He left Mya struggling to do up the clip of her bra while he headed for the door.

When he got there, he flung it open, ready to tell whoever was there to leave, but his mother stood on the veranda, smiling and holding grocery bags.

"Mum, what are you doing here?" He surreptitiously checked his jeans to make sure they were fully fastened before raking a hand through his hair.

She tilted her head to the side, and her lips flattened. "Do I need a reason to see my son?" she asked as she walked past him into the house.

Just as she reached the living room, Mya scurried out of the library, her T-shirt askew and her hair mussed. She straightened her glasses as if she was trying to verify what she was seeing was real. "Nancy, hi. How are you?"

His mother smiled at Mya, and Aiden could see her notice Mya's disheveled state. When she turned her gaze on Aiden, her eyes gleamed with understanding, and her mouth turned up in a decidedly smug grin. "I hope I haven't interrupted anything?" Her voice was the pinnacle of feigned innocence.

"No!" Mya blurted. "I was just… just… going to check on Noah." She pointed to the stairs.

"Oh, your son is here? Wonderful. Can I meet him?"

Oh please, God, no.

But it was already too late. At the top of the stairs, a little voice said, "Mummy, who's that?" Noah looked down at them, rubbing sleep from his eyes.

Mya jogged up the stairs and picked him up. "Did you have a good nap, sweetie?"

He nodded as he continued to look at Aiden and his mother.

Setting him back on his feet, Mya held his hand as they walked over. "Noah, this is Aiden. This is who we'll be living with for a little while. And this is his mother, Miss Nancy."

"Do you live here too?" Noah asked Nancy, his eyes wide.

"No, I'm only visiting. How old are you, Noah?"

Noah held out his hand to show five fingers.

"Wow, you're a big boy." His mother's eyes brightened as she cooed over the boy. "Do you go to school yet?" she asked.

He shook his head. "Mummy said I can go to big school next year."

There was a faint pillow line on his face, and his hair stuck up in different directions. His eyes were bright and

SONIA STANIZZO

chocolate brown—like his mother's. A tightness squeezed
Aiden's chest, and he had to look away.

"Are you hungry? I brought food," his mother asked
Noah.

"I'm staaarving." He held his stomach like he had
hunger pangs.

Mya and his mother laughed.

"Why don't you come into the kitchen and help me
make a snack?" His mother held out her hand. The little
boy hesitated and looked at Mya—who nodded her
permission—before taking it.

"I'll be there in a minute, sweetie," Mya said, watching
them walk from the room.

"We need to finish what we started."

She shook her head. "No, we do not. It was a mistake. I
don't know what I was thinking."

"The only mistake is if we don't act on this attraction.
And in there"—he pointed in the library's direction—"you
wanted to get laid just as much as I did."

"Well, I've changed my mind." Her gaze dropped to
her feet.

He put a finger under her chin and tilted her face up.
"Really?"

"Yes." She tried to say it with conviction, but the truth
was obvious when she pressed her face into his hand.

They both knew that she wanted him. Still, he would
respect her words and not press any further. "Then I'll just
wait until you're ready," he said, slipping his finger from
her chin.

"I won't ever be ready. This was a mistake. A mistake
that we won't be repeating," she replied, turning her back
on him and walking deliberately to the kitchen.

Chapter 17

*M*ya paused before entering the kitchen. Her hand shook as she slipped a hair elastic from her wrist, brushed her hair back, and pulled it into a ponytail. She drew several deep breaths to calm her racing heart.

God, I almost had sex with Aiden in the library with my son asleep upstairs! Why was she so weak whenever Aiden came near her? Was it because it had been so long since anyone touched her? Was it because he made her feel like a woman again? After her man drought and his expert hands, it wouldn't be unreasonable for her body to react so strongly.

Once she had her heart under control, she walked into the kitchen. Noah sat at the breakfast bar peeling potatoes and passing them to Nancy to chop. Aiden was nowhere to be seen.

"Mummy, I'm making mashed potatoes." Noah beamed with pride.

"I bet they're going to be the best mashed potatoes I've ever tasted." She kissed the top of his head.

"He's peeling the spuds faster than I can chop them," Nancy said with a wink and a smile. "By the way, I've invited myself over for dinner. I hope you don't mind."

"Not at all. I'd love the company." Seeing salad fixings on the counter, Mya pulled out a cutting board and started prepping a salad.

"Thanks for doing that." Nancy plopped the potatoes into a pot of water and waited for Noah to peel the next one. "So, Mya, is my son giving you much trouble?"

Mya thought for a moment, trying to choose her words carefully. She didn't want Noah learning what kind of man Aiden was. "We had a rough start, but I think we've come to an understanding."

Nancy chuckled, then said, "Aiden can be pigheaded and will do the opposite of what he's told. I know I've told you this before, but I'm glad you're here. You're good for him."

Mya shifted on her feet, uncomfortable hearing that again. Was Nancy holding on to hope that she could help her son become the man he once was before the lies and deceit had torn apart his life? It had taken a toll on him, and it was hard to look his mother in the eye, knowing the reason his life had spiraled out of control. Aiden should have confided in his family. Told them the unvarnished truth. They loved him and would have supported him through his darkest days. Maybe if he'd spoken up, he wouldn't have fallen so far.

"I'm not so sure about that." Mya nodded her head toward Noah. Surely Nancy knew Aiden's feelings about children.

"This is exactly what he needs," Nancy said firmly. "Aiden used to love kids. When he was a teenager, he used to talk about having a big family. He was so excited when he found out Madeline was pregnant. Then Madeline and the baby died, and suddenly he hated kids. This will force him to see that children are a beautiful gift and it doesn't always end in tragedy."

For Aiden's sake, Mya hoped it was true. It couldn't be easy going through life with such a broken heart.

Once Noah and Nancy finished peeling the potatoes, Nancy left to summon Aiden while Noah bounded over to where Mya was working. "I like her," he said in a faux whisper.

"I do too."

And it was the truth. If Nancy convinced Aiden to join them for dinner with Noah, it would be a miracle. She saw the way he'd looked at Noah earlier—like he was some kind of scary monster. Noah was such a great kid, most people who met him loved him, and she was gutted that he could have such a negative effect on anyone like he seemed to have on Aiden.

Nancy stormed back into the room, a deep line creasing her forehead.

"He's not joining us?" Mya didn't need to be a mind reader to figure out that's what had caused Nancy's ire.

Nancy shook her head. Mya could tell she had something to say about Aiden, but she glanced at Noah and her lips flattened into a thin line. Whatever she wanted to say wasn't appropriate for five-year-old ears.

Despite Aiden's no-show upsetting Nancy, they enjoyed their meal and talked about Nancy's career as a makeup artist, which fascinated Noah. He asked Nancy dozens of questions about making movies. His eyes lit up when she told him she was doing the makeup for a horror film and was tasked with turning actors into zombies.

Two hours passed with no signs of Aiden.

"Okay, sweetie, it's time for bed," Mya said.

"I'm not tired." His words would have been more convincing if he hadn't said them through a yawn.

Mya and Nancy giggled.

"Say good night to Miss Nancy, then go to our room and get ready for bed. I'll be up soon."

"Okay." He dropped his head and slid from the chair. "Night, Miss Nancy."

"Good night, Noah. Thanks for helping me with dinner."

He smiled and ran from the kitchen.

"That kid only has two speeds, go and stop—and that's only because he's asleep," Mya said.

"He's a beautiful boy. You're lucky."

"Thank you. I'm so grateful he's in my life. I wasn't planning on having a kid so young, but now I can't imagine what I'd do without him."

"I'm sorry Aiden didn't join us for dinner," Nancy said with a frown as she prepared to leave.

"I know where he stands with kids."

Nancy shook her head. "It doesn't mean he can be rude! I taught him better than that."

"He's making progress. He let Noah live here. That's a huge step. I don't want to push him too much. He's been through a lot."

With sad eyes, Nancy said, "Yes, he has. I know I've said it before, but I'm really glad you're here. You're good for him. You both are."

Mya hoped that would be the case. As she headed upstairs to tuck Noah in, she had to come to terms with some pretty uncomfortable truths. She liked Aiden. Really liked him. And if Nancy hadn't interrupted their make-out session, they'd have done a lot more than just kissed. Aiden had said he wanted to finish what they started. What's more, so did she, and that scared her more than she'd like to admit.

Aiden Doyle was trouble. A trouble she just couldn't seem to resist.

———

Aiden waited until his mother left and he heard Mya go upstairs before he poked his head out of the library. It was ridiculous hiding in his own goddamn house! But what other choice did he have? No way would he sit down to dinner like a happy family. His mother had made it clear he was being unreasonable, but she couldn't change his mind.

His stomach growled so loudly he was afraid he'd woken the neighbors, and he went to the kitchen in search of leftovers. Knowing his mother, there'd be plenty. In the fridge, he found plates filled with chicken schnitzel, salad, and mashed potatoes.

He placed two pieces of chicken and a huge spoonful of potatoes on a plate and stuck it in the microwave. While it spun, he pulled out some juice from the fridge. He could grab a bottle of wine from the stash he had hidden in the island counter and hadn't touched, but he didn't feel like it. After two years, not wanting alcohol felt strange.

When the microwave beeped, Aiden pulled out the plate, sat at the breakfast bar, and dug in.

A quiet rustle behind him caused Aiden to spin around. Mya's kid, wearing red Spider-Man pajamas with a book tucked under his arm, stood in the doorway, staring at him.

"Shouldn't you be in bed?" Aiden snapped. He'd thought he'd been safe. Unbidden, memories of life with

Madeline threatened to surface, but Aiden shoved them aside ruthlessly.

The kid's eyes grew round at his harsh tone, and Aiden felt like a prick for scaring him. "Where's your mum?" he asked in a gentler tone of voice.

"She's asleep."

"Do you need something?" Why was he wandering around the house?

The kid glanced at the fridge, then back at Aiden, biting his bottom lip like he wanted to say something but was afraid to speak.

"Are you hungry?" Aiden asked when he peeked at the fridge again.

He nodded.

"There's leftovers."

The kid shuffled to the fridge.

Aiden got up to leave but noticed the boy standing on tiptoes struggling to get the dish filled with schnitzel from the shelf. With the book still tucked under his arm, the plate wobbled in his hands. Aiden hurried around the counter and caught the food before it crashed on the floor, averting a potential disaster.

The kid smiled his thanks, scooted onto a stool at the counter, and didn't move.

"What are you waiting for?" Aiden frowned.

"It's cold," he said.

"Then heat it up."

"Mummy doesn't let me use the microwave."

"Why not?" Aiden asked.

"Because she thinks I'm too little"—the kid leaned forward in his seat—"but I'm not."

Aiden wanted to wake up Mya so she could deal with her son, but then the little boy said, "Can you teach me?"

Aiden rubbed the back of his neck. He should get

Mya, but when he looked down, Mya's big brown eyes looked up at him and some unfamiliar emotion skittered down his spinc. It wasn't the terror he typically felt seeing kids, but something else.

"You look big enough to me." Aiden put his finger and thumb on his chin in thought. "How old are you… ten?" He knew Noah's age but was curious to see if he'd tell the truth.

Noah giggled, "I'm five."

"Ok, you're old enough. I'll show you. But you have to promise you'll only use the microwave if your mum or your aunty is around."

"And you?" he asked.

Hopefully, he'd never be alone with him again. "And me, sure. Put your book on the counter and stand next to me."

The kid did what he was told and stood with his head tilted back, staring at the microwave.

"Do you know your numbers?"

He nodded.

"You press the one, the three, and the zero and this big button. It says Start."

"I can't see. Pick me up."

A shiver ran down Aiden's spine. He froze, staring at the child.

The boy held up his arms and waited.

Shoving aside the sheer terror that had wrapped around his heart, Aiden placed his hands under the kid's armpits and lifted him up, keeping him at arm's length.

The boy kicked his legs and laughed like they were playing a game.

His arms started to shake. Whether it was from the fear or the strain, he wasn't sure. Mya would never let him hear the end of it if he dropped her son, and he knew he couldn't hold a squirming child at the end of outstretched arms forever, so he propped him on his hip.

His throat tightened, his body stiffened, and his heart raced. The kid was waiting for him to show him how to use the microwave, unaware of the turmoil raging through his body. It was the same feeling he felt when he had to be in a scene with one of his child costars. Aiden took a deep breath and went through the instructions again. "Have you got it?"

"I think so."

Aiden set the kid onto his feet and got a plate from the cupboard. "How many pieces do you want?"

The kid scrunched up his face in thought. "Five hundred and sixty billion."

An unexpected laugh burst from Aiden's mouth. "Wow, you must be hungry. How about we start with two?"

He shrugged. "Okay."

Aiden put the schnitzel on a plate and placed it in the microwave. "Do you remember what to do?"

"Yep." And he held his arms up again.

Aiden sighed as terror once again welled up inside. He should have gotten Mya straight away to deal with her son. But maybe the boy should do something that didn't always involve his mother. Even if it was learning how to use the microwave.

Picking Noah up, Aiden propped him on his hip and watched him press the right numbers and hit the start button. The microwave lit up and the turntable began spinning.

"Good job." Aiden held up his hand for a high five and the kid slapped him as hard as he could.

Aiden shook out his hand like he got hurt, and the kid laughed and wiggled down his body onto the floor.

"Enjoy," Aiden said once he'd gotten the kid situated with hot food and a fork. He turned to leave.

"Where are you going?" Noah asked around a mouthful of food.

"To bed."

Rejection and hurt settled onto his features. "You're not staying with me? I don't want to be by myself." Had he forgotten he'd come to the kitchen on his own?

As much as he wanted to escape to the safety of his own rooms, he shouldn't leave the kid by himself. He wasn't a complete monster. Resigned, Aiden slid onto a stool next to him. Noah smiled and dug into his meal.

The book he'd been carrying caught Aiden's eye. He read the title—*Wally the Lost Whale*—and flipped it open. Although it was a storybook with colorful illustrations, it hadn't been purchased from a shop. The pictures were hand-painted, and there was no evidence of a publisher's imprint, ISBN, or barcode.

"That's my mum's book. She writes me heaps of stories," Noah said around a mouthful of food.

Aiden noticed her name and her sister's on the bottom of the cover. "I didn't know she wrote books." It was something else to add to the enigma that was Mya.

Pride shone on the kid's face. "She writes them specially for me, and Aunty Amelia paints the pictures. She has a room filled with paintings. She lets me play in there sometimes until I get paint on everything and she gets mad." Noah paused, glancing at him hopefully from under his fringe of blond hair. "Can you read it to me?"

Stifling a growl, Aiden said, "Doesn't your mum do that?"

"She fell asleep right before the good part. Wally finds dolphins to play with, but they're not very nice."

"Sounds interesting."

"She writes the best stories. So"—another glance —"will you read it to me?"

"You should go to bed." He ran a hand through his hair.

Noah's face scrunched up. "But I can't sleep unless someone reads me a story."

Aiden took a deep breath and released it slowly. "Okay."

The kid fist-pumped the air. "Yes!"

Feeling like he'd been played, Aiden opened the book to the first page and began reading. The kid scooted as close as he could to him without falling off his stool and leaned his head on Aiden's shoulder. Aiden's first reaction was to shrug him off, but something stopped him. Maybe it was the softness of the little body pressed against his arm or the smell of the apple shampoo in Noah's hair, but this was almost... nice.

Aiden read about the adventures of a young whale wandering away from his mother and getting into lots of trouble. The illustrations were charming, and he got so caught up in the story that he started to wonder if Wally would ever find his way home.

"The end," he said once Wally had been reunited with his mother. "Are you—"

"What's going on in here?" Mya said from the doorway. They both glanced over their shoulders to look at her. "You should be in bed." Whether she was talking to Aiden or her son was unclear. Probably the five-year-old, though from the look she shot in his direction he could be wrong.

"I got hungry and Aiden helped me use the microwave," the kid explained, assuming his mum was talking to him.

"Did he?" Her unimpressed gaze flicked to Aiden once

again then back to her son. "Put your plate in the sink and go back to bed."

The kid slid off the stool and tugged at Aiden's arm. "Thanks for reading me a story. Next time Mummy falls asleep, you can do it again."

As he watched the Spider-Man pajamas disappear from view, Aiden promised himself there wouldn't be a *next time* because he planned to do a better job at staying away from the kid.

"I'm sorry Noah disturbed you," Mya said.

"He didn't." The words came out before he could censor them.

She searched his face, trying to detect a lie. If he was honest, it hadn't been so bad, but that didn't mean he wanted to make a habit of it. He still didn't like kids— didn't like the memories they brought up—but Noah hadn't been that bad.

Seemingly satisfied with his answer, she nodded. "Good night."

"Good night." She turned to leave, but he stopped her with a word, "Mya?" She turned around. "Can I kiss you?" She'd made it clear earlier that they weren't going to do anything sexual, but that didn't mean he couldn't ask. She hadn't forbidden asking yet.

At her hesitant nod, he crossed the distance between them in two long strides. He cupped her face in his hands and kissed her long and deep. She melted against him, placing her hands on his waist.

Why he needed to touch her, feel his lips on her lips, he didn't want to analyze. He only knew that he wouldn't be able to sleep without kissing her. It was like he was starving for air, and she was the oxygen.

When he let go, she stumbled back a step with a dazed expression, her mouth plump and begging for another kiss. It took some effort, but he managed to restrain himself.

"Good night," he said again, heading for his room.

Maybe the reason he hadn't reached for wine earlier was that Mya was more intoxicating than anything he could pour out of a bottle.

Chapter 18

*F*or the next two days, Mya avoided Aiden. The kiss in the kitchen confused her more than almost having sex with him. Sex was about two bodies wanting to find release with each other; the kiss had been more personal—intimate. The thought frightened her. Safer to stay away so there wasn't a repeat.

Not like there would be a repeat. Not with Aiden spending most of his time in his room or in the library, probably regretting what had happened. Mya had absolutely nothing to worry about.

Besides, keeping Noah busy, entertained, and away from Aiden was a challenge. When he wasn't playing in the makeshift toy room or kicking a ball outside, he asked questions about Aiden. Noah wanted to invite Aiden to join their games. Telling her son "no" over and over again made Mya feel like a broken record. If they played with cars, Noah would tell her only boys knew the different models and he should ask Aiden which ones were better. When they played a game of one-on-one soccer, he complained that girls couldn't kick a ball as hard as boys and he should get Aiden to play.

Sick of hearing Noah talk about Aiden, she kicked the ball so hard it went flying over the fence and disappeared into the surrounding bushland.

Argh!

This was the first time Noah had been around a man capable of doing all those things a son would do with a father, and Noah clearly wanted it to continue forever. Every time she had to remind him that Aiden didn't have time to play with them, she died a little inside.

They didn't even eat at the same time. Mya would always leave leftovers in the fridge for Aiden, and she'd taken to locking their bedroom door to stop Noah from making any more late-night trips to the kitchen, considering how the last one had gone.

Still, she couldn't stop thinking about the first time he'd gone to the kitchen for a midnight snack…

Neither of them had heard her come down the stairs, and she'd stayed in the doorway, watching them with voyeuristic joy. Aiden had been reading *Wally the Lost Whale*, and Noah's attention had been on Aiden the whole time, enraptured not by the story—which he'd heard a hundred times—but by the man reading it.

For a second, she'd thought, *What a perfect moment*. The little family Noah deserved. When the book had closed, it had snapped her out of her musings. The scene had been far from *perfect* because Aiden could never—would never—fill the role of Noah's father. He'd been very clear on that. Several times. But when Aiden had kissed her with a passion that melted her bones, she couldn't help wondering what a life with him would be like.

She told herself over and over that she needed to forget about Aiden. He wasn't her future husband or

Noah's future father. She needed to manage her rampaging libido. In a few weeks, she could reactivate her dating apps and begin her search for a partner in earnest with Aiden Doyle and his sexual magnetism firmly in her rearview mirror.

The front door buzzed while she sat on the floor doing a puzzle with Noah.

"Who's that?" he asked.

"I don't know."

"Aren't you going to get it?"

"Aiden's downstairs; he can."

But when the bell buzzed again and then for the third time, she sighed, "I better see who it is. Stay here and finish the puzzle, okay?"

Jogging downstairs, she opened the door. The last person she'd expected to see stood on the veranda. "Mr. Masters, is there a problem?"

"No problem. I wanted to see how things are going. Where's Aiden?"

"I think he's in the library," she said.

He raised an eyebrow. "You *think*?"

"Mr. Masters, I know you want me to watch him twenty-four seven but I'm not following him around the house all day. We both deserve some privacy. He's been out of the spotlight like you wanted, and he's not been drinking in a while." She struggled to keep her tone professional rather than defensive. Aiden was home. There hadn't been any more midnight escapades, no tabloid photos, and no social media shenanigans; she'd set up alerts and had been checking for those. Nothing had come up. She didn't need to babysit a grown man like Aiden like he was a child the same age as her son.

But from Mr. Masters's expression, it was clear he didn't feel the same. His lips pressed into a flat line, and he let out a little "hmph" of disapproval. "I'd like to assess that for myself."

Frustrated with Mr. Masters, she gestured for him to enter the house before leading him to the living room. "Take a seat, and I'll get him."

"I think I'll come with you. See for myself."

Unable to disagree, Mya shrugged her shoulders and headed toward the library. When she got there, she knocked on the door and waited for Aiden's response. Nothing. She knocked again, and this time she didn't wait for a response before sticking her head in the room. But the library was empty; Aiden wasn't there.

Huh. A trickle of dread slithered up her spine and settled in her belly. This wasn't looking good.

Putting on a brave face, she turned to her boss. "He must be in his room." Before Mr. Masters could say anything, she hurried up the stairs and knocked on Aiden's door.

Again, there was no answer. Frustrated, she tried again, her eyes drifting toward the stairwell where Mr. Masters was no doubt waiting. "Aiden, are you in there?" But when she poked her head in, the room was empty.

Oh crap!

Mr. Masters watched her walk down the stairs without Aiden. He frowned. "I assume he wasn't in his room." It wasn't a question.

Why did her boss have to show up now? Having to search for her charge was making her look incompetent. To cover her feelings of growing dread, she said, "This house is huge. It often takes me forever to find him. Won't be long." She scurried into the kitchen, then every other room she could think of where Aiden might be, but he was nowhere to be found. She even knocked on all the bathroom doors, peered into the showers, and checked the closets just to be sure. Out of desperation, she checked the backyard, which was populated entirely by songbirds. Her stomach fell into her shoes. Maybe he'd left, exactly as he'd promised he wouldn't.

She had to make sure the car was in the garage. If he'd been in there working out, he'd have had his music blasting like usual, and she wouldn't have wondered for a second where he was. It was possible he'd discovered the joy of headphones, possible… but not likely. Still, she held out hope that he'd be there. But unfortunately, to get to the garage, she had to walk past Mr. Masters again.

"Is there a problem?" he asked, his eyes narrowed. "Has Aiden slipped out of the house without you noticing?"

"No, he's promised he wouldn't do that again." She prayed it was the truth.

When she opened the door to the garage, the gym equipment was unused, as she'd expected.

Aiden's car was gone. Panic bubbled in Mya's chest. She knew better than to trust him! And now Mr. Masters would know she'd messed up again and Aiden would be out of a job. Probably her too, since she couldn't imagine looking Mr. Masters in the eye ever again.

Leaving the room, she shut the door behind her and took a deep breath, ready to tell Mr. Masters Aiden wasn't home and prepare herself for the lecture. Getting fired would soon follow. Ready to face the music, she headed back to where she'd left her boss when something stopped her. A sound. Cocking her head, she waited to see if it would happen again. It did: Noah's giggle followed by Aiden's deep chuckle.

Could Aiden be with Noah? The playroom was the only room she hadn't checked because it was the last place she'd ever thought Aiden would go.

Without explaining to Mr. Masters why she was going upstairs again, she took the steps two at a time. Huffing when she reached the toy room, she stopped suddenly at the open door.

Noah and Aiden were piling colored blocks on top of each other. The tower, almost as tall as Noah, tilted to one side, and Noah held his breath as he put a red block on top. He snatched his hand back and waited with wide eyes. When the tower didn't topple over, he sagged down on the floor.

Aiden took his turn next, and he placed a yellow block on top of the red one. The tower wobbled and smashed to the floor.

"Oh no!" Noah squealed and pointed to Aiden. "You lose again."

"I don't have a steady hand. How do you do it?"

"With practice," Noah said proudly. "Don't worry, Mummy's not good at it either."

Aiden's chuckle speared Mya through the heart. For the second time, visions of a family that looked just like this one flashed before her eyes. Aiden smiled at Noah, giving him his full attention. Noah basked in it. They didn't even notice her standing in the doorway.

Finding her voice, she said as she stepped into the room, "I've been looking everywhere for you. Mr. Masters is downstairs."

Two heads swung toward her. Noah's smile held a hope that melted her heart. One day she'd give him what he craved. But just as Noah's smile bloomed, Aiden's smile faded. Was it because he'd been busted playing with her son or because Mr. Masters was here?

"Your car's not in the garage, I thought you'd left," she said. He must have slipped into the toy room when she was searching downstairs.

"I had my mechanic pick it up early this morning for a service."

"Mr. Masters thinks you're not home. I don't even think he wants you for anything, he just wants to see you with his own two eyes." She left unsaid what the repercussions of Mr. Masters getting the wrong idea might be.

Understanding dawned in Aiden's eyes. "Gotta go, kid." He levered himself to his feet.

"Will you come back?" Noah asked hopefully.

"Aiden is busy," Mya said before Aiden could answer.

A frown flitted across Aiden's face before he could hide it, but he played along with her suggestion. "That's right, kid, I've got to talk to Mr. Masters. Private conversation." His eyes flicked to Mya. "No babysitters or tower builders allowed."

Noah giggled, but Mya felt like she'd done something wrong. Before she could ask, though, Aiden left the playroom and headed for the living room. She waited at the top of the stairs until she could hear the murmur of voices downstairs.

"Can Aiden play later?" Noah asked from behind her.

Turning, she shook her head. "It will just be you and me."

Noah's face fell, but it was best he didn't get too attached. This situation was temporary, even if a part of Mya's soul desperately wanted it to be forever.

Chapter 19

"*I* have news," Amelia announced over the phone. When Mya didn't ask her to elaborate, she continued, "I've fixed you up with a date tonight."

"You did what?" Mya had to whisper because Noah was asleep on the bed beside her. Usually, he slept through anything, but yelling at Amelia would almost certainly wake him up. What was Amelia thinking?

As if hearing her unasked question, Amelia explained, "You got this amazing guy messaging you wanting to chat."

Mya slid out of bed, slipped her feet into her UGG boots, and wrapped herself in a dressing gown. She let herself out of the bedroom. Noah would be awake in about an hour, so she went into the kitchen to make coffee so she could drink it in peace and maybe scream at Amelia for doing something so stupid.

"You said you'd delete my account!" She'd left it for Amelia to cancel her dating profile because Amelia had been the one to sign her up for it in the first place. Turning on the coffee machine, she stared at it, wishing for it to brew faster. She had a feeling she was going to need it after the call with Amelia.

"Well, I was going to, but…"

Mya sighed heavily. "But what?"

"I was checking out your hits, and this guy stood out so I sent him a message and we got to chatting. And Mya, you have to meet him. I think he's the one for you. That's unless you've changed your mind, and you're going to snag Aiden?"

No, she hadn't changed her mind about Aiden. He wasn't a family man, no matter how much her wild imagination wanted it to be otherwise.

"Nothing is going to happen with Aiden." She usually told Amelia everything, but she couldn't tell her she'd almost had sex with him on his desk. That stuff only happened in movies, didn't it? Amelia would have a fit if she found out.

"Then go out with Caleb. He's good-looking, too."

"If he's so great, why don't *you* go on the date?" She poured herself a cup of coffee, added a spoonful of sugar, and went to the living room. Kicking off her UGG boots, she plopped on the couch and curled her legs up under her.

"Not my type," Amelia said quickly. Almost too quickly. Something was up.

Mya shook her head. "Why do you think he's mine?"

"He has a successful career as a construction manager, loves kids, and wants to settle down and start a family. If I wanted that right now, I'd go out with him, but I don't, so he's all yours."

"That's it?" She couldn't believe her sister had decided that this Caleb was the one for her with that little information. Did Amelia really think she was that desperate? "From that description, you think he's great? Did you even bother checking out his personality?"

Amelia scoffed. "Of course I did. He enjoys going to the gym, watching movies, and hanging out with friends."

"Wow. Sounds fascinating," Mya said in a voice dripping with sarcasm.

"There's more; you just need to meet him and find out for yourself."

Mya blew the steam away from the mug before sipping her coffee. "Even if I wanted to go on this date, you know I can't. I have to stay home with Aiden."

"It's sorted. The twin swap worked with Noah's grandparents. We'll do it again!"

"Bad idea. Bad. Horrible. Wretched idea."

"Oh come on, it's not that bad."

"Yes! Yes, it is! What if Aiden finds out? I've been telling him he's not allowed to sneak out of the house. It's a bit hypocritical if I do it. This is a terrible idea!"

"You're not the one who's under house arrest. Besides, how will he find out? I won't tell him I'm not you, and Noah will keep the secret just like he did before."

"I don't know…"

"You can't cancel," Amelia told her when she hesitated. "You've agreed to meet him, and the restaurant's booked. What if he's the love of your life and you've stood him up?"

Mya's heart pounded with dread, but she said, "Fine. What time do I have to be there?"

Mya and Amelia made plans and worked out how the twin swap would happen without Aiden noticing. Mya still didn't think it was a good idea, but when Amelia was set on something, it was hard to change her mind. It was easier just to go along with her off-the-wall ideas.

By the time Noah had woken up and walked downstairs, Mya had cooked his favorite breakfast: pancakes with strawberries. A full Noah would hopefully be a more obedient Noah.

Aiden sauntered into the kitchen. It surprised her that he hadn't waited for them to finish and leave the room like he'd done every other morning. He fixed himself coffee and something to eat before sitting down at the counter.

Her gaze trailed over his body. The way he made faded denim jeans and an old T-shirt look so sexy was a crime. Maybe even a sin, because when she looked at him, her thoughts were anything but pure. *Stop checking out Aiden and think about your date tonight.* Caleb could be the love of her life. Aiden was a pretty distraction. A huge distraction—in more ways than one—but not the long-term commitment she and Noah craved.

He poured himself a second cup of coffee and leaned a hip on the counter. "What are your plans today?"

Plans? Did he somehow know about her dinner date? Play it cool, Mya. Pulling out her best nonchalant shrug, she said, "Just hanging out with Noah."

He nodded once. "Cool. That's what I thought. I want to go for a drive up the coast. I'm going stir crazy inside these four walls."

Oh no. Bad idea with a capital *B*. She needed to nip this idea in the bud. "What if Mr. Masters comes back again and you're not home? He'll think you've gone off to some cheap bar to cause trouble." Maybe that was his plan. God, she hoped not. Not because she'd lose her bonus and extra pay if he did, but because the idea of him with other women made her sick to her stomach.

He tipped his head to one side. "We could all get out of the house."

"Even Noah?" He had warned her to keep Noah away from him. Now he wanted to go for a drive?

"You can't leave him home alone."

Of course, she couldn't. That wasn't what she'd been asking. But she couldn't very well ask Aiden why he'd suddenly changed his mind about being around kids in front of said kid.

Speaking of which, her son turned to her, a broad smile on his face, and asked, "Can we go, Mummy, please?" Noah bounced on the stool, unable to contain his excitement.

"Are you sure?" she asked Aiden.

He nodded.

Not wanting to disappoint her son, she decided to relent. "Okay, we'll get cleaned up and meet you in half an hour."

After all, nothing could go wrong going out for a drive, could it?

Chapter 20

*W*hat the hell had he been thinking? He'd had no intention of leaving the house. He'd come into the kitchen for coffee, and then planned to lock himself in the library. But the idea of spending another day cooped up surrounded by Madeline's boxes of books had him spewing out words he couldn't take back.

Did he want to take back the invitation for a drive? What he *wanted* was to keep his distance from Mya's son. Somehow, on multiple occasions, he'd found Noah underfoot, asking him to do something with him like read stories or build block towers. The kid was okay in small doses. But this wouldn't be a small dose. He hoped he wouldn't regret spending most of the day with him.

Or with Mya. He still hadn't figured out what had possessed him to kiss her in the kitchen the other night. He hadn't even really meant to. The strangest part was that it hadn't felt sexual at all. When he'd left the room, he hadn't been full of regret that they'd both still had their clothes on. Instead, he'd been satisfied with the sensation of her in his arms. He'd never experienced anything like it before—not even with Madeline.

For the past two days, he'd been avoiding Mya, and she appeared to be avoiding him, too. Maybe her son was a convenient excuse to be somewhere Aiden wasn't.

Soon enough, the three of them were cooped up in Mya's car, driving across the Water Valley Bridge. When Aiden glanced in the mirror, he saw the kid in his car seat, his face pressed to the window staring at the water.

"I can see boats!" Noah pointed out the window at them.

"The big ones are called ships, and the little ones are fishing boats," Aiden explained.

"Can we go on a fishing boat one day, Mummy?"

Mya glanced at him over her shoulder. "I don't know anyone who owns one."

Aiden heard a sigh from behind him.

"I know someone who has a cool boat. Maybe we can borrow it." Why had he said that? He didn't like kids! Or at least he didn't anymore. Even if this particular kid seemed pretty great sometimes.

"Today?" Noah said with hope.

"No, Noah. Not today. You need a license to drive a boat, and Aiden doesn't have one. So he can't take you."

Aiden glanced toward Mya and caught her *don't make promises you can't keep* glare. The daggers she was shooting him were a good indicator that he should keep his mouth shut.

Aiden pulled into a car park next to a beach. Swimming was out since the air was on the cool side and the breeze was definitely a bit nippy, but people were still walking along the sand or sitting on beach towels, taking in the autumn weather.

"Want an ice cream, kid?" He turned toward Mya. "That is, if it's okay with your mum."

"Please, Mummy?" Noah turned puppy-dog eyes to his mother.

"Only if Aiden buys me one too," Mya said with a smile.

The kid unbuckled his seat belt, placed his hands on the front passenger and driver's seats, and stood between them. "Can she have one too?" he asked Aiden.

Aiden pulled a face like he was thinking. "I don't know…"

"Oh please! Please! Double please!"

"Well when you put it like that"—he shared a surreptitious wink with Mya—"sure."

"Yay! Ice cream!" he cheered.

They each chose their favorite flavor from the ice cream truck and sat on the warm sand to eat. Every flick of Mya's tongue on her chocolate gelato sent waves of heat through his body. He had to concentrate to keep from groaning out loud.

When they finished their ice cream, they took off their shoes and strolled along the water's edge. The kid *accidentally* got splashed by a wave and squealed with excitement as the water curled around his ankles.

"He'll be soaked through if I don't get him away from the water." Mya's husky laughter arrowed through his chest.

A flyaway strand of hair blew onto her lip, and he reached out to sweep it away, his finger tracing the line of her jaw. Her eyes fluttered closed. He wanted to kiss her more than anything. Damn it, she was a drug, and he was hooked. He leaned in and—

"Look what I found!" Noah bounded over to them,

breaking the connection. They stepped away from each other much to Aiden's dismay.

Mya bent down to see what Noah held in his hands. "Wow, that's a beautiful shell! We should build a sandcastle and put it on top."

"Okay!" The kid dropped to his knees and began piling sand into a heap. Mya joined him. Before they got started, Noah looked up at Aiden. "Will you help us?"

Aiden hesitated for a moment. This was resembling a family day out. Sure, it had been his idea to go for a drive, but this was all too much, especially with the spark of electricity that zapped him every time he got close to Mya. But how could he refuse those big brown eyes?

He couldn't. It was as simple as that. This kid had managed to worm past layer upon layer of protection around his heart. With an internal sigh, he sat and began pushing sand onto the castle.

"Excuse me." He turned and glanced up at the elderly woman who'd spoken. Two little girls peeked out from behind her. "Are you Aiden Doyle?"

He rose and dusted sand from his hands. "Yes, I am."

"I told my granddaughters it was you, but they didn't believe me." She grinned, nudging the two young girls knowingly. "I'm a huge fan of your show! I watch it every week without fail. I'm even watching reruns until next season. Can you give out any details?" she asked, her eyes sparkling with excitement.

"I'm sorry, I'm sworn to secrecy," he said, making a lip-zip motion across his smile. Even if it wasn't a violation of his contract, the next season of *Family First* might not go as planned. That all depended on him.

"I can see you're a great dad, just like the show." She gazed fondly at the sandcastle. "You have a beautiful family. I'll let you get back to them."

Aiden's blood turned to ice as she walked away. "Let's go," he said sharply.

Noah's face fell. "But we haven't finished the castle!"

Mya looked at Aiden, her eyebrows drawn together in a silent question. She noticed his tension. "Aiden's right, Noah. We should get going. It's getting late," she said as she stood her son up and brushed off the sand.

"But I don't wanna go yet!" He stomped his foot, and his lip quivered. Aiden turned away, not wanting to see the disappointment on the kid's face. Anyway, it wasn't his problem. Let Mya deal with the kid's tantrum. It wasn't his son. This wasn't his family.

It never would be.

Noah's face fell. "But we haven't finished the castle!"
The car ride back was quiet. Tense. Even Noah, who liked to fill the air with chatter, sat in silence as he stared out the window. He'd tried a couple of times to ask Aiden a question about something he'd seen out the window, but when Aiden had only grunted unintelligible answers, he eventually gave up.

Something had changed at the beach after he'd spoken to the lady with the two girls. The wind had been coming off the water, so Mya hadn't heard more than a few random snippets from either of them. Had she said something to upset him? Or was spending time with Noah more than he could handle? It had been his idea to get out of the house, and he'd agreed to Mya and Noah coming to keep him out of trouble. She hadn't forced him to do something that made him uncomfortable. It had even seemed like he was getting used to Noah—she'd caught them playing together, for heaven's sake!

So what had happened?

But no answers appeared to be forthcoming on their trip back to Aiden's house. She'd have to talk to him later. Glancing at Aiden's face she amended that to: much later.

When they arrived at Aiden's house, Mya sent Noah upstairs to clean up. She needed to get ready for her date. Why had she agreed to it? Maybe she could call Amelia and have her cancel it.

Yeah, right. As if Amelia would take no for an answer.

Mya needed to tell Noah what was happening—not the part about her going on a date, she'd make something else up—and make him promise not to say a word. She hated lying to him and making him lie, but from the amount of times he'd told her the story from the time they tricked his grandparents, he thought that covering for twin swap was the best game he'd ever played.

She needed to shower and do her hair and makeup *and* sneak Amelia into the house. Just thinking about everything that had to be done weighed heavily on her shoulders. And for what? A date that would probably be a waste of time anyway? She bet Caleb wasn't nearly the perfect match Amelia had built him up to be.

No, she needed to think positively. Amelia had said he was great and that they had a lot in common. What if he had real potential and she never gave it a chance? Her gaze flicked over to Aiden as he walked into the library and shut the door behind him.

He would have kissed her at the beach if Noah hadn't interrupted. And she would have let him. So caught in his eyes, she'd forgotten they were standing on a beach surrounded by people. How could she have explained to Noah why she'd kissed the man she was looking after? Worse yet, how could she explain that to Mr. Masters when the inevitable pictures made it to the gossip sites?

Thankfully, it hadn't gotten that far. She should leave

Aiden to brood in the library and start preparing for the date, but instead of going to her room she stood in front of the library door. He probably wanted to be left alone, but she knocked and walked in anyway, wanting to make sure he was okay after his sudden change in mood earlier.

The setting sun filtered orange and yellow light through the windows. Little motes of dust floated in the air, reflecting the diffused light like diamonds or pixie dust. It was almost like a fairy tale—complete with a beast with a troubled past. Aiden sat in a chair that overlooked the backyard and the adjoining bushland.

"Aiden," she said, waiting for him to turn around. When he didn't, she said his name again, but he didn't move.

When she walked over, she found him sleeping. She stopped to study his face. The creases around his mouth had softened. His full lips were slightly open, and though they looked hard, she knew from experience they were warm and supple. It was the first time she'd seen him so relaxed. Her heart fluttered behind her ribs. God, he was beautiful. If only things were different. If only he didn't come with so much baggage. If only she hadn't. Then maybe...

No, she had to stop thinking that way, or she'd be in big trouble. She tiptoed from the room and let him sleep.

Hopefully the nap would put him in a better mood in case he saw Amelia later and figured out what they'd done.

Oh God, what was she thinking? Tonight was going to be a disaster on every possible level.

Chapter 21

Getting Amelia into the house was easier than Mya had expected. Aiden's library nap meant they didn't have to be clever about getting Amelia into the nursery.

Noah was happy to see his aunt but more excited about playing the twin-swap game again.

Amelia came prepared, wearing clothes Mya had left behind. Mya gave her a spare pair of glasses and hoped Amelia wouldn't trip over her feet trying to focus through them.

While Amelia applied Mya's makeup, she recapped the day's activities—leaving out the almost kiss at the beach—and gave her a rundown of the layout of the house. Noah offered to be her guide so she wouldn't get lost.

Mya wore one of Amelia's dresses, because according to her sister, she didn't own anything appropriate for a date. Taking a deep breath, Mya looked at herself in the mirror. She wore a silky green camisole-style dress with spaghetti straps that flowed over her curves and flared inches above her knees. A pair of nude strappy heels, gold hoop earrings, and a matching clutch rounded out the outfit.

"I'm overdressed," Mya said worriedly.

"You look great. Caleb is going to drool all over you," Amelia countered.

Mya shot her a wry look. "That's not the kind of date I'm hoping for."

"There's got to be some kind of sexual spark, otherwise what's the point?" Amelia bopped Mya on the nose with a knuckle. "Now hold still."

Holding still, Mya thought about the *sexual spark* she had with Aiden. Sexual spark? More like a sexual lightning strike. But a good relationship needed more than just sex. Sure, that was important to her, but so were things like love, loyalty, and trust. Aiden didn't do any of those.

"Okay, it's time." She didn't know whether she was more nervous about meeting a stranger for dinner or having to sneak past the library on her way out. "And you parked your car where I told you to on the street?"

"Yep." Amelia tossed Mya the keys.

Leaving Amelia in the bedroom, she made her way quietly down the stairs. She held her breath when she tiptoed past the library doors and didn't take another breath until the door to the house shut behind her.

Aiden awoke with a crick in his neck and the urgent need to pee. He glanced out the window to note the sun had set fully—where had the time gone? Apparently he'd napped the evening away. That never happened. He wasn't the napping type, but after everything today, he guessed his brain needed a rest. And since drinking was out of the question with Little Miss Follow The Rules around, sleep was his only viable option. Stretching his arms over his head, he felt a few vertebrae crack.

His stomach rumbled, reminding him that he hadn't eaten anything since the ice cream on the beach. He was hungry. Hungry for both food and Mya if he was honest with himself.

Even after finding out she had a kid and meeting said kid, he still wanted her. In fact, he wanted her more than ever. There was something about the way she wouldn't let him walk all over her while not shutting him down completely that appealed to him.

There was only one thing to do: find Mya.

Thankfully, it appeared that finding her wouldn't be that hard. From out in the hallway, he heard the kid complaining that he was hungry and Mya's voice answering. Or at least it sounded like Mya. Aiden was too far away to hear the words through the sturdy wooden door, but there was something off about her voice. He frowned.

Crossing the room and opening the door, he found the pair still in the hallway on their way to the kitchen. The two froze. He opened his mouth to say hello when something odd struck him.

The woman in front of him wasn't his Mya.

Oh, she looked like his Little Miss Follow The Rules. Same hair. Same brown eyes. Same baggy clothes. But the woman wearing them looked like she was wearing a costume instead of sinking into them like they were both armor and an old friend like his Mya did. His gaze traveled from her face down to her feet and back up again.

The fake Maya stiffened for an instant, her hand tightening around a beaming Noah's hand as she checked him out. And she was checking him out, but there wasn't the same barely suppressed passion in her eyes and his dick didn't get hard like it did under the real Maya's scrutiny. As if a light switch had been flipped, the woman's posture changed, becoming an exaggerated likeness of his Mya.

She fake smiled at him and said, "I'm making dinner for Noah. Would you like something?" There was a little quiver in her voice, and more, the tone in her voice wasn't quite right.

His eyebrows drew together, and he crossed his arms over his chest. "Who the hell are you?"

Chapter 22

*A*melia was right; Caleb was perfect. Not only handsome with dark-blond hair, piercing blue eyes, and a strong jawline, he was tall, and his muscular body looked like he knew his way around a gym.

Check.

Even better, he had a great personality. He asked her questions and seemed genuinely interested in her answers and made her laugh with funny stories.

Double check.

Amelia had chosen her date well. But if Caleb was so perfect, why didn't she feel a spark? She'd felt nothing, not even a flicker of interest. When he'd introduced himself, he'd put a hand on her arm as he'd kissed her cheek, and crickets. Most women would celebrate hitting the jackpot with this date, but all Mya could think about was how things were going at Aiden's house.

"So, when he asked me if I knew his name, I stood there with my mouth open in shock. He slapped me on the back and laughed," Caleb chuckled.

Mya realized she'd zoned out and only heard the last part of the story but laughed along with him.

When the waitress arrived with their desserts, she wondered if Amelia had fed Noah. Should she call her? No, her son always vocalized when he was hungry; he'd let her know.

What if Amelia was alone with Aiden? Would he try to kiss her? Or worse, lay her down on his desk and have sex with her? Amelia would never let that happen. Even though she'd told her sister there wasn't anything going on, she trusted Amelia wouldn't let things get out of hand. But Aiden could be hard to resist.

"Is something wrong?" Mya's attention jerked to Caleb. He stared at her with concern.

"Oh, umm, no. I was trying to figure out if that guy sitting over there is Aiden Doyle." Oh crap! She could have used dozens of other names. Aiden's name slipped off her tongue.

Caleb turned in his seat to look. "No, that's not him."

The end of the date could not have come quickly enough. She wanted to enjoy her time with Caleb, but all Mya could think about was what was happening at Aiden's.

"Would you like to go for a coffee?" he asked as they stood outside of the restaurant.

"I'm sorry. I have to get back to my son. Maybe another time?"

He arched an eyebrow. "Will there be another time?"

Mya was about to say *of course*, but her shoulders sagged, and she sighed. "I'm sorry. I had a great time and I should say yes, but…"

"You're just not feeling it."

She shook her head. "I'm sorry." The guy was perfection incarnate, but she couldn't keep the image of

Sir Imperfection, Mr. Rule Breaker himself, Aiden Doyle, out of her head.

"That's okay." He leaned in and gave her a kiss on the cheek and again, no zing. "Nice meeting you. Whoever you're thinking about is a lucky guy."

Mya gasped, "I wasn't—"

"It's okay. Good luck."

Even though he was right, Mya felt unreasonably offended that he'd given her the brush-off. She had half a mind to chase him down and kiss the hell out of him. The other half of her mind was still thinking about Aiden.

Mya got in the car and drove home. She parked in the spot Amelia had left her car earlier, pulled out her phone, and dialed her sister's number. After a few rings, it went to voice mail.

That was weird. Why hadn't Amelia kept her phone on her in case Mya needed to check on Noah? She redialed the number. Still no answer.

Mya frowned. Maybe Amelia was putting Noah to bed. Sometimes that took a while. She sat in the car and waited fifteen minutes before dialing again.

Amelia didn't answer.

She glanced at the time. Noah should be in bed by now. Why wasn't Amelia answering? Then thoughts from the restaurant came flooding back. Aiden and Amelia could be doing all the things Mya had been fighting against. It wouldn't take much for Aiden to seduce her sister. Mya knew firsthand how hard it was to resist him. Was Amelia strong enough?

Leaping from the car, she raced up the driveway and let herself into the house. The living room was dark and quiet, but she heard giggling and a low, deep chuckle coming from the library. With no hesitation, she opened the door with so much force it slammed back on the wall.

She'd forgotten about the twin swap, and she'd just ruined their ruse. All she wanted to do was break them apart.

Amelia and Aiden flinched and swung their heads in her direction. Instead of finding them as they lay naked in each other's arms like she'd imagined, they sat cross-legged on the floor doing one of Noah's puzzles. A gush of relief escaped her lungs. She'd overreacted. She should have known her sister would never do anything sexual with Aiden.

"Mya, you're home early," Amelia said and got to her feet. "How was your date?"

Aiden's gaze traveled over her. Deep lines creased his forehead.

"Umm, okay, I guess," Mya said. "What's going on?" She motioned to the puzzle.

"Aiden saw straight through our trick. Can you believe he knew I wasn't you the second he saw me?" With her back to Aiden, Amelia widened her eyes and mouthed, O*h my God. No one can do that*. "So-o-o," Amelia dragged out the word. "Was Caleb as good as I predicted?" Her sister smiled widely and wiggled her eyebrows suggestively.

Mya's gaze flicked to Aiden, whose face had darkened like a storm. "Maybe we should talk about this later." An eyebrow rose as she tried to convey a message to Amelia to drop it.

Ignoring her, Amelia said, "And is he as hot as his photo? Please tell me he's a great kisser." Amelia bit her lip, trying not to laugh.

"And I said, we'll talk about this *later*. It's getting late. I'll call you tomorrow." Mya grabbed Amelia by the arm and ushered her from the room. "What was that all about? Why grill me about the details of my date in front of Aiden?" Mya whispered through gritted teeth.

"Why not? If there's nothing happening between you

two, why would he care?" Amelia arched an eyebrow, waiting for Mya to contradict her, but she kept her lips sealed. She rolled her eyes. "Please. You expect me to believe that? When he cornered me, I had to tell him where you were, and when I told him you were on a date, I thought he'd rush out of the house and drag you back here. I had to point out he was acting like a ridiculous cartoon caveman before he'd calm down. But sure, there's *nothing* between you."

"He wasn't jealous. Only mad because I did something I've been telling him he can't do."

"Whatever you say." Amelia shrugged, but Mya could tell her sister wasn't buying her excuse. With a playful grin, Amelia said, "He knew I wasn't you the second he saw me! No one can tell us apart like that!"

"So? Gran used to—sometimes."

"And who else besides Gran and Noah? Do you know what this means?"

"It means nothing."

"It *means* Aiden is *the one*." Amelia's eyes lit up with excitement. "Forget about dating apps, and grab that man because he's a keeper."

Mya opened the door. "Good night, Amelia." She pushed her out of the house.

Amelia spun around. Her mouth opened to say something, but Mya slammed the door in her face.

Hanging her head for a beat, she stood facing the door. She needed to confront Aiden and explain.

But how could she explain without being a hypocrite? For days, she'd been on his back about leaving the house and nagging him about following the rules in case Mr. Masters found out. Now, she was the one sneaking out. Had she just undone all the progress she'd made with Aiden? Like Amelia had pointed out, Mya wasn't the one on house arrest, but she was still being paid to stick with Aiden twenty-four seven. Because of this incident, would he think he was justified in going back to his wild ways?

Better to face him now and get the argument over with. From the expression on his face when Amelia had mentioned Caleb, Mya knew Aiden was angry.

Taking a deep breath, she pulled her shoulders back and walked into the library to face the music.

Chapter 23

*A*iden sat at his desk with his feet propped on the top, a book open in his lap. He hadn't read a word. Gripping it so tight, Aiden was surprised the pages hadn't crumbled in his hands.

Why the hell had she gone on a date? She should've been home making sure *he* followed the rules. But she'd used her sister as a decoy. Did she honestly believe he wouldn't know the difference? They looked nothing alike. Yes, they had the same hair color and style. Their eyes were a similar shade of brown, but Mya's were slightly lighter, like a silky caramel. Even he had to admit that their facial features were identical, but Amelia's lacked a certain essential Mya-ness, and from the moment he'd laid eyes on her, he'd known she was an impostor.

Amelia had initially tried to laugh it off and ask him if he'd been drinking. Her laugh didn't have the same playful husky sound that sent arrows of pleasure to his groin every time he heard it, and her eyes lacked the desire that he so often saw in Mya's.

He had to give her credit; she played Mya beautifully,

but not so perfectly that he'd believed it. When she'd eventually given up the charade and told him about Mya's date, the only thing that had kept him home was his car still being at the mechanic's.

Why had he reacted like that? Mya was free to date whoever she wanted. Surely he'd been pissed not because of her date, but because she'd set rules for him that she hadn't abided by herself.

He looked up when Mya rapped softly on the doorjamb. "May I come in?" she asked.

He nodded.

She was still dressed for her date. Gone were the baggy, ill-fitting clothes. She'd replaced them with a silky number that flowed over her body like water. She had pulled one side of her hair up with a shiny clip above her ear exposing the creamy length of her neck and sending golden waves cascading down her back. Damn, he hated how the sight of her made his body ache with desire. Every muscle screamed to get up and pull her into his arms.

He reminded himself she'd been on a date. His jaw clenched tight.

She stood in front of his desk with her hands clasped in front of her. "I'm sorry I went out. I shouldn't have. I can't expect you to follow Mr. Masters's rules if I don't. That was selfish of me, and I apologize."

"Are you seeing *Caleb* again?" He could barely spit out the man's name.

A line creased between her brows. "No."

"Why not?" He tossed the book on the desk and stood up.

She evaded the question. "Look, Aiden, you don't have to worry about me sneaking out again. It was a stupid thing to do. I should never have listened to Amelia."

But he wasn't about to let it go. "Why aren't you seeing

him again?" He couldn't explain why he was so desperate to know the answer. But he needed her to answer his question. "Amelia said he was perfect for you."

Her frown deepened. "She should've kept her mouth shut."

"Was he perfect?" he asked, taking another step.

"He was nice," she answered. Her gaze flicked to his mouth. There was that look that made his heart race. The look that even Amelia hadn't been able to imitate.

"Why did Amelia think he was perfect?" he pressed.

She shrugged. "Because he ticked all the boxes of what I'm looking for in a man."

"And what are you looking for?" Aiden knew before she even told him that he wouldn't qualify.

She shook her head. "It doesn't matter."

"Tell me."

She sighed. "I want someone who is loyal, kind, and wants a family… especially one already made. I want someone to love Noah and be the father he's aching for."

All the things he steered clear of. She and Noah deserved to have those things; he knew that. But damn it, why did it twist like a knife in his gut knowing he couldn't be the one to provide them?

"Just to love Noah? What about you?" Surely, she wouldn't be so selfless as to enter a loveless and passionless relationship just to give Noah the father he wanted. But he didn't have to look at her to know it was true. Mya would always put her family first.

"Yes, to love me too." Her eyes flicked away, and he wondered if she'd ever been anyone's top priority before. She deserved to be someone's top priority.

"Did he fit the criteria?" He couldn't let this go; he had to know. Even if the truth would be like a knife in his heart.

"I don't want to talk about this." She turned to leave, but he put a hand on her arm to stop her. Her head tilted up to meet his gaze, and they stood there for a moment in silence.

"Did he fit the criteria?" he repeated, saying each word slowly.

"Why do you care?" A flicker of anger but also desire leapt into her eyes.

"Answer the question." He paused for a beat. "Please."

She blew out a long breath. "Yes, he did, and he was gorgeous too."

"Why aren't you seeing him again?"

Her hands fiddled with the hem of her dress. "Because…"

"Because why? He trailed a finger up her arm, along her neck, and down her jaw. Her lips quivered, the flicker of desire morphing into a raging bonfire.

"Because I kept thinking about you!"

Aiden's hand dropped to the silky fabric at her waist, and she pressed her body into his. Her lips opened willingly against his, and they kissed like lovers who'd been apart for years.

His fingers wound in her hair, tipping her head back, allowing him access to kiss her jaw, neck, and the tops of her breasts. Nudging her backward, he pressed her against the desk, letting her go only long enough to unzip her dress. The zipper caught, and he pulled hard enough to rip the seams instead.

"That was Amelia's dress!"

"I'll buy her a hundred more," he growled as the material slithered down her body to pool on the floor.

Her strapless bra was light pink with dark pink rosettes embroidered in silk. She wore matching panties too. He paused. Had she worn this for her date in case it went further than dinner? He clenched his teeth. Even though he had no claim over who Mya slept with, the thought of Caleb putting his hands on her sent a surge of jealousy through his veins.

Like she'd read his mind, she said, "I'm not one to have sex on a first date, but Amelia said I should be prepared, and it was easier to just do it and keep her happy."

"What about me? Will you sleep with me?"

She nibbled her bottom lip as she looked at him.

He caressed her cheek. "Don't overthink it. It's two people attracted to one another. Don't make it more than that."

He knew the moment she'd decided because her eyes smoldered. Her hands went to the hem of his T-shirt and pulled it up his torso. She trailed kisses up the newly exposed skin, pouring fuel on his fire.

Lifting her so she could sit on the desk, he spread her legs and stepped between them. Out of all the rooms in the house, there was something about the library. When she left, he'd never be able to look at the desk—or the room—the same way again.

The sudden jolt at the thought of her leaving snapped him upright. When her time here was over, she would be gone. Forever. Out of his life. Never to return. Wasn't that exactly what he wanted?

Then why did his heart ache so much?

Mya blinked, a questioning look in her eyes. "Aiden, are you okay?" she asked, uncertainty in her voice.

He wanted this, wanted it more than he'd ever wanted anything, but he had to make sure he and Mya were on the same page. "I can't tick your boxes. I'm not the perfect man for you."

"I know."

"If we do this, I won't change my mind." He needed to say that out loud, more for himself than for Mya.

Her hand slid to the nape of his neck, bringing their mouths a hairbreadth apart. "I *know*. It's okay. I want this."

They were all the words he needed.

He didn't know who moved first, but their lips locked and their hands roamed over each other's bodies. He ran his palms over her breasts, hips, and legs, and to the heat between her thighs. She hissed and arched her back when he stroked, putting her breasts within easy reach of his lips. Wasting no time, he kissed her nipples.

Her pleading gasps spurred him on to touch even more of her. Belly. Thighs. Arse.

Her hands grabbed the waist of his jeans and tugged him closer. She wrapped her legs around him and rocked her groin against his.

Her fingers found the fly of his jeans and unfastened them. She slid her hand inside, wrapping her fingers around his cock. Oh God, she felt so good. He pumped into her hand once, twice, then stopped so the fun didn't end too soon.

He lifted her up and carried her to the couch. Unsteady on her feet, she sank down onto the cushions, eye level with the hard-on straining at his underwear. She nibbled her lower lip, and her eyes flicked up to his face, full of need. The question in her eyes was obvious.

He groaned out loud. As much as he'd love her mouth on him like that, he was desperate to be inside her more.

Grabbing his wallet from his back pocket, he pulled a condom out and tossed it on the floor beside him. When she lay back on the couch, he took no time removing his jeans and underwear and diving on top of her.

The feel of their bodies, skin on skin, set a fire within him. He stripped her of her undies as she undid her bra clasp and tugged it free of her breasts. He lifted himself up to admire her nude form. Was there anything so beautiful? So sexy? He couldn't think of anything. He bent to lave his tongue over the column of her neck.

She squirmed and thrust against him. "Hurry." Her voice shook as her hand slid down the length of his back and grabbed his butt, pulling him toward her. She was as desperate for him as he was for her.

But just before he entered her, he pulled away.

She groaned, "Where are you going?"

"Condom." Christ, so desperate to fuck her, he almost forgot the most important thing. He never forgot to use a condom. Mya was screwing with his mind. Picking up the foil packet, he tore it open and slid it on.

She cried out as he entered her, and they both paused, breathing deeply as they stared at each other. Then Mya moved, and his mouth claimed hers as he moved along with her, the rhythm slow and languid. She locked her legs around his waist like she didn't want him to leave. There was no way in hell he was going anywhere. He'd found his new happy place. Being with Mya, being inside her, felt like paradise. A paradise with only the two of them. She arched underneath him, encouraging him to go faster. And he happily complied. Their tempo picked up, becoming hard and fast. She bucked under him as he drew a nipple into his mouth.

"Oh, God, Aiden, I'm going to… to…" She couldn't seem to find the words.

It didn't matter; he knew what she was trying to convey. "Honey, let go." He switched his attention to the other breast, drawing the hardened nipple into his mouth. She was on the brink, and so was he. He didn't know how much longer he could hold off. He slipped a hand between them, and a finger circled around the button that would help her climax.

"Yes… Aiden…" she panted right before she exploded in his arms. As she pulsed around him, he came too, thrusting deep a few more times before collapsing, remembering at the last second to prop himself up on one arm so he didn't accidentally squish her. Her heated flesh quivered underneath him. Or was it him quivering? Too spent to judge, he nestled his face in the curve of her neck, breathing in the scent of jasmine and sex. He wanted to savor this moment, sear it into his brain, to replay over and over in his dreams.

When he got his breath back, he eased his weight from her. She sat up and reached for her bra. The moment had passed to be replaced by the morning-after awkwardness. "I should check on Noah," she said, pink coloring her cheeks. Was she embarrassed by what had happened? She shouldn't be. She'd been magnificent. Amazing.

She found her panties next to her feet and slid them on. His cock twitched at the display. Did she know how fucking sexy she was? How much he wanted her?

Before she found her dress, he held on to her hand and turned her toward him. Her eyes looked everywhere but directly at him.

"Are you okay?" He'd hate for her to regret what had happened because he couldn't—wouldn't—regret this night.

She gave a shy smile. "Yes, but I should go."

Still sitting on the couch, he tugged at her waist so she fell into his lap. She squealed, "What are you doing?"

He was ready to go again. As much as it killed him, he didn't move. "Do you regret what we did?"

She took a moment before she answered, "No."

Aiden let out a relieved breath. Yes, it was only sex.

Nothing more, but he had a strong feeling he'd never forget it.

"Wanna do it again?"

She slid her hand between his legs and felt his hardness, then swung around so she was straddling him.

He guessed that was a yes.

Chapter 24

*M*ya checked on Noah, who she said could sleep through a bomb explosion, and then joined Aiden in his bed for round two. Spent and sweaty, she lay over his chest as they tried to catch their breath.

Normally this was the time when the woman he slept with would leave. They knew there weren't any cuddly sleepovers. But as Mya started to slide from bed, he hooked onto her waist and anchored her to him.

"I should go," she said, lifting her head to look at him but making no more effort to leave.

He brushed her hair from her face tenderly and stared into her eyes. "Tell me why it's so important to find the *perfect* man."

"Why?" she asked, tearing her gaze away to fumble at the night table for her glasses.

He shrugged like he wasn't interested, but damn it, every fiber of his being needed to know about the man who might fill that place in Mya's life. "Just curious."

Settling the frames on her face, she sprawled on his

chest and rested her chin on her forearms. They were so close and comfortable it was like they'd been doing this for years, not one night.

Her breasts pressed against his chest, her heart beating in tandem with his. He tucked his hands under his head to stop himself from touching her.

"I don't think there's such a thing as the *perfect* man. But it's important to find the *right* man," she said finally.

"You've never mentioned Noah's father."

She sighed. "Daniel died in a car accident."

"Shit. I'm sorry." He knew firsthand how difficult it was growing up without a father. His dad had died in a boating accident when Aiden was young, and his life had never been the same. "You both must miss him."

Mya shook her head. "Noah never met him. He died before he was born."

The poor kid. No wonder he hung off him every time he was in the room. He was starving for a father figure. Unfortunately, he'd set his sights on the wrong guy. Aiden could never be that for him.

"It must have been hard raising him on your own." He knew how much his mother had struggled.

"Gran helped, and Amelia is like his second mother."

"What about your mum and dad?"

She turned her head, her hair falling in front of her face. Brushing the locks back, he tilted her chin so he could see her.

"I never knew my father," she answered after a long minute. "He took off when he learned my mother was pregnant. As for Mum, she died a week before my seventeenth birthday."

What kind of arsehole left a pregnant woman? Then he gave an inwardly mocking laugh. It happened more than he'd thought. If the father of Madeline's baby hadn't taken off, maybe he wouldn't have had to cradle another man's dead baby in his hands.

"What happened to your mother?" he asked to remove the image he'd conjured from his mind.

Mya's voice grew distant. "One night she was out drinking, stumbled onto a busy street, and got hit by a car."

This conversation kept getting worse. God, how much had this woman been through in her life? He pulled her off his chest and leaned them both against the headboard to cradle her against him. His hand caressed her arm. "I'm sorry that happened to you. You must miss her."

She shrugged. "She wasn't around much. Having us at eighteen wasn't easy for her. We got in the way of her partying and carefree lifestyle. Gran raised us. Mum came home now and then to check on us, but she wasn't the maternal type."

"You haven't taken after your mother. I see the way you love Noah. You'd do anything for him."

"I was *exactly* like my mother," she scoffed. "The partying. The drinking. The mindless, meaningless sex. I did it all."

Aiden gazed down at her with surprise, but she kept her eyes downcast. "You don't look like the drinking and partying kinda girl."

"I'm not now." She started tracing lines and curves onto his skin aimlessly. "Not since I fell pregnant with Noah. After Mum died, it messed me up. I had no father and no mother. I never got to experience what a real mother did for their children. I figured if she neglected us for parties, there must have been a good reason. So I followed in her footsteps to see what was so great about it."

Aiden hummed, a nonjudgmental sound. He linked their fingers together and clasped her hand to his chest.

She squeezed his hand and continued, "For three years I put on revealing clothes, partied, got drunk, and hooked up with guys trying to understand why my mother chose that life over her family. But I never found the answer I was looking for." She took a deep breath. "I should have stopped. Gran and Amelia begged me to, but I wanted that answer. She abandoned us for that lifestyle, so it must have been worth it. I searched and I searched. Went to party after party, drank so much that I often couldn't walk home, but still I never got any closer to the truth." Mya met his eyes. "The day I found out I was pregnant, I stopped. I had my answer."

"What was it?" he asked.

The deep, shuddery breath she took vibrated against his side. "No amount of *fun* was worth leaving your kids for. Mum was selfish. She didn't care for us or about us like a mother should, and I would never make my baby endure the things Amelia and I went through. That's when I promised I'd give Noah everything I missed from my mother."

"A family with the perfect man," he stated.

"A family, yes. And a man who will love my son like his own."

"And what about you? You don't mention wanting love."

She shifted on the bed and sat up, dragging the sheet with her to cover her breasts. "I should go to my room. I don't want Noah to wake up and come looking for me."

She didn't want to answer the question, but he let it go. It was none of his business.

Gathering her clothes, she quickly dressed and slipped from the room.

He wanted to stop her and pull her back to bed and have her stay the night. With his unsettled thoughts, feelings, and the taste of her in his mouth, it was better to let her leave. He'd gotten what he wanted; now it was back to normal. Well, as normal as his life had become.

The next morning, Mya stayed upstairs for as long as possible, not yet ready to face Aiden. She didn't want to take any chances of running into him. She hadn't processed what had happened last night and how she felt about it. Hopefully he was locked away in the library like usual.

That library had some serious vibes. Something about the room switched on the sexual chemistry between her and Aiden. Avoiding it might keep her out of trouble. But the library hadn't been to blame when she'd followed him to his bedroom. That had been all her. And all Aiden.

He'd asked if she regretted sleeping with him, and she'd told the truth when she'd said no. How could she regret such a magical night? She was a woman with needs. Maybe, Amelia was right; she needed to clear out the cobwebs and have a fling before she focused on finding the right man to make a family with. But when she tried picturing what that man looked like, the image of Aiden filled her mind. She shook her head. Impossible. He even admitted he was the wrong kind of man.

She'd never opened up so much about her life after her mother died. Something about the way Aiden listened with no judgment in his eyes had had her spilling her guts.

Keeping it buried was her way of dealing with it. If she didn't talk about it, she could pretend she hadn't spent three years throwing her life away. Every time she'd left the house she'd put stress on her grandmother and Amelia, who'd wondered if she'd make it home. She should never have done that. And she would be forever sorry for causing them pain.

"Mummy, I'm staarrrving." Noah stretched out the word as he held his stomach and rolled on the bed, bringing Mya out of her musings.

"My poor son is fading away. I need to feed him," Mya said, pretending to examine him. "Lift your shirt, I need to see if your belly is still there."

Noah giggled. "Bellies can't go away." But he lifted the shirt anyway.

"Hmmm. This is serious." She bent over him to take a closer look, then blew raspberries on his exposed stomach. Noah twisted, wiggled, and laughed as she tickled him.

"Come on," she said when he couldn't take anymore, "let's have breakfast."

"Yes!" Noah bounded from the bed and ran from the room.

"Careful on the stairs," she called, rushing after him to make sure he was safe.

When she reached the bottom of the stairs, she heard voices in the kitchen. The deep one she would recognize anywhere. It had whispered things in her ear last night that made her whole body blush. The other voice was female. Her heart skipped a beat. Would he invite a woman over after the night they'd had? While they hadn't promised each other any kind of exclusivity, the thought still rankled. Then she heard Noah's little voice. Surely Aiden wasn't doing anything inappropriate with her son in the same room?

Taking a deep breath and pulling her shoulders back, she walked into the kitchen. Three sets of eyes turned to stare at her. She sagged with relief when the mystery woman proved to be Aiden's sister, Chloe.

"Morning, Mya. Sleep well?" Chloe smiled, and Mya had to wonder if she knew she'd spent most of the night in Aiden's bed.

Mya's gaze snapped to Aiden. She couldn't read his poker face. Had he said anything to Chloe? Why would he talk to her about his sex life? Maybe they were really close—Amelia overshared sometimes. Her cheeks grew warm.

She played innocent. "I did. Except this little wiggly worm likes to kick me." She messed up Noah's hair. He squirmed, trying to pull away from her.

Picking up a mug from the counter, Aiden took a sip of coffee, hiding his lips, but she could see the smile in his eyes.

"What are your plans today?" Chloe asked.

"Catching up on some work and babysitting this guy." She pointed to Aiden, who scowled at her with a hint of mirth in his eyes.

"Excellent. Then you can help me," Chloe said to Aiden.

"Doing what?" He stared at her warily.

"Industry stuff. I need someone to bounce ideas off of, and you've been chosen."

Mya would love for Aiden to spend the day with Chloe. It would give her more time to work on Wally the Whale's next big adventure. Noah had been begging for more. As an additional bonus, it would keep her away from Aiden.

"I'll leave you to it." She put Noah's empty cereal bowl in the dishwasher. "Get dressed, buddy, and don't forget to brush your teeth."

"Okay," he said, sliding off the stool and racing from the room. Did that boy ever walk?

"Cute kid," Chloe said.

"Thanks. Some days, that's the only thing saving him from being tied to a chair," she joked. "I'll be in my room if you need me." Mya directed this to both of them.

Aiden's lazy glance sent lightning down her spine. "I'll let you know."

That hadn't been what she'd meant, but she couldn't say she minded the insinuation.

Chapter 25

*I*n the library, Aiden sat on one side of the desk while Chloe pulled up a chair across from him. Casting briefs and headshots lay between them. Chloe held the photos up for his opinion.

"Him." He pointed to the actor on her left.

She glanced at it and frowned. "Really? He's not too rough-and-tumble? He's supposed to be part of a bachelor auction in a rom-com, remember?"

Aiden sighed. This was the fourth time Chloe had questioned his choice. If his sister already knew who she wanted, why was she asking for his opinion? "Give him a haircut and shave, and he'll be great. I've worked with him; he's good." Aiden scrubbed a hand through his hair. "Besides, it's not like he's the leading man."

Placing the picture on the table, Chloe studied it closely. "You're right."

Aiden rolled his eyes.

Before Chloe held up the next picture, Mya ducked her head into the room. "Would you like coffee or something?"

Aiden thought of *something* he'd like: her sprawled over the desk.

Every time he looked at the desk he couldn't help thinking about Mya—hell, he thought about her no matter what room he was in. After Madeline, no woman had held his attention for more than the few hours they'd spent in bed together. They'd been forgotten the moment they walked out the door. But Mya... God, she'd gotten under his skin. Every gasp, pant, and moan replayed over and over in his mind. He wanted—needed—to hear those sounds again. Hopefully once more would be enough to purge her from his system.

"Aiden?" Chloe snapped her fingers in front of his face, bringing him back to the task at hand. "Are you still with us? Mya wants to know if you want anything."

Even from across the library, he could see the color flood to Mya's cheeks, and he'd bet his left nut she was thinking about what had happened in here too.

"No coffee for me, thanks," he said.

Mya nodded and left the room.

"Wow." Chloe fanned her face with the headshot. "Is it getting hot in here?"

"Open a window." Aiden ignored the smirk plastered on his sister's face and gave his full attention to the next batch of photos.

"You've worked your charm on Mya too, haven't you?"

Something about the way she said it made his jaw clench. Sure, they'd agreed to keep things casual. But Mya wanted a family. He didn't. There would never be anything serious between them. But he hadn't worked his charm. Instead, she'd bewitched him. Made him want to listen to his heart instead of his head.

Chloe must have sensed the turmoil inside him. "She's been wonderful for you. I haven't seen you smile or look so relaxed since before Mad—" she broke off, nibbling her bottom lip.

"Before Madeline died," he finished for her. "You can say her name, you know. I won't fall into a broken heap on the floor."

"But you used to, see?" She gestured at his head. "That's what I mean when I say Mya's been good for you. We couldn't mention Madeline without you biting our heads off or going off to sulk. It's the first time you've said her name in ages, and I think it's because of Mya. And in the kitchen with Noah…" She pointed in the general direction of the kitchen. "For months you couldn't look at kids, and now you're making one breakfast and telling jokes?" She leaned forward and put her hand on his arm. "This makes me so happy for you."

Aiden picked up a casting brief. "You're reading too much into it. They're living with me. I can't avoid them twenty-four seven."

She propped her head on her hand and said, "I think there's more to it."

"Stop trying to read too much into my life and concentrate on work," he said, shuffling the headshots.

"You like her more than you're willing to admit."

He tossed the photos on the desk with a huff. "Yes, I like her. And yes, the kid isn't so bad either. But we want different things from life. She wants a family. I don't."

"I remember a time when a family was all you wanted, even more than you wanted to be an actor. You wanted the family Dad missed out on with us." She poked him. "Don't let one tragedy ruin the rest of your life." She poked him again for added emphasis.

Aiden batted her hand away. "Thanks, Dr. Phil. Are we working or not?"

Chloe narrowed her eyes. He knew she had more to

say, but thankfully she just sighed and picked up another two photos. "Mean teacher in uplifting teen drama."

"The left one," he said even though the actor on the right was just as talented. He wanted to see if Chloe would question his choice.

Right on cue, she screwed up her nose and asked, "Really?"

Aiden threw his hands up. "If you don't need my opinion, why the hell are you here?"

"I wanted to spend some time with my big brother." She gave him an innocent look that didn't fool him at all. More like she wanted to get some juicy gossip on his situation and report back to Mum and Ethan. He'd bet Mum would stop by in the next few days, just as fake casually as Chloe had.

Chloe pulled a book from under the glossy pictures on the desk. "What's this?" She flicked through the pages. "This is beautiful."

"Mya writes children's books for Noah, and her sister illustrates them."

She flipped to the front of the book to check for the copyright. "Has she published this?"

"No; she writes them only for him."

"There's more?" Chloe's eyes lit up, and he wondered what she was thinking.

"He said he has thousands but I'm guessing it's a bit less than that." He smiled, remembering the proud expression on the kid's face when he told him how much he loved the stories his mum made.

Chloe started flipping through the book again. "She should publish these."

"You're an agent, get it done."

"An agent for actors, not writers." Her bottom lip quirked thoughtfully as she ran her hand over the handmade cover. "Can I take this? I know someone who might be interested."

He paused. Technically the book wasn't his, but Mya deserved more than just babysitting washed-up actors like him or working for producers like Lionel. If this turned into an opportunity for her to shine, he wanted to do everything in his power to make sure she succeeded.

His sister cleared her throat, and he waved a hand at her. "Sure," he said, hoping no one would miss it.

Chloe slipped the book in her bag, and they continued with the briefs.

After Chloe gave him the rundown of a small budget gangster movie set in Australia in the early 1930s, Aiden straightened in his chair. "That sounds interesting. I want this." For the first time in months the thought of working excited him.

"Oh, umm… you don't fit the description of what they're looking for."

"I don't want the role. Who's directing?"

"Tom DiFazio," Chloe said, frowning slightly.

Aiden knew the name. Ethan, normally one to watch his words, had nothing good to say about DiFazio—his skills or his personality. It didn't surprise Aiden that all he could get was a small indie film. "I could do a better job than he could."

"They've already picked their director. Besides, you've never directed a movie before."

"Plenty of episodes of *Family First*, though." He'd enjoyed being behind the camera more than in front of it. "C'mon, Chloe, you know people. Let me talk to the producers."

"You're not my client, and besides, your reputation—" She bit off her sentence.

"What? You think I'll fuck it up? Look, I'm sober and

staying out of trouble like a good little boy. I'm getting my life back in order." Something about this movie felt like a fresh start. He wanted it more than he'd wanted anything in a long time.

"It's a big job," Chloe said. "How can you even do that around *Family First*?"

Aiden shrugged. "They've already got the script to kill me off."

"So, you're just going to flush it right back down the toilet by ditching your show and breaking your contract."

"I'll work it out with Lionel! And it's not like they're going to start shooting tomorrow anyway." He grinned. "Besides, unlike Tom DiFazio, I've never punched a PA for bringing me a lukewarm, flat white."

The conflict was clear on Chloe's face. Finally, with a groan, she said, "Okay. I will make some calls, but I make no promises. But I am not your agent."

"You were Ethan's agent."

"That was one time!"

"He won an Oscar!"

"He's also not a pain in the arse!" She shook her head. "You're a pain in the arse, but you're my pain in the arse. I'll see what I can do."

"Did I ever tell you you're my favorite sister?" He grinned.

She rolled her eyes. "I'm your *only* sister. But I love you too."

Chapter 26

*T*wo days. That's how long Mya had been avoiding eye contact with Aiden. They only spoke when necessary and spent as little time as possible in the same room. And if togetherness was unavoidable, Mya always made sure Noah was with them.

If she kept getting distracted by Aiden, she'd lose sight of what was important: making a happy family for her and Noah. But every time Aiden entered a room, the temperature rose, and she got a not-unpleasant tingling in her lady parts. God… it was hard keeping her hands to herself. She had to, though—sleeping with Aiden again would be a mistake.

Aiden stretched for a mug in the cupboard, and his T-shirt rode up, giving her a glimpse of his lower back. Two nights ago, her hands had raked over his bare skin and he'd shuddered under her fingertips seconds before he fell apart. She choked on her coffee at the memory.

"You okay?" Aiden asked as he poured coffee into his mug.

Making a fist, she pounded on her chest, and Noah

slapped her back. Maybe she should smack herself in the head instead so she'd stop reliving that night.

"Coffee went down the wrong pipe," she croaked between coughing fits.

He grabbed a glass from the cabinet, filled it with water, and slid it in front of her. "Drink this."

"Thanks," she rasped and took a deep gulp.

"Better?"

She nodded.

Once she trusted herself to speak without swallowing her tongue at the sight of Aiden's bare skin, she said, "I have to take Noah to preschool." She glimpsed at Aiden as she gathered their breakfast dishes. The way he stared at her with hooded eyes told her what was on his mind: the same thing that was on her mind.

They'd be alone for the day.

Mya would be strong. She was a freaking grown woman, not some horny teenager whose undies melted away at the sight of a gorgeous guy! *And* she planned to fill the day with errands, so she kept busy. Just in case.

"I need to do a few things and I want to see Gran, so it will take a while. Maybe even until I need to pick Noah back up."

His lips tilted into a small crooked grin. It made him look sexy as hell. The expression told her he knew she was keeping busy on purpose so they wouldn't be alone. "I'll stay home and do stuff here. I'll see you when you get back."

Mya turned to her son. "Noah, sweetie, put your lunch in your bag and go brush your teeth. We'll leave in a few minutes."

He clutched his Justice League lunchbox and left the room.

"You can't stay home without me," Mya said to Aiden.

"I promise I won't go anywhere." When she opened her mouth to tell him that's not what worried her, he quickly added, "Or have anyone over."

She'd skin him alive if he had a woman here after their night together. But why should it matter? They'd had no-commitment sex. Made no promises. They knew where they stood. But why did the thought of him with another woman burn like acid in her stomach?

"You can't stay home. If Mr. Masters drops by and I'm not here, he won't give us a second chance. Third chance? I forget what we're up to."

Noah raced into the room with his backpack on his back.

"Ready, sweetie?" Mya asked.

"Yep, but I can't tie my shoelaces." He stared at his shoes. How he hadn't tripped over them in his rush, Mya didn't know.

Before Mya could bend down to tie them, Aiden was already kneeling in front of him. Showing him how to do the loops and tuck them so they made a bow.

"Try doing the other one," Aiden encouraged him.

Noah's little fingers twisted and turned, holding the laces, and his tongue stuck out from the corner of his mouth as he concentrated. The finished product wasn't quite as tidy as Aiden's, but it was still tied. Noah peeked at Aiden hopefully.

"Good job, kid." Aiden rose and ruffled his hair, making it stand up in spikes.

Noah grinned ear to ear looking at Aiden with adoration in his eyes. "This is way easier than how Mummy shows me."

Mya's breath caught in her throat from something other than misplaced coffee. This was what she wanted from the man who would make their family complete.

Someone who wouldn't hesitate in helping her son tie his shoes, learn how to use a microwave, and build towers from blocks.

But that missing puzzle piece wasn't shaped like Aiden. How could he be a father figure to Noah when she'd never even heard Aiden say Noah's name?

When they arrived at Noah's preschool, Mya helped him unbuckle from his booster seat and grabbed his backpack.

"I'll be five minutes," she said to Aiden, who was sitting in the front passenger seat.

"Aren't you coming in too?" Noah asked Aiden.

"No, sweetie, we won't be long," Mya told her son.

"But I want to show him where I put my bag and the paintings I made." His head tilted back to look at his mother with pleading eyes.

"Aiden doesn't—"

"I'd love to see your paintings," Aiden interrupted, getting out of the car. He smiled at Noah, but it didn't reach his eyes.

"Yes!" Noah did a little hop and ran to the gate.

"You don't have to do this." She kept her voice low.

"It's fine."

"I can give him some excuse."

"Come on, Aiden," Noah yelled from the gate.

"It's fine," he repeated, even as the muscle in his left cheek fluttered from the strain.

Mya gave a heavy sigh. She needed to have a talk with Noah. Spending too much time with Aiden was giving him false hope. It didn't go unnoticed that he wanted a father figure in his life just as much as she wanted to give him one. From what she could see, he'd set his sights on Aiden.

She hated to crush his hopes, but doing it sooner rather than later hopefully wouldn't hurt as much.

Hopefully.

Inside the preschool, Noah's teachers turned to greet them. When Aiden walked in, they froze. Their mouths gaped open, and their eyes widened. The few parents in the room had similar expressions on their faces. It wasn't every day a celebrity sauntered into their school.

Noah held on to Aiden's hand, tugging him around the room, showing him the paintings he'd made, toys he played with, and where he sat for lunch. Then he introduced him to three of his friends and announced, loud enough for the entire room to hear, "Me and Mum live with him."

Shocked faces all turned toward Mya. She wanted to slink into a hole in the ground. She didn't dare look at Aiden, assuming that his expression was one of horror. Not only was he in a room filled with small children, but Noah's statement might have everyone believing they were a family.

Spencer, one of Noah's teachers, broke away from the children gathered around him and sidled up to Mya.

"Oh my God," he whispered, "how on earth did you get involved with Aiden Doyle? How long have you been living together? Are we going to hear wedding bells soon?" Spencer fired off questions, his eyes sparkling with excitement.

Mya risked a glance at Aiden. He sat on one of the tiny chairs made for children, doing a puzzle with Noah. He didn't show any signs of distress over her son's announcement, nor did he run screaming from the room. But that didn't mean it wasn't eating away at him.

"It's not what you think. I'm…We're…" How did she explain to Noah's teacher why they were living together? Her babysitting duties—getting Aiden sober and keeping him out of the tabloids—weren't public knowledge. If she told Spender, could she trust it wouldn't get out? She didn't want to risk it. Any damage to his reputation and they were both in seriously hot water. She couldn't even claim that she was Aiden's personal or executive assistant since that would lead to even more uncomfortable questions. Even saying that she wasn't at liberty to discuss it was a bad idea. That would just fuel the rumor mill even more. Where was the studio publicist when she needed her? Mya sucked at spin.

Spencer's eyebrow arched, waiting for an explanation.

"You'll be the first to know when we get married." Oh God, she was going to hell.

Before Spencer asked any more questions, Mya called, "Noah!" He and Aiden turned to look at her. "We have to go. I'll see you this afternoon," He ran to her and gave her a quick hug.

"Will you pick me up, Aiden?" Noah asked.

Mya wrestled with the question. She should come back alone to avoid another scene, but what if she left Aiden at home alone and Mr. Masters showed up?

"Sure. I'll be with your mum all day," Aiden said to Noah, then turned to another teacher, Deb. "Mya can't let me out of her sight." He grinned and winked at her; she giggled like a young girl instead of the grandmother she was.

Little did they know the real reason he was hanging around Mya. It was much less of the romantic movie scenario they were envisioning. She hooked her hand around his elbow and tugged him from the room before he said anything else.

When they reached her car, safe from eavesdroppers, she hissed, "Why did you say that to Deb?"

He shrugged, smiling playfully. "It's the truth."

"Yes, I know that. But they think we're *living* together."

"We are." The playfulness lingered in his tone.

She pressed her eye sockets with the heel of her hand. Was he being obtuse on purpose? "You know what they're really thinking."

His chuckle sent desire rippling under her skin even though she was determined to be mad at him. "Yeah, that we've shacked up, and we're having hot sex every night."

Mya sucked in a startled breath and checked over her shoulder in case anyone was lurking nearby and listening.

As she leaned closer, the musky scent of his aftershave filled her nostrils, and she wanted to bury her nose in his neck and breathe him in. Self-control won out. "That's not true."

"It kinda is," he disagreed.

"We're living together. Not shacked up. And we are not having… having… every night." The word *sex* clogged her throat.

Knowing exactly what she meant, he leaned even closer, his warm breath fanning her face. "But we could," he said with a smirk.

She groaned.

He was teasing her, that's all, but that didn't stop the warm feeling from spreading through her. Damn it, he had her wanting him every night. If only he was the man she and Noah needed him to be, she'd break the land speed record into his bed.

She took a step back, out of reach of that delicious aftershave scent. Maybe, just this once, she could get one over on him. "Just so you know, I told Spencer we're getting married."

With that, she sashayed around the car to the driver's side and slid onto the seat, leaving Aiden slack-jawed on the sidewalk.

Chapter 27

$\mathcal{M}$ ya hadn't been joking when she'd said she had errands to run that would take up most of the day. They drove from one side of the city to the other and seemed to stop in every shop in between. She probably planned it that way so they wouldn't be home alone, although he bet she wouldn't admit to that. It was obvious she'd been avoiding him, but it hadn't stopped the heated glances she threw his way when she thought his attention was elsewhere.

She wanted him.

And damn it, he wanted her again too.

There was no reason he couldn't have stayed home while she ran her errands. When he'd said she could trust him, he'd meant it. If Lionel turned up to check on them —like she worried about—he didn't have to answer the door, and Lionel would assume they'd gone out. He couldn't expect them to live like hermits.

Being home alone was unappealing. He wanted to spend the day with Mya, even if she did drag him around town. He enjoyed her company. When had shopping for groceries become more fun than brooding in the dark with alcohol?

He'd also discovered that he hadn't been freaked out by being surrounded by kids in the preschool. It hadn't felt great, and his palms had definitely been sweaty. But for a few minutes, he'd forgotten he had told himself to stay away from small children. Going to the preschool hadn't eliminated his aversion to kids, though. Madeline's betrayal had ripped the nurturing instinct right out of him. Of all the things he resented her for, that was the one that burned most deeply in his gut.

"We're here," Mya said, turning the ignition off and unbuckling her seat belt. Thankful for the distraction, he got out of the car. He'd been so deep in thought, he hadn't noticed they'd arrived at the nursing home.

As they walked inside the building, Mya's movements became jerky and stiff. She wasn't looking forward to this.

"Hey," he said, putting his hands on her shoulders before they entered her grandmother's room. "I know this is hard for you. Maybe you should call Amelia to visit with you?"

She shook her head and swallowed hard before she spoke, "That's okay. Sometimes she gets confused with both of us in the same room together. Like she's seeing double. The hardest part is not knowing how I'll find her. Will she recognize me or mistake me for my mother or sister? Or worse, not know me at all?"

He drew her into a comforting hug. He wanted to take away the pain of watching a loved one fade, but he couldn't. All he could do was hold her, let her know he was here for her.

She shuddered against him, and he glanced down at her. Tears shimmered in her eyes. After a moment, she pulled away and brushed at her damp cheeks. "Sorry

about that. I've had no one comfort me about this before."
She stared at her feet and twisted the hem of her shirt in
her fingers.

"What about Amelia?" He held on to her hands,
stopping the fidgeting.

"She's in the same situation as me. We help each other,
but it was nice to have someone who's not involved hand
out some love—" Her eyes widened. "I mean… not love
—*definitely* not love… I meant support."

Aiden chuckled. "I'm happy to hand out *support*." It
wasn't love. It was only a slip of her tongue, even if it did
make him feel warm inside.

"Thank you," she said.

"Any time." Without thinking, he placed a featherlight
kiss on her lips. They broke apart and stared at each other
with wide eyes. Aiden cleared his throat. "Ready to go in?"

She nodded and led the way.

Once inside the room, they found Mya's grandmother
sleeping in an armchair next to the window. Aiden glanced
at Mya, a question in his eyes.

"We'll sit and wait for a few minutes. She might wake
up," she whispered. "I need to talk to the nurse. I'll be back
in a minute."

"What if she wakes up?" Waking up with a strange
man in her room could confuse her even more.

Mya searched Celia's face. "She looks fast asleep. I
won't be long." She hurried from the room.

Aided picked up a chair and moved it farther away
from Celia. In case she woke up, he didn't want to frighten
her by being so close.

Who would have thought he'd be going to preschools,
grocery shopping, and visiting nursing homes? Even when
he'd been married to Madeline, they'd never done normal
everyday things. They'd been so caught up in the celebrity

life. Madeline had loved parties and socializing, not the mundane business of running a household—she'd hired people for that. She had blamed him for working so much, leaving her feeling neglected, but she'd never once complained about the money and status his work provided.

"You've come back for a visit," a small, croaky voice said. Surprised, he turned to find Mya's grandmother blinking sleepily at him.

He wasn't sure who she thought he was, and he doubted she'd remember him from his first visit. "How are you?"

"I'm better now you're here." She smiled. "Why are you sitting so far away? I can barely see you. My eyesight isn't like it used to be."

Aiden pulled his chair closer, hoping the good day she seemed to be having lasted until Mya returned.

"Where's Mya?" she asked. Maybe she did remember him?

"She'll be here in a minute. There was something she needed to talk to the nurse about."

"That girl worries too much about me," she scoffed but couldn't hide the proud look on her face.

"She loves you," he said.

"And she loves you too. Oh," she said, and reached into a wicker basket at her feet. "I finished the baby's cardigan." She pulled out a tiny white sweater.

Rattled by Celia's declaration that Mya loved him, it took Aiden a moment to realize she was holding the baby outfit toward him. He took it from her. The yarn was soft and delicate in his hands.

"I hope you give her lots of babies." She shook a playful finger at him. "Have I told you how happy I am that Mya has finally found a good man?"

"You did," he answered.

"Mya is special. She always helps the family." She stared off into the distance. "And now I've made it difficult for her."

Celia was lucid today, except for thinking Aiden was Mya's husband. "Why do you say that?"

"The girls have had to put me in here, and Mya doesn't believe it's a good enough place. She wants something better, but I'm comfortable here. I don't need much. She says she's saving for a fancier place. I don't want her working so hard for me."

That would explain why Mya was so strict about following Lionel's rules. If she lost her job babysitting Aiden, that would mean she couldn't put her grandmother in a nicer nursing home. Guilt twisted in his gut. He hadn't made it easy for her.

She shook her finger at him again. "That girl has a heart of gold. Don't break it." Then she smiled. "I know you won't; you love her too much. And you've stepped up to be Noah's father. You're a good man. It warms my heart knowing Mya will be okay."

Even though Celia didn't know what she was talking about, her words smashed into him like a wrecking ball. He opened his mouth to say something but couldn't form any words.

"You're awake," Mya said as she walked into the room.

He sighed with relief at the interruption.

Celia blinked rapidly as she looked at Mya, then tears brimmed and spilled down her cheeks. "Helen, where have you been? You've not visited in years. I thought you'd forgotten about me."

"I haven't forgotten you." Mya's smile wobbled as she spoke.

"My daughter is always too busy to visit her old mother," she said to Aiden.

Wanting to give the women some privacy, Aiden rose from the chair and turned to leave.

"Jonny, are you leaving without kissing me?" Celia looked at him with confusion.

He turned back. "Never." He leaned over her and placed a kiss on her powdery-soft cheek.

"I've left a list of things I need at the shops on the kitchen counter," Celia told him. "Don't forget the milk like you did last time."

Heart aching, he patted her hand. "I won't. I'll see you soon."

Mya wasn't sure what they'd talked about while she'd spoken to the nurse. But when she'd walked into the room, Aiden's face had turned white as a sheet, his eyes wide with shock.

It hadn't been a good idea to bring him here. Next time, she'd leave him in the car. Gran didn't appear upset, so it wasn't anything Aiden had said to her, but what had she said to him? Last time, Gran had thought he was Mya's husband. Today she must have believed Aiden was Mya's grandfather, Jonny. But why did that seem to scare the crap out of him? He'd practically left skid marks on the tile from leaving the room in such a rush.

There had been a small white cardigan on the chair he'd been sitting in. Had Gran said something about babies that upset him?

She sped through the rest of her visit with Gran. While part of her felt guilty for not spending more time with her grandmother, another part—a bigger part—was concerned about Aiden. She didn't want this visit to trigger a setback. She really hadn't thought this through at all!

Outside, Aiden leaned against her car. The color returned to his face, and the deer-in-headlights daze was replaced with an expression she couldn't read.

"Is everything okay?" She searched his face, trying to penetrate his inscrutable veneer.

His eyes flicked over to her. "Yes. Why wouldn't it be?"

"You rushed from the room so fast, I worried Gran might have said something to upset you. She doesn't know what she's saying half the time." She played with the hem of her shirt. "I hope you didn't take offense."

"She's sweet. What could she say to upset me?" His tone gave nothing away.

"Last time she thought you were my husband and was knitting a cardigan for our baby." The vision of the happy family she hoped for flashed before her eyes. In it, Aiden was by her side with Noah perched atop his shoulders and a little girl reaching up to hold his hand. Butterflies fluttered in her chest, and she needed a moment to settle her racing heart. "I know it's difficult hearing stuff like that."

"I wanted to give you time alone with her, that's all." Mya didn't believe him but let it go.

He flicked out his wrist and looked at his watch. "Don't we need to go back to the preschool soon?"

Mya nodded. She wondered if she could convince him to stay in the car as they drove over.

She doubted it.

Chapter 28

The next morning, Mya packed an overnight bag for Noah and dressed him for his monthly visitation with his grandparents. As much as she didn't like Bob and Julie, these regular sleepovers kept them from pursuing full custody—at least for now.

"Do I have to go?" Noah whined, fiddling with the laces of his shoes.

"What's the matter? You love spending the night with Nanny and Poppy." She tried combing his hair, but he kept wiggling around. The messy look would have to do. At least it looked adorable.

"I do," he said, looking down at his shuffling feet, "but I want to stay here with you and Aiden."

Living here with Aiden had to be hard—this was the family Noah saw represented on TV and with his friends, and he must want so badly for it to be real. She couldn't blame him. She'd had similar thoughts, but she was older and wise enough to know Aiden was not right for their family.

Mya knelt in front of him so they were eye level.

"Sweetie, when you told your friends at preschool we live with Aiden, you know it's not forever, right? I'm here to help him for a few weeks, then we'll go back home with Aunty Amelia and Aiden will live here by himself."

Noah's lower lip trembled. "Why can't we keep staying here? Aunty Amelia can come here too?"

The poor child. He wanted so desperately to have Aiden fill the role of father, but Mya couldn't let him keep his hopes up only to be dashed by the realities of life. Aiden wasn't father material. There wasn't a happy ending for them.

Mya brushed back a lock of Noah's hair. "We can't stay here because we have our own house to live in."

"Then Aiden can live with us!" His big brown eyes filled with hope.

Disappointment at not being able to give Noah what he wanted, what he *needed*, sat heavy on her shoulders. As soon as this was over, she'd try harder to have the family Noah longed for.

She put a hand on his shoulder. "No, sweetie. When I finish helping Aiden, we'll live in our house and he'll stay here."

"But *why*?" His face turned red.

"Because… because… that's how it is." Wow, she was doing an awesome job explaining the situation to her son. "Maybe we can visit." It was unlikely, but right now, she just needed to appease him. When they were gone, he'd hopefully forget Aiden.

"I don't wanna leave!" He stomped from the room and down the stairs.

Mya followed. She found him in the kitchen, sitting at the counter, arms crossed over his chest and his lower lip stuck out so far she worried Aiden might trip over it.

"Everything okay?" Aiden asked Mya.

"Yes," Mya answered at the same time Noah snapped, "No!"

Stepping back, Aiden held his hands up, palms out in a placating gesture. "Whoa, kid. Did you get up on the wrong side of the bed this morning?"

Noah screwed up his face in confusion. "I got up on the same side as I always do."

Aiden chuckled. "Has something upset you?"

"Mummy won't let us live here forever or let you come live with us," he grumbled.

Aiden took another step back, but this time his eyes were wide with shock. "Well… We… Uh…"

From the look on Aiden's face, the thought of living with Noah terrified him. A ball of lead sat heavy in her gut. She liked Aiden—had even imagined a life with him—but that expression said it would never happen. Stifling the urge to sigh, she stepped in to save Aiden from her son. "We have to take Noah to my house so his grandparents can pick him up. Can you be ready to leave in ten minutes?"

Aiden's relief was palpable. The ball of lead tripled in size. Her logical brain had known that Aiden wasn't "daddy" material, despite his role on *Family First*, but her heart had held out hope—hope that was now being dashed.

"Why can't they get him from here?" Aiden wanted to know.

That was another conversation that was going to be oh so fun. "I'll explain later." Bob and Julie had made plenty of threats to take Noah away if she didn't meet their conditions, but Noah didn't need to know any of that. When she picked the overnight bag up from the floor, Aiden's gaze zeroed in on it.

"What's the bag for?" he asked.

"Oh." She glanced at it. "Uh… Noah is staying the night with his grandparents."

His stare practically melted her clothes off and left no questions about what was on his mind. Would she be strong enough to resist him? So far she'd been doing a good job, but only because she had Noah as a buffer. Was her willpower enough to stay away from Aiden while Noah was gone?

Oh, God. She was screwed.

Half an hour later, they arrived at Mya's house. Mya gave Aiden a quick tour. It had to be quick because the entire house was the size of his kitchen and dining room combined.

"Are there any toys you want to get from your room to take to Nanny and Poppy's?" she asked Noah. She needed a minute alone to talk to Aiden—just talk—when Noah wasn't listening in. Thank God Amelia had an art show today; Mya didn't need her sister's matchmaking right now.

She had already explained to Noah not to mention to his grandparents that they were living at Aiden's house. It tore her up, making him lie so much lately. But if he didn't keep their secret, his grandparents would use Aiden as an excuse to gain custody of Noah. Aiden's reputation was the ammunition they'd need to follow through with their threats.

When Noah went in search of toys, she turned to Aiden. "His grandparents don't know I'm living with you. If they did, it would cause a lot of trouble."

An eyebrow raised in question.

She glanced pointedly at the clock and then in the

direction Noah had gone. "I'll explain later, but I need you to stay out of sight. When they get here, wait in the kitchen until they leave."

Mya was thankful when he nodded and didn't ask questions. The crunch of tires as a car pulled into the driveway turned her attention to the window. Right on time.

Shoving him in the kitchen's direction, she whispered as if they could hear her from outside, "Please don't make a sound."

They knocked on the door, and she checked to make sure Aiden was nowhere to be seen before she answered it. Then she plastered on a smile and greeted Noah's grandparents. "Julie. Bob. How are you?"

"Hello, Mya. I'm well, thanks." Bob gave her a warm smile.

"Mya," Julie said in a clipped tone.

All in all, it was a typical start to one of these monthly visitations. "Take a seat; Noah will be down in a second."

Right on time, he dragged his feet down the stairs.

"We'll have him home tomorrow at lunchtime," Julie stated. Mya had learned early on that trying to get them to accommodate her schedule resulted in more threats. "Before we go, I need a glass of water. I've got a tickle in my throat."

"Are you getting sick? Maybe Noah should stay home," Mya suggested, worried.

Julie waved off her suggestion. "Not at all, it's just your neighbor mowing their lawn. Fresh-cut grass always sets me off."

"I'll get it for you," Mya said, heading for the hallway leading to the kitchen.

Julie brushed past her. "I know where the kitchen is."

Crap! She needed to think of a reason to keep her

from discovering Aiden. Latching onto the first excuse that popped into her brain, she said, "But… it's a mess."

Julie gave Mya a critical glare. "Not surprising."

Well, that didn't work. Time for more direct action. Mya scampered after her toward the kitchen. She nearly bumped into Julie, who'd stopped short upon seeing Aiden leaning against the kitchen counter.

Mya hung her head in defeat. There was no way this was going to end well.

Chapter 29

"*W*ho are you?" The woman with the pinched expression raked her gaze from his head to his toes.

Aiden pushed off the counter and glanced at Mya, who had a look of utter despair etched into her face. Right, this must be the kid's grandmother, the one Mya didn't want him running into.

Returning his gaze to Pinched Face Person, he slipped on his movie star persona. "I'm Aiden Doyle." He offered her his hand to shake, but she gave it a disdainful glance and looked away, sniffing.

"And what are you doing here?" she asked, her voice filled with equal parts suspicion and anticipation.

"Aiden is here because… because…" Mya rushed to stand beside the woman, trying not to panic and failing.

Whatever was going on, he wouldn't make it worse. "I'm a client of Amelia's. I commissioned a piece from her for my mother, and I've come to pick it up." He flashed his award-nominated grin.

It landed like a dead fish. The woman's eyes narrowed.

It was clear she didn't believe him. Why the fuck did Mya let the kid's grandmother come in here and act this way?

"I know who you are. You're that actor"—she said the word *actor* like it was a dirty word—"who keeps getting himself into trouble. It's not surprising you want to buy Amelia's rubbish."

Aiden saw red. This woman didn't deserve to share the same planet as Mya and Amelia. Hell, he wasn't sure if she rated being in the same galaxy. And why was Mya letting her get away with being so rude? He wasn't about to stand for it. Ready to defend both Mya and Amelia, Aiden opened his mouth to give the woman a piece of his mind.

But Mya stepped between them, and in an obviously false cheerful voice, said, "Noah's ready to go!" She reached into the fridge, pulled out a bottle of water, and handed it to the woman. "Don't forget your water." She slapped it into the woman's hand with a thwack.

The woman took the water, gave Aiden one last scathing glare, and sauntered from the room.

Mya mouthed, "thank you," and hurried after her.

Aiden stayed in the kitchen. It was safer that way, because if he had to listen to that woman and watch Mya grovel at her feet, he couldn't help what he might say or do. No one got to put down Mya. No one.

After a few minutes, he heard the front door shut. A few heartbeats later, Mya called out, "They're gone."

He joined her in the front room. She was sitting on the couch with her elbows on her knees and her head in her hands. Taking a seat beside her, he removed her trembling hands from her face.

"Want to explain why the fuck you let that woman into your house? And worse, let her near your son?"

Her back stiffened. "I wouldn't put Noah into the

hands of someone who didn't care for him. She may be awful to me, but she loves Noah."

"Why is she such a bitch to you?"

Mya tilted her head to look at him, anguish etched on her face. "Because I killed her son."

Mya had never been so scared in her life. Her whole body shook. She was sure Julie would see through Aiden's lie and storm straight to her lawyer's office, announce Mya's involvement with a known degenerate, prove she was an unfit mother, and petition for her and Bob to get custody of Noah.

She'd never been so grateful for Aiden's acting skills and quick thinking. When Julie walked in on him in the kitchen, Mya's mind had gone completely blank.

"Wasn't it an accident or something?" Aiden said as he held her hands and calmed her shaking. "That's what you told me."

"She blames me for causing it."

Aiden waited for an explanation.

"The day I found out I was pregnant with Noah was the most terrifying and happiest day of my life." She shook her head. "It's hard to explain the mixed emotions. Anyway, Daniel and I weren't in a serious relationship. I could have walked away, and he would never have known about the baby. But I didn't know my father, and I always wished I had him in my life. I'd never keep Noah away from his."

Restless, she let go of Aiden's hands, instantly missing the strength and warmth from them, and rose from the couch to pace a trench in the carpet. "Daniel's life was about parties and having fun. Every weekend he got drunk, and I was right there with him. But when I saw the positive pregnancy test, it was like a slap in the face. My mother chose partying over me and Amelia, and I resented her for it. I didn't want my baby to feel that way about me. I knew I had to change my life. I hoped when Daniel found out he'd be a father, he might put his child first too."

Through her trip down memory lane, Aiden never said a word. His expression was unreadable. Was he judging her for her past, even though it wasn't so terribly different from his own recent history? She ran a hand through her hair and slid her glasses up the bridge of her nose. "I went to see him, and he'd already had a few drinks with his mates. I wanted to talk to him in private, but he did that *whatever you have to say, you can say it in front of my friends* speech. So I told him."

She stopped at the fireplace and brushed a finger over a picture of Noah with a soccer ball that sat on the mantel. He was three in that photo. God, he was growing up so fast. Where had the time gone?

Staring at the photo, she continued, "His friends thought it was hilarious. Made a bunch of jokes about dirty nappies and screaming kids. He put on this macho mask and told me it could be anyone's baby and that I just wanted to hook my claws into his family's money."

She glanced at Aiden. "He was wrong. I never wanted a cent. Just a committed father. I tried telling him I hadn't been with anyone else, but with his mates goading him, he wouldn't listen. So I went home. One of his friends later told me that after I left, Daniel had a change of heart and went looking for me. He was drunk and wrapped his car around a telephone pole. Fortunately, no one else was hurt, but he didn't make it."

"How is that your fault? Why would his mother blame you?"

Mya turned to look at him. He was on his feet and stood mere inches away from her. "He was her only child. She needed someone to blame. If I hadn't told him I was pregnant while he'd been drinking, then he'd be alive. At least, that's how she sees it." She laughed nervously. "No one said people had to make sense."

He dropped his hands on her shoulders. "That's bullshit. You didn't hold a gun to his head and make him get in the car."

"I know."

"You don't blame yourself, do you?" He ducked his head, and their eyes connected.

She bit her lower lip. "Maybe if I'd picked a better time—"

"No." He squeezed her shoulders. "The baby was his responsibility as much as yours. He should have believed you and stepped up and done the right thing. He made his choices; you didn't make them for him." Anger burned bright in his eyes.

Was he thinking about his wife and her lover? The man who'd abandoned a woman while pregnant? Was he thinking about himself? She didn't know.

Over the years, Amelia and Gran had told her Daniel's death wasn't her fault. He'd chosen to drive drunk; she hadn't forced him behind the wheel. She'd heard that over and over again. It hadn't assuaged the guilt. But hearing the truth from someone who wasn't family, it was more believable. And it was like someone had lifted a weight from her chest.

"And because they blame you for his death, you let them walk all over you and treat you like crap?"

His hands were sweeping from her shoulders to her elbows and back up again. The gesture made it hard to concentrate. "They've also accused me of leading Daniel down the path of substance abuse. Little do they know he'd been getting drunk and high long before he met me. If I do anything to suggest that I'm not behaving like a respectable mother to their grandson, they'll petition for custody of Noah."

"Can they do that?"

She shrugged. "I'm not sure. I've done some research, but I don't understand all the legal jargon." She glanced at the pictures of Noah again. "From what I could find, a lot of it would depend on the judge and the case Bob and Julie make. They have loads of money and can hire fancy lawyers to get what they want. I can't afford to risk it."

His eyes narrowed. "Having them pick Noah up from here and getting me to hide in the kitchen was all because they've threatened to take Noah away from you if you're not living a *wholesome* life?"

She nodded, her chin wobbling as she struggled to hold back tears.

"Fuck," he snapped and pulled her into a tight embrace.

Mya soaked up the heat radiating from his body. Took comfort from his strong arms wrapped around her. For a minute, she felt protected and loved and believed that no one could ever tear away her family.

"You're a wonderful mother. Your kid's lucky to have you." Aiden pressed a kiss on her temple, then another on her cheek and continued to her lips.

Mya lifted her chin, and the kiss deepened when he opened her mouth with his tongue. She shivered with delight. There was nothing she wanted more in that moment than Aiden. It didn't matter that he was the wrong man for her future. He was the right man for *right now*.

She slid her hand down his arm, linked their fingers, and led him from the room.

"Are you sure?" Aiden asked.

Her mouth quirked up into a grin. "You're about to get lucky. Do you object?"

"No fucking way." He smiled and followed her up the stairs.

In Mya's room, she turned into Aiden's arms, kissing him long and deep. Her heart pounded so hard and fast, she was sure he could feel it.

"Thank you," she said between kisses.

"For what?" He pulled back and frowned.

"For not judging me by my past."

"I'm hardly qualified to judge someone by their past. And yours is small change compared to mine," he said with a sly smile.

God, his grin was the devil tempting her. Would she ever have enough of him? The way she felt at the moment, probably not.

She wrapped her arms around his neck, drawing their bodies together. Aiden's hands landed on her waist, and he eased up her shirt. She broke away so he could pull it over her head. He skimmed a hand over her bra-covered breasts and down to tease the skin at the top of her waistband. He was waiting for her to take the next step. Reaching out, together they flicked open the top button of her jeans, undid the zip, and slid the denim down her hips and thighs to puddle on the ground. Mya kicked them away, absently.

As she stood in front of him in her underwear, Aiden's gaze traveled over her body. "God, you're beautiful," he rasped.

"So are you," she replied, taking in the muscles and long lines elegantly hidden under his clothes.

He covered her mouth with a kiss. God, she could kiss

him all day. Every day. His kisses were like a drug, and she was addicted. Her hands slipped under the hem of his shirt to feel the heated flesh underneath. She wanted to see all of him, taste all of him. Right now!

"Strip," she ordered, tearing her mouth away from his.

They made quick work of removing his clothes and her underwear. If he thought Mya was beautiful, Aiden's muscular physique and tanned skin were every woman's dream. She ran her hand down his chest and abs, feeling every muscle under her fingertips.

"I want to touch every inch of you." She followed her fingers with soft kisses, and he quivered from her touch. "Taste you."

"Yes, please!"

Mya went to remove her glasses.

He stopped her. "You don't have to do that if you don't want to. You look fucking sexy wearing them."

"Really?" She and Amelia had been teased for wearing glasses in school, and a lot of the guys she'd dated had told her she looked better without them. The glasses were like an armor—a protection—in her post-party life.

"You're my boss-and-secretary fantasy come to life," he said, nibbling on her neck.

She giggled and tilted her head to the side. "Technically I don't work for you."

"Who cares about details? Now shut up and kiss me."

"Whatever you say, boss."

She pressed her mouth to his, sliding her tongue along the seam of his lips. He tasted of coffee and something more, something that she could only identify as Aiden. She wanted more. She pressed her body to his, trying to feel every inch of him all at once. He lifted her up by the waist, walked her to the bed, and gently lowered her down, covering her with his body. She felt so protected, and, of course, really turned on.

Aiden pulled away, and she mourned the loss. But she didn't mourn long; he kissed her beating pulse, laving kisses to her neck and down, down, until he reached the top of her breasts. Smiling, he trailed his tongue over the top of her right breast, down the side, and under in an ever-tightening spiral. But he stopped before reaching her nipple. With a self-satisfied smirk, he shifted his attention to her left breast, repeating the sensual teasing. Over and over, he switched back and forth, teasing each breast by coming infinitesimally closer to her now aching nipple. God, how she wanted to feel his mouth close around them. She wanted it so much. As if hearing her internal thoughts, he did just that, capturing her right nipple in his mouth. Her back arched off the mattress, and she cried out, "Oh God, Aiden!"

A soft chuckle was his only response.

Moving on from her breasts, he trailed open-mouth kisses over her stomach and hip bones. He lingered there, tracing the thin silvery stretch marks from when she'd carried Noah. He seemed to worship them and her not so perfectly flat stomach. No one had ever paid so much attention to her body. No one.

His tongue slipped into the heat between her legs to flick at her core.

"Oh fuck, yes!" She clamped onto the back of his head, holding him in place.

Again, he chuckled, but this time the vibrations sent little shivers of pleasure straight to her center. Before she could even think of asking him to continue, he dove in, worshiping at her core. He drew her clit into his mouth, sucking on it. The sensation had her shaking with pleasure, her mind and body focused on only one thing: his mouth and tongue on her. After a few mind-blowing minutes of him lapping and sucking gently at her clit, she tugged his hair, bringing him back to her because she was ready to shatter under his magical tongue.

He looked at her askance.

"I want to finish together," she answered his unasked question.

A slow, sexy smile slid over his features, and he lay down next to her. It was an invitation, one she wasn't going to refuse.

It was her turn to explore his body. And she couldn't wait. After all, turnabout was fair play. It was time to tease him to the brink. Climbing on top of him, she leaned down to place little kisses along his jaw. Her tongue flicked over the rapid pulse in his neck. Her lips skimmed over his chest to his abs and farther south, taking his hardness into her mouth.

Aiden's hips bucked off the mattress, and his fingers twisted in her hair. "You're killing me," he groaned.

Mya pulled away, looked up at him, and smiled. "Wouldn't want to do that—I'm not done with you."

Lifting Mya up, he growled as he flipped her onto her back. "I'm not done with you either."

He positioned himself between her thighs, and as he entered her, their eyes locked and he went still, a flood of emotions flickering across his face.

"Aiden?" Mya cupped his face in her hands.

Her voice seemed to bring him back to the moment, and whatever concern she had was replaced with heat as he moved his hips. Her eyes fluttered shut, and all thoughts were scattered in the wind. Her body burned with desire for him. No man had ever made her feel so alive. She was on fire for Aiden. A wild, whirling blaze that grew hotter and hotter with each stroke.

Aiden thrust deeper, faster, harder, and she met him every step of the way. Hips thrusting to meet his. Their deep breath mingling with lips and tongue. Her hands clenching his shoulders as she strove to bring herself, and him, to climax.

When she could take it no longer, Mya wrapped her legs around Aiden's waist and clung to his back. "Aiden, now… please," she panted.

He slipped his thumb between them and slid it across her clit as he picked up the pace. There was time for one last intoxicating kiss before they both fell over the edge.

Aiden and Mya lay on their sides facing each other. While Aiden slept, Mya took the time to soak him in. Long, thick lashes fanned his cheeks, and his breathing was deep and even. His dark hair needed a trim, but she liked the tousled look, made messier from her fingers. He appeared so peaceful, like he wasn't being chased by the demons of his past.

Her gaze dropped to his chest and followed the fine trail of hair to where the sheets covered his waist. Only moments ago, she'd followed the trail with her tongue.

"If you keep looking at me like that, I'm going to do something about it," he said with a low, gravelly voice.

It was a tempting offer. Why couldn't she control herself around this man? On the surface, it was because he was gorgeous and sexy, and she'd never experienced such mind-blowing sex before. But it went deeper than that. She liked him. Enjoyed his company when he wasn't trying to wind her up. Behind his gruff exterior was something soft and caring. If she wasn't careful, she could fall for him—but falling for someone who couldn't love her back was a big mistake. She'd been down that road before; she wasn't going to travel it again.

She started to get up, but he dropped a hand on her waist. "Where are you going? I haven't finished with you."

Her insides melted as he stroked the curve of her hip, but she needed to be strong. She motioned to the clock. "Amelia will be home soon."

This time, he let her go and fell on his back, tucking a hand behind his head. "Be prepared for a busy night." The smoldering look in his eyes told her exactly what he had in mind, and her whole body tingled with excitement for the night to come. The sheet covering him slid lower down his body as he moved, dangerously close to exposing him, and her wicked mind prayed it would drop farther. When had she become so shameless? Turning her back to him, she retrieved her clothes from the floor and dressed.

When she faced him again, he hadn't moved from the bed. He looked like a sex god displayed for her enjoyment. "Why aren't you dressed?" she asked.

"I'm enjoying the show."

She picked up his shirt from the end of the bed and tossed it at his chest. Instead of putting it on, he sat up, held on to her hand, and pulled her down next to him.

"So, Amelia's the artist, and you're the writer. Why does she get to showcase her creativity while your books are hidden away?"

It wasn't the conversation she was expecting, but she ran with it. "I'm not as talented as my sister, and they're not hidden away. I get to read them to Noah."

He caressed her cheek. "You *are* talented. Never sell yourself short. Your imagination is incredible."

She couldn't hide her broad grin.

"Why haven't you published your books?" he pressed, cupping her jaw.

She leaned into his hand. "I don't have time to look into that. And it's just a hobby, anyway." She tried to get up.

But he stopped her, turning her head to meet his eyes. "You put time aside for your sister, grandmother, the kid, and now *me*, but you don't make time for yourself?" He shook his head. "Celia was right."

Mya blinked. Where had that come from? "Gran… What did she say? You know she doesn't always make sense."

"She told me you look after everyone around you and forget about yourself." He placed a kiss on the tip of her nose. "And I agree."

She fiddled with the hem of her shirt. "I have responsibilities I can't ignore. What else did she say?"

He took her hands into his, running his thumbs over her knuckles. "She's happy in the home she's in. She hates that you're working so hard for a better place." He lifted her hands to his lips to place a kiss on each one.

She pulled away, crossing her arms over her chest. This conversation hurt, and she wasn't going to let herself be distracted by a sexy, naked Aiden in her bed. "She's never made a fuss about anything her entire life, so of course she wouldn't criticize the nursing home. She took in two young girls and worked hard to raise us without a single word of complaint. I know she doesn't want us to worry, but she deserves to be somewhere better, and we'll get her there just as soon as I can raise the money."

"As soon as *you* raise the money? Doesn't Amelia help?" Aiden asked.

"She does. But her art doesn't provide her with a steady income, so she pitches in when she can. Like with this art show that she's going to be back from at any minute," she said, dropping a Sydney-sized hint that it was time for Aiden to drop this subject and get dressed.

But he ignored the hint, his eyes narrowing as he assessed her. "So that leaves you paying the bulk of the bills. You don't complain about it because you think the responsibility is your penance for your past behavior."

Ouch. Before she had the chance to disagree, Mya heard the front door open and close downstairs.

"Hello! I'm home. Is everyone decent? If not, I can come back later," came a singsong voice.

"Oh crap, Amelia's home! Hurry and get dressed before she thinks we've... we've..." Mya indicated the bed with a frantic wave of her arm.

"Had sex?" he said, amused. "What's your problem with the word *sex*? She just said, *is everyone decent*, which implies that she has a good idea of what we've been doing." He chuckled as he reached for his jeans.

Mya buried her face in her hands and groaned, "She's going to make such a big deal out of this. I'm sorry."

This is a big deal.

Aiden froze for a moment as the words ricocheted through his mind. Where the hell had that thought come from? This was *not* a big deal. It was two people enjoying each other with no commitments or expectations. But something had squeezed his heart when they'd made love —no, not making love—it was just sex. Fucking. He didn't *make love*. But when he'd looked down at Mya, his feelings had shifted from indifference and uncommitted to something deeper.

Fuck! This couldn't be happening.

Aiden ran a hand through his sex-tousled hair. He had

no room for feelings and didn't want a relationship, especially with a woman who had a kid. Those were the rules he'd set for himself, and he wasn't about to change his mind. What he needed to do was shove his feelings back into the dusty cardboard box in the mental closet where he'd kept them for two years. That and keep his distance. Well, as much as he could while they lived together.

How many more weeks did they have? Five? Six? He couldn't remember. Besides, one more day was one too many.

These were going to be the longest weeks of his life.

Chapter 30

Mya had rushed Aiden from the house before Amelia made a scene about them coming out of her bedroom looking disheveled. On the ride home, they'd sat in silence. Mya had tried multiple times to start a conversation, but Aiden had kept his responses short, just this side of rude. Eventually she'd given up. Was he upset with her because she'd raced him from the house like a dirty little secret? She would have thought that wouldn't bother him since his life was so detached from commitment. It didn't make sense.

When they'd arrived home, she'd asked him if something was wrong. He'd told her he had a headache and needed to lie down for a while. That had been several hours ago.

Leaving him to rest, Mya spent the rest of the afternoon writing—well, trying to write—Noah's next book. She kept getting distracted by thoughts of Aiden. Earlier, when they'd had sex, she had been sure she'd seen something more than lust in his eyes. If she didn't know him so well—and surely they could consider each other friends now—she'd mistake the look for affection, maybe even love.

But that couldn't be it, could it?

She sighed. Wishful thinking got her nowhere. Aiden had made it clear that he didn't fall in love, and even more importantly, he didn't want to be a father. Whatever she thought she'd seen in his eyes had been her imagination, nothing more.

Unable to concentrate, she gave up on Noah's story to get ready for the night. Mya showered, shampooed her hair, and shaved her legs. If she'd owned any sexy lingerie, she would have worn them, but the most alluring thing she had was the extra-large T-shirt she used as pajamas. That would have to do. She didn't bother with underwear. He'd only rip them off.

What had happened to fighting the attraction and keeping her hands to herself? Her self-control simply flew out the window whenever he got near. He knew just what to do to make her body hum with pleasure. Who knew when she'd get to experience anyone like Aiden again? Why shouldn't she enjoy the way he made her feel when they were together? It would end soon, and they'd go their separate ways, even if the thought of it made her heart sink.

Waiting for him to come to her room, she paced the carpet. When midnight struck and he didn't show up, she wondered if it was because he didn't want to be in a bedroom filled with uncomfortable memories.

Taking a deep breath, she padded barefoot to his bedroom and turned the handle. It was locked. Why had he locked the door? Was he sick? He'd complained of a headache. Maybe it was something serious. Should she check that he was okay? Before she had time to knock, a light flicked on, shining through the gap under the door.

Dropping her hand, she held her breath with excitement. He was finally coming to her.

After a few moments, the light flicked off without Aiden making an appearance. Pressing her ear to the door, she heard the rustling of bed covers, then the chime of a phone. She knew she shouldn't eavesdrop, but she couldn't help herself, pressing her ear to the door. Aiden's deep voice rumbled when he answered the phone.

She couldn't hear who was on the other end of the line, but whoever it was Aiden seemed to like talking to.

Step away from the door.

She took a step back. Followed by another. And another. She knew it was unreasonable to assume that he was talking with another woman, but there was something about the change in his voice. She couldn't imagine him laughing like that with Mr. Masters. Had he gotten a booty call?

Mya slunk back to her room. Of course she shouldn't have expected intimacy, even though he'd been hinting at it all day. But clearly he had more of a connection with whoever he was talking to on the phone, which shouldn't have been surprising. He'd made it clear he just wanted sex, not an emotional bond. She thought she'd been okay with that, but her heart had other ideas. She wasn't a casual fling kind of girl, and Aiden and all his sexiness had lured her in nonetheless.

Mya couldn't tell whether she was glad or relieved when she didn't hear Aiden come out of his room before falling into a restless slumber.

Only a few hours later, she stumbled out of bed, had a quick shower, and headed downstairs, hoping she wouldn't bump into Aiden. Her emotions zigzagged all over the place, and she worried he'd take one look at her and read too much into what she was feeling toward him. Feelings she hadn't figured out herself. For now, she'd keep her distance and wait for Amelia to drop Noah off. It wasn't unusual for Bob and Julie to leave him—albeit begrudgingly—with Amelia on days Mya worked. It was one benefit of having a sister who worked odd hours.

The library door was shut, and she prayed Aiden would stay in there all day like he normally did. She needed time away from him to sort out her feelings and get her head and heart on the same page.

A few quick knocks came from the front door, and before Mya could answer it, Chloe came sailing in with a takeaway coffee cup in her hand.

"Good morning!" she said with a chipper voice. "You're just the person I want to talk to."

"I am?"

"Yes. I'd love to see more of those gorgeous books you write for Noah."

Mya started and blurted out the first thought that popped into her brain, "How do you know about the books?"

"There was one in the library when I visited last. I hope you don't mind, but I took it." Chloe gave Mya a conspiratorial wink.

"Why?"

"I have a friend who's a literary agent," Chloe explained, wrapping an arm around Mya and steering her toward the sofa. "She doesn't represent children's book authors, but she knows people who do. I showed her your book, and she passed it around and someone would like to see more."

Mya heard the words coming from Chloe's mouth but couldn't quite understand what she was saying. "Why would a literary agent want to see my books?"

"To publish them, silly!" Chloe chuckled. "I can't

understand why you haven't done so sooner; *Wally the Lost Whale* is lovely. The illustrations are so gorgeous too. Please pass my compliments to your sister."

Publish them? This was all moving way too fast. Mya couldn't keep up. "Writing them is only a hobby," she protested. "I just got tired of reading the same ones to Noah over and over again. He loves them, but surely they're not good enough to publish."

"Of course they are! I wouldn't have shown them to my friend if they weren't." Chloe bumped Mya's shoulder conspiratorially. "And if you play your cards right, Noah won't be the only one who loves them." At Mya's stunned silence, Chloe's eyes widened. "Oh my God, I never thought to ask you if it was okay for me to show them to my friend. I'm sorry. I should have asked. Can you forgive me?"

Mya waved her apology away. "I'm flattered you think they're good enough."

"They're great. Awesome, even, but if you don't want me to go any further with them, I'll back off."

Mya nibbled her bottom lip. It wasn't every day an opportunity like this fell into her lap. Or Amelia's— illustrating children's books might be a steady source of income if people liked her art. "Okay. Let's do this. I'd love to see what you can do."

Chloe clapped with excitement. "Wonderful! I have a good feeling about this. You're going to be the next Maurice Sendak!"

She doubted that her stories would rival *Where the Wild Things Are*. She wrote silly stories about silly animals. If nothing came of it, Mya would still write them for her son.

"Are the books in the library?" Chloe asked, heading in that direction.

"No!" Mya practically shouted. She wasn't ready to face him. Not yet. Not after being abandoned last night.

Chloe raised an eyebrow.

"The books are in my room. I'll go get them." Mya led Chloe away from the library door.

"I'll come with you." Chloe followed her up the stairs.

They entered Mya's bedroom, and she picked two books off the bedside table: *Gertrude the Grumpy Hippo* and *Pete the Brave Parrot*. They were Noah's favorites. Mya turned to hand them to Chloe, but the other woman had stopped at the threshold, mouth agape as she scanned the room. "Is there something wrong?" Mya asked.

"He makes you stay in the nursery?" Chloe's voice was aghast.

"This is the only room with furniture. Noah and I share it."

Chloe flew past Mya and flung open the wardrobe doors, gasping as she saw the baby clothes and Madeline's outfits hanging like they were ready to be worn. She gently fingered a pink dress, then shut the door. Next, she went into the bathroom and stared at the cosmetics and medical detritus Mya had pushed to a corner of the counter.

After a moment, she turned to face Mya. "I assume that's not your stuff in there?"

Mya shook her head. "No."

"Why are Madeline's things in the nursery? It's like she lived in here too."

Mya shrugged. "Maybe she did while she was sick so she didn't disturb Aiden?" She couldn't betray Aiden's confidence and tell his sister the real reason.

Crossing her arms over her chest, Chloe continued to look around the room, tapping her lower lip as she went. "No. There's no way he'd want to be away from her. Not even for a minute. God, he loved her," she said with a heavy sigh. "He can't bear to donate her clothes and pack away her personal belongings. The house should have been sold months ago, and here he is still living in it and holding on to her things. Surrounded by the memories of a life he had with his wife and the children they were going to have." She brushed away a tear. "This isn't healthy. For a moment, I thought he'd moved on." She averted her gaze, and Mya knew she was referring to her. No, he wasn't moving on with her. She was just like the rest of the women he used to put a Band-Aid over how he really felt.

Because Chloe was right: Aiden still loved Madeline. As much as she'd hurt him, as much as he denied it, it was clear in this room and all the boxes he hadn't been able to part with.

What the hell was she doing? She was supposed to be having fun before she settled down with a man she could depend upon. Aiden had told her he was emotionally unavailable, and she hadn't really believed him. Not until now, realizing how tightly he was clinging to the old memories. The painful ache in her chest told her she'd already taken a step too far and lost her heart to Aiden.

"What are you doing?" Chloe shot at Aiden as she blew into the library.

Aiden raised an eyebrow. "Catching up on emails."

Putting her palms on the top of the desk, she leaned forward. "I mean with this house. With the room you've put Mya in, surrounded by Madeline and the baby's things —which, by the way, I think is creepy as fuck! I know it takes time to heal from a love like you had with Madeline, but I was hoping something was happening between you and Mya. I was praying you were finding your way back to us, back to being happy again! And then I saw the memorial upstairs."

Aiden closed his laptop and leaned back in his chair. "This is my house. I can do whatever I want with it."

"How are you going to move on with your life if you're constantly reminded of everything you've lost?"

He hung on to Madeline's things precisely so that he wouldn't forget. They were constant reminders to never open up like that again. He refused to make himself vulnerable. No one else would ever get close enough to rip out his heart.

During the last few weeks with Mya, Madeline's betrayal had slipped his mind. He'd begun feeling things in the space where his heart used to be. It was like Mya was putting the heartbeat back inside his cold, dead heart. And when she left in a few weeks, those feelings would be gone, and he'd be all the better for it.

"I'm moving on with my life just fine," he said.

"With Mya?" Hope filled Chloe's voice.

Aiden slammed his lips shut.

She blew out a breath. "You could be so good for each other if only you'd let her in!"

"No, we're not 'good for each other.'"

"Why would you say that?"

"Mya has a specific kind of man in mind, and I don't fit the criteria."

Chloe frowned, tilting her head. "She's falling for you. I'd say you fit perfectly."

His heart skidded to a stop. Mya couldn't be falling for him. He wouldn't let her. There was no denying they had a physical connection, and if he were honest with himself, an emotional connection he'd never felt with another woman, not even Madeline. But it could never go further than friendship. "No, we don't, so drop it."

Her eyes widened at his harsh tone. "Excuse me for wanting my big brother to be happy! And if it's with Mya and you throw it away, you'll be making a huge mistake."

Aiden sprung from the chair. "What will make me happy is for you to butt out of my business! Got it?"

"Oh, okay, fine." She threw her hands in the air. "I'll stay out of your *business*. But before I go, I was coming to tell you about that directing job you wanted. They not so politely rejected my suggestion of hiring you. Apparently even Tom DiFazio's reputation is better than yours. So next time you have a crazy idea and need my help, you'd better come crawling on your knees with flowers in your teeth." With that, she marched from the room.

He followed her out and found Mya, Amelia, and Noah sitting in the living room. Mya saw his face and asked with a frown, "Is everything okay between you and Chloe? She didn't look happy when she left."

"I have to go out," he said instead of answering her question.

"Oh, okay. Just give me a minute to say goodbye to Amelia."

"I don't need a babysitter," he snapped.

She rose from the couch and crossed her arms over her chest. "Actually, you do."

"Aren't you sick of following me around like a puppy dog?"

Tossing her head back, she gave a mirthless laugh. "Oh, I am. But that doesn't mean I'm going to let you leave without me."

Aiden was about to say something, then his gaze landed on the kid, who'd glued himself to Amelia's side with concern etched on his face. Noah's eyes flicked between him and Mya, and Aiden bit back his comment.

"I'll stay with Noah while you go with Aiden," Amelia offered.

"Are you sure?" Mya asked.

Amelia nodded. "Go."

Aiden spun on his heels and stomped into the garage, not waiting to see if Mya followed.

Chapter 31

*a*iden drove along the windy coastline. He was going faster than Mya liked, but when she glanced at his stony face and his white knuckles on the steering wheel, she kept her mouth shut and watched the blue ocean and white sandy beaches fly past. Now was not the time to distract him with her questions.

After twenty minutes, Aiden slowed the car, and Mya breathed a sigh of relief. He pulled into a small clifftop parking lot overlooking the sparkling ocean. Any other day, Mya would think this spot beautiful and romantic, but at this moment, with the air thick with tension, it was far from a secluded romantic rendezvous.

They didn't speak for a few minutes; Aiden just gazed at the view. When Mya couldn't take a moment of silence any longer, she said, "What's wrong?"

Aiden flicked a glance at her, then stared out of the windshield. "Nothing."

"I don't believe you."

He didn't respond.

"What happened between you and Chloe?"

Instead of answering, he shot from the car and slammed the door.

Like the puppy dog he'd accused her of being, she followed him and leaned on the bonnet next to him. The wind blew through her T-shirt, and she regretted not grabbing a jacket.

There was a family sitting on a grassy area on a picnic blanket eating fish and chips while their toddler chased seagulls. Mya would have enjoyed watching the little girl squeal and play, but instead she focused on Aiden.

"Aiden, you can talk to me." She put a hand on his arm, and he jerked away like she'd burned him.

What the hell was going on?

When he didn't answer, she shoved off the car and positioned herself in front of him, careful not to stand too close in case he pulled away from her again.

"Something has upset you. Is there anything I can do to help?" she asked.

"You've done enough." His jaw clenched as he spat out the words.

Mya flinched like she'd been slapped. "Excuse me. What the hell have I done?"

He crossed his arms over his chest and averted his gaze. "Forget it."

With hands on hips, Mya narrowed her eyes. "Oh no, I will not *forget it*. You can't accuse me of something and then not explain."

He pinned her with a hard stare. "What's going on between us?"

Mya frowned. "What do you mean?"

"You were supposed to live with me and keep me out of trouble."

"And that's what I've been doing." She was confused. She'd emptied the house of booze and booty calls. Aiden no longer went clubbing or partying. According to the alerts she had set up, there weren't any new tabloid stories on him. She'd kept him out of trouble. She'd kept him from breaking the rules. She didn't know what he could possibly mean.

Aiden placed a hand at her elbow, trailing it up her arm and stopping with his palm resting at her neck. Stepping closer, he searched her face. She leaned forward, wanting to kiss him, wanting to forget why he wasn't good for her, and wanting to take away whatever stressed him. Because that's what you did for someone you loved.

No, no, no. Not love. *Cared* for, yes, but love? The answer blasted into her chest like a bullet.

She loved him.

What had she done? This wasn't supposed to happen. She had planned on finding a loyal, reliable man who loved kids and wanted to settle down. Aiden was none of those things, so why had she allowed herself to fall in love with him?

"Are you falling in love with me?" he asked. Could he read her thoughts, or was it written all over her face?

"No." But it was a lie, and she had always been a terrible liar.

A finger brushed over her lips. "Tell me the truth."

Mya shuffled her feet and glanced away, but when she looked back into Aiden's eyes, she knew she couldn't lie to him. "Yes, I'm falling in love with you." But that was a lie in its own way, wasn't it? Closer to the truth, but still a lie. She wasn't falling in love with him, she had already fallen in love with him. Somehow she couldn't admit it out loud.

All the color drained from Aiden's face, and his eyes grew round with shock. His hand dropped from her face, and he stumbled away so fast that his foot caught the edge of the curb. He grabbed onto the car to stop himself from sprawling in the gutter.

From the looks of it, she should have lied and kept her feelings to herself. Utter horror wasn't generally the desired reaction to a declaration of love. Quite the opposite.

And what a dirty trick he'd used to pull the answer from her. Her back stiffened, and she jabbed a finger in his direction. "How dare you play on my feelings with your tender touches and adoring eyes. But they're not really adoring eyes, are they? They're only lusty. For a second, I got them confused." She took a breath. "I didn't mean for my feelings to change. I especially didn't mean to have feelings for a man who can't bear to part with his wife's belongings because he still loves her." She bit her trembling lip, determined not to cry.

Aiden's eyes widened. "What? No... I don't—"

Cutting him off because her heart was too broken to hear him try to deny it, Mya said, "You don't need to lie to me. The truth is right in front of me." She forced herself to stay calm, stay sane. "When this is all over, you'll never see me again."

"Mya," he said, reaching his arms out and placing his hands on her shoulders, "I'm sorry I can't give you more." Genuine regret shone from his eyes, but he didn't deny that he still loved Madeline.

Yanking out of his grasp, she took a deep breath and squared her shoulders. "Don't be sorry; it's my fault. Just take me home." Without waiting for a response, she returned to the car.

She had to remind herself that Aiden's house wasn't really home. She'd lived there for a few weeks, and it had started to feel like it. But home wasn't a place full of someone else's ghosts. Home was with Amelia and Noah.

Home was a place filled with love and laughter and family. Aiden's house was the antithesis of home.

Aiden dropped his head for a beat as he stared at the ground, then scrubbed the back of his neck. After a moment, he slid into the driver's seat, started the engine, and put the car in gear. Tears threatened to spill, and Mya held them back. It wasn't until she was in her room, sitting in the bathroom, out of sight of Noah, that she let them fall.

That evening, Mya and Noah were lining up his cars on the floor of the toy room when a loud banging came from the front door.

"What's that, Mummy?"

"Sounds like someone's at the door," she said and continued playing with the cars.

"Aren't you going to answer?"

"Aiden will." She'd spent the afternoon with Noah in the playroom, avoiding Aiden with her phone on silent. She didn't know how she'd make it through the next few weeks living together. She imagined she'd be spending a lot of her time in her room.

A familiar but angry voice reached her ears, and she got to her feet.

"Pack up the cars, sweetie, I'll be back soon," she said to Noah.

Mr. Masters was back, and he wasn't happy. What had gone wrong?

She hesitated at the top of the stairs and watched Mr. Masters's face turn red as he pointed his finger at Aiden. "This was your last chance, and you blew it! I can't sacrifice the careers of dozens of people because you can't keep it in your pants—you're fired."

Mya squeaked in shock. Had Aiden been talking to a woman the night before and somehow sneaked out without her hearing? But she'd been awake most of the night!

Both heads swiveled in her direction.

"You're the next person I need to speak to," Mr. Masters growled.

With feet like lead, she trudged down the stairs.

"I had a high opinion of you, Mya. I never thought Aiden would lead you astray. I'd hoped you could do your job without getting yourself involved in his lifestyle."

Mya frowned. "I'm not sure what you mean."

He dug his phone from his pocket, swiped the screen a couple of times, and held it out to her.

She took it with trembling hands. Would she see photos of Aiden with another woman? A wave of relief washed over her—not another woman.

Aiden walked over and stood behind her, watching over her shoulder as she swiped through the photos.

Someone had taken pictures of them earlier that day while they had been talking in the car park by the ocean. The gossip sites had turned an innocent conversation into a sordid affair.

Aiden Doyle's Newest Conquest—Who Will It Be Tomorrow?

The pictures showed Aiden's hand resting on her neck, and her standing too close for comfort when she'd been fighting the urge to kiss him. They were undeniably intimate.

They'd caught Aiden's stumble on the curb too, and called him out for drunk driving, even though he'd been stone sober and had merely slipped. As if Mya would have gotten into a car with someone who'd been drinking! But of course the tabloid didn't know about Daniel. On one hand, at least Aiden hadn't been out with another woman, but on the other hand, Mr. Masters didn't look like he was done firing people for the day.

"This isn't what it looks like," she said, passing the phone back.

"Oh, so you haven't been fucking Aiden?" He snapped.

"Don't you *dare* speak to Mya like that." Aiden took a menacing step toward Mr. Masters.

Mr. Masters's eyes widened at the threatening tone in Aiden's voice. He adjusted his tie and cleared his throat. "Anyway, it no longer matters what's going on between you two. You're both fired."

"Mr. Masters, please let me explain," Mya pleaded.

He turned to Mya with flushed cheeks. "What's to explain? You had a job to do, and you failed."

"But this isn't what you think," Mya said. "We've been doing what you asked. He isn't drinking anymore. I've stopped the parties, and he's staying home. There haven't been any strange women or anything!"

Mr. Masters shook his head. "The deal was Aiden stays out of the tabloids. The actor who plays the patriarch on *Family First* must be squeaky clean. We've given him plenty of chances to toe the line, and he hasn't. The only difference is that this time, you helped get him in hot water. But the show must go on."

Mya swung her attention to Aiden, waiting for him to step up and defend himself. Defend his job. *Their* jobs. But he sat in an armchair and crossed an ankle over his knee, looking like he didn't have a care in the world.

"Can't you just give him another chance?" Mya needed the money for Gran.

"I've given him enough chances." Mr. Masters turned

to Aiden. "Good luck getting another job in the industry. You're going to need it."

Mya watched Mr. Masters's retreating back, then pivoted toward Aiden. "Why didn't you say anything?"

"Nothing I said would have changed Lionel's mind. He's wanted to get rid of me for months." He gestured toward the door. "He got his wish."

"You could have tried!" The money—and her job—had just walked out the door.

"I don't want the job anymore." He said it as calmly as if he were commenting on the weather.

Mya's blood boiled. She had a son to raise, a sister to help, and a grandmother who needed a better nursing home to live in. And he didn't fight for them because *he* didn't want the job!

She might have chucked a knickknack at his head if the room hadn't been empty of anything that made the house look lived in. The whole place was as barren as Aiden's heart. Madeline had broken him. Perhaps it was best that she'd lost this job. Now he could live here in this museum of betrayal all by himself since nothing else mattered to him anymore. Not his family's concern for him, not his job, and certainly not falling in love.

All the anger deflated from her, and she wanted to sag down onto the couch, but she locked her knees and stayed standing. "I needed that job, and you've ruined it for me."

"I'm sorry."

"*Are* you sorry?"

He looked at her as if she'd asked a stupid question. "Of course I am. I know what the money meant to you. It was my fault this happened, so I'll pay you what Lionel would have. Celia can still get her nice nursing home, and you won't need to struggle until you find another job."

Mya's jaw hit the floor. "I am not a charity case."

"I know that." There was something odd in his tone that she couldn't place.

"Or some disposable woman you can pay off once you're done with her," she continued, still furious about the lost job and Aiden's nonchalance.

He rose from the chair and stood in front of her. "You've never been *disposable*."

"But you're still going to throw me away!" The words spilled out before she could stop them.

"Mya, we both knew this was only…"

"Temporary? Fun? No strings attached? Yes, and in my head I wanted all those things too." She clapped a hand to her chest. "My heart had other ideas." Her mouth couldn't control itself.

Aiden scrubbed a hand over his face. "Mya—"

She held up a hand, stopping him from saying anything because she knew his words would tear her heart out and hurl it to the floor. It was already breaking into pieces. She didn't need him finishing the job. "It's okay. I knew where you stood, and I was happy to go along. But somewhere along the way, emotions got in the way and things changed for me. This is my problem, not yours. But I thought we were at least friends."

"We are friends."

"You didn't help me fight Mr. Masters to keep my job!" Why couldn't he understand?

He blew out a breath and jerked his fingers through his hair. "That's because you don't deserve to work for someone like Lionel. Lionel walked all over you. It's how you ended up with this shit assignment. With the money I'll give you, you'll have time to look for something better."

"I'm not taking your money," she gritted through clenched teeth.

"Why not? You need it."

"Because I love you! And you're treating me like every other woman you've been with since Madeline died! Like sex is all you—or they—need. Offering me money makes me feel like a cheap whore." She willed the tears that pricked at her eyes not to fall.

Aiden's face grew pale, and his eyes darted around the room like he was a scared rabbit trying to find a safe place to hide. She waited for him to say something.

But he didn't.

Fine. If this was how things ended between them, this was how they ended. She could pick herself up again and start over. But first, she needed to get out of this house.

"I'm getting Noah and going home." She turned away from him. She couldn't look at him a moment longer without tumbling into a blubbering heap.

Aiden finally found his voice. "Mya, I never thought of you as a… as a…"

She turned back. "But you don't love me either."

His lips pressed into a thin line.

His silence was all the answer she needed. With a heavy heart and tears threatening to spill down her cheeks, she went to her room and packed.

Chapter 32

"*I* don't want to go home," Noah complained from the back seat of Mya's car.

"My job with Aiden is finished." His name on her lips was like a knife to the heart.

"You didn't let me say goodbye," he whined.

Mya heard the sulky tone in her son's voice and glanced in the rearview mirror. Noah sat with his arms crossed, a frown creasing his face as he stared out of the passenger side window. She wished he hadn't gotten so attached to Aiden, and she hated that she couldn't give her boy what he wanted. Maybe she never would. The thought of jumping back into the dating game left a bitter taste in her mouth.

When they arrived home, Bob and Julie's car was parked on the street. It wasn't a visitation day with Noah, and they were the last people she wanted to deal with today.

As they got out of the car, Amelia rushed from the house. "Hey buddy," she said to Noah, "I made some brownies. They're in the kitchen and still warm."

Noah took off into the house, leaving Mya alone with her sister.

"I've been trying to call you to tell you Bob and Julie are here," Amelia hissed.

"I was driving," Mya said. "You know I won't answer the phone if I'm driving." There was no way she'd put Noah at risk by being distracted. She knew better than anyone the consequences involved.

"Well, Julie's super pissed. More pissed than I've ever seen her before."

When was Julie ever happy with Mya? "Why is she upset?" Even as she asked the question, she knew what must have happened.

"She's seen the photos of you and Aiden—cute outfit in them by the way—and she's blabbering on about you putting Noah in an unstable environment and not giving him proper care and attention." The last few words were said in an over-the-top impression of Julie's voice.

Mya's blood ran cold. "Oh God, I've given her the ammunition she needs to take Noah away from me."

Amelia clapped her hands on Mya's arms. "No, you haven't. You are a great mother. Those photos don't prove a damned thing—Noah wasn't even in them, so as far as they know, Noah and Aiden didn't spend more than a few minutes together the other day when they picked him up here."

"You're right. You're right. I better get this over with." Mya tried and failed to calm her racing heart.

Inside the house, Bob sat on the couch and Julie stood ramrod straight with an expression like she'd been sucking lemons. "You've been a busy woman."

"Hello, Julie. Bob. Nice to see you too. Thank you for the lovely and polite greeting." Her tone was sarcastic, and she didn't bother trying to hide it. There was no point being nice to this woman. She didn't dislike Mya because of anything she'd done, and Mya suddenly realized that meant there was nothing she could do to change Julie's mind. All the time she'd spent trying to prove that she was a good mother had exhausted her for nothing. "Is there some reason you've dropped in without calling? Kind of rude and inconsiderate, don't you think?" This was the first time Mya had been anything other than deferential to the other woman, but she was done. Done with the accusations, the insinuations, she was just plain done and not willing to take Julie's abuse anymore.

Julie's eyes widened, and huge splotches of pink appeared on her cheeks. But she gathered herself together to say, "We've seen those trashy photos splashed all over the place. How dare you associate yourself with a man like that? A man whose life is tainted with alcohol and drugs and women." After a bark of harsh laughter, she continued, "Oh, you've been trying to hide behind a squeaky-clean lifestyle but underneath you're just as rotten as the day you killed my son. You're not fit to look after my grandson. You'll be hearing from our lawyer."

Even though the threat was expected, it didn't stop a red haze from clouding Mya's vision. Her body vibrated. Her hands shook. She was so bloody tired of Julie looking down her nose and accusing her of being an unfit mother. So *so* tired of it. She wanted to say something, shout something, but her rage was so great that it had lodged in her throat, preventing her from speaking. Sending a death glare at Julie would have to suffice for now.

On the other side of the room Bob rose from the couch and put a soothing hand on his wife's back. "Julie, let's talk about this—"

"There's nothing to talk about. She is an irresponsible mother and Noah needs to live with us," Julie snapped and shrugged away his hand. "I won't have her ruining him like she ruined our son!"

Shoulders sagging, Bob tried again, "Taking Noah away from his mother isn't right."

"Not right?" she asked, pursing her lips. "What's not *right* is that our grandson is living with a slut!"

"Julie, you're being a bit harsh," Bob said.

"It's the truth; she's a slut. A horrible, no-good slut. She drinks and sleeps around and our son is dead because of her!" She pinned Mya with a stare full of hate.

The knot in her throat eased, so Mya drew herself up to her full height and said, "Your son is dead because he got drunk and then got behind the wheel of a car."

Julie recoiled like she'd been slapped. Even Bob looked uncomfortable.

But Mya didn't care. She'd told them the unvarnished truth. Talking to Aiden had helped Mya see that Daniel's death hadn't been her fault. She could have told him about the baby at a different time, she could have stayed instead of leaving him with his friends… But ultimately, it had been Daniel's decision to drink and drive that day. Mya was done carrying the guilt for his poor choices, and more than done letting Julie hold it over her head.

Mya continued, "I'm a good mother—a great one! I love Noah, and he loves me. He has a safe place to live with people who care about him, the fridge is full, and he's never wanted for anything. He is a well-adjusted kid who laughs, plays, and loves his friends and family. You're included in his affections. Go to your lawyer if you must, but let me make myself clear: I will fight you with everything I have. Those pictures prove nothing about my ability to be Noah's mother. You will lose, and then you'll never see your grandson again."

Mya and Julie stared long and hard at one another.

Neither was willing to back down. But Mya knew she was going to win this battle. Knew it in her gut.

Someone else seemed to know it too. Bob sidled up to his wife. "Julie, you need to stop this. Daniel made a mistake. I realized that ages ago; why can't you? It's not Mya's fault. I don't know about you, but I'd rather see Noah grow up than escalate this situation and have our only grandchild resent us. Please, Jules, let's go home." Her shoulders stiffened, and her jaw clenched. For a second Mya thought she would continue to fight, but instead, she slumped and leaned into Bob. As he steered Julie out of the house, he said to Mya, "I'm sorry. We won't try to get custody. We'll see you next month, okay?" The last was said in a hopeful yet pleading tone, like Bob knew things had gone too far and was unsure about the future.

Mya nodded. She wouldn't stop Noah from seeing his grandparents although there would be new boundaries put in place. But they could discuss them later.

After Bob and Julie left, Mya deflated like a balloon and collapsed onto the couch. No longer did she have the anchor of their expectations hanging around her neck weighing her down, threatening to drown her if she set a foot wrong. She could breathe again knowing that Noah was safe and secure with her and no one could ever take him away.

Amelia walked into the room and sat down. "I'm so proud of you."

"You were listening?"

"Of course I was! I had to know if I needed to jump in to help you hide the bodies."

That was so like Amelia, willing to protect and help the people she loved. The swirling emotions of the roller coaster last few days crashed over her. Leaning her head on her sister's shoulder, Mya burst into tears.

"Hey." Amelia pulled away to look at her. "You won! You should celebrate, not cry."

"I know. I know. But… Oh God, I could have lost Noah too." Her body shook as she spoke.

"What do you mean, *too*?" Amelia rubbed Mya's back gently.

She took a huge gulping breath and answered, "Those photos got back to my boss. He came by Aiden's house earlier and fired us both."

"He what?" Amelia's screech could have shattered glass. "He can't do that! You've been keeping Aiden out of trouble."

"That's not the way he sees it. Aiden made the gossip sites, and the photos make it look like we're having more than an innocent conversation."

"We'll sue the studio. This can't be legal."

The thought of contacting lawyers for another fight was too draining to even contemplate. Not to mention she had no idea where she'd get the money for a lawyer. "I knew what I was getting into. I knew the rules. I didn't hold up my end of the bargain, and now I'm paying the price."

"What did Aiden say about all this?"

It was a reasonable question. One she should have expected. But at the mention of Aiden's name, more tears sprung from Mya's eyes as she tried to hold back a sob.

"Oh Mya, what's wrong?" Amelia put an arm around Mya's shoulders.

"Aiden didn't even try to help us keep our jobs," she wailed, not even bothering to hold back the tears. "He doesn't want his anymore and didn't care that I'd lost mine, even though Mr. Masters never said that my job as his assistant was on the line."

"What a bastard," Amelia spat. She paused for a beat before adding, "The both of them."

"He offered to pay me the money Mr. Masters would have paid when the job was done. But I refused to take it."

"Why? He's the one who caused the problem."

Mya stood up and wiped the tears from her cheeks. "Giving me money is like a slap to the face. I poured out my heart to him, and he's pulling out his wallet like I'm someone who can be bought. I don't want charity. I want someone who will put me first! And Aiden wouldn't even consider it."

"Oh, Mya. You love him." It wasn't a question. Amelia's eyes turned sympathetic. "I should never have encouraged you to have *fun* with him. That's not who you are. I'm so sorry."

She waved Amelia's apology away. "This isn't your fault. It's mine. I knew what I was getting into, and I thought that's what I wanted too. He wasn't relationship material. But I… I…"

"Fell in love."

Nodding, Mya's face crumbled, and the tears poured out again.

Amelia pulled Mya into a hug and patted her back comfortingly. "Did you tell him how you felt? Maybe he feels the same way."

"He knows," Mya wriggled out of her sister's embrace, walked to the window, and stared into the distance. "And he doesn't feel the same way. But that's not important." She knew that was a lie, but she soldiered on anyway. "I have to find another job and get the money to move Gran into a better nursing home." Focusing on Gran was better than remembering the look of fear on Aiden's face when she told him how she felt.

"Gran has told me more than once she's happy where

she is. Maybe we should leave her," Amelia said tentatively. "If we relocate her now, who knows how confusing it might be for her."

Aiden had said she'd told him the same thing. But Mya needed to take care of her family the best way she could, and putting Gran in a better facility was the best thing to do.

"She'd get better care somewhere else," Mya insisted.

"Sure, the facility is old and dated, but the nurses are lovely. She's made friends and knows the staff." Amelia added, "Isn't it better to keep her with her friends than to move her in with strangers?"

Her sister had a point, but Mya's brain was so overloaded with the day's events that she couldn't think straight. "I can't talk about this right now. I'm going to shower and lie down for a bit. Do you mind keeping an eye on Noah?"

"Sure, take your time."

Mya trudged to the bathroom and stripped out of her clothes. Under the hot spray of the shower, she slid to the floor and tucked her knees to her chest as the water beat down on her head, mixing with the tears falling down her face.

Chapter 33

*a*iden's hand clenched the bottle of Jack Daniel's. He twisted off the cap, and the pungent alcohol tang burned his nose. He couldn't recall why he'd ever found it pleasant enough to crave the stuff. Now the stench caused his stomach to churn.

Pouring it down the drain, he threw the bottle in the bin. He placed his hands on the counter and let his head drop. *I love you.* Mya's words played on repeat through his brain, making him want to reach inside his head and pull them out. The last woman who'd told him she loved him had betrayed him in the worst possible way. How could he believe anyone again? Was it all an act? He knew Mya was looking for someone to play happy families with. Someone who'd take on the role as father for her son.

The kid had gotten under his skin. It wasn't hard to tell Noah craved a father figure in his life, and he'd set his eyes on Aiden. Even though he'd enjoyed spending time with him, he wasn't the man for the job. Mya and her son needed a man they could rely on, who'd stand by them no matter what and fight their battles. Aiden couldn't even stick up for Mya and help her keep her job. She deserved better.

Memories of Madeline in the house had been replaced with memories of Mya, and her absence made the house feel emptier than it had even after Madeline's death.

Not able to stay home a moment longer, he jumped in the car and took off with no destination in mind. He just drove. Trees and buildings whizzed past, but he didn't see them. His thoughts were still filled with Mya.

After driving around for an hour, he pulled up outside Chloe's house. If she was surprised to see him at her door, she didn't say, but concern was etched on her face as she trailed her gaze over him. "Hey, I'm glad you're here. I feel awful for upsetting you about the nursery," she said as they made their way into the living room. Chloe sat in an armchair while Aiden stared out the window. "I'm sorry I delivered the news about the directing job so harshly. I'll help you if that's what you want, and I won't even ask you to crawl—although, flowers in your teeth might be a nice touch." She giggled, then turned serious when she said, "I should never have told you to move on with Mya, especially if you're not ready. I can't imagine what it's like to lose someone you love so soon after losing your baby."

Aiden's spine stiffened. He was sick of keeping Madeline's dirty little secret. Sick to the teeth. It was time for the truth to come out. "It wasn't my baby."

"What?" Chloe gasped.

Without turning around, he said, "Madeline had an affair."

Chloe stood and closed the distance between them. She placed a hand on his shoulder. "Why didn't you tell us?"

He shrugged her hand away. "Because you all loved her, and when she got sick… Well, I didn't want to upset the family more."

"You cared for her until the end, knowing she cheated?" Chloe shook her head in obvious disbelief. "I don't know if I could have done that. I don't know how you could. How anyone could."

"Don't make it sound like I was all noble. I wasn't." He turned away from the window, unable to watch as a mother and child walked by. "When I found out about the affair, I wanted a divorce. Then she told me she was pregnant with my child, and like a sap, I believed her." He ran a hand through his hair. "I was so stupid. I should've known better. If she could cheat on me, she could lie about the pregnancy too. I didn't even think about asking for a DNA test."

"It was a lot to take in. You weren't thinking clearly. She'd been in your life for years; of course, you'd believe her," Chloe said, her voice soothing. "How did you find out?"

"When she got sick and needed to be induced to receive treatment, she finally told me I wasn't the father. The man she had the affair with left her when she told him she was pregnant."

Chloe put a hand to her mouth. "How awful! And after what she put you through, you stayed by her side. Oh, Aiden, you should never have carried this burden on your own. We love you and would have helped you through it." She slipped her arms around him, holding him to her like he was a child.

"No one could do anything." He pulled away to go back to the window.

If his sister was annoyed at his brusqueness, she didn't show it. "We would have understood that what you were dealing with was more than just losing your wife. It would explain why you buried yourself in such a deep hole, why you threw away your career, and why you wouldn't let anyone get close to you. I wish you'd trusted us."

"Better to keep it to myself." He didn't bother explaining.

But Chloe didn't let it go, she wormed herself in front of him and stared at him with her hands on her hips. "How was that better? We've always stuck together and helped each other in good times and bad. If I'd known what she did to you, I would have… have…"

Seeing Chloe's fierce expression, Aiden smiled softly. "And that's why I didn't tell anyone. If you'd all turned on her…" He trailed off, letting her draw her own conclusions. "She was sick, dying. She didn't need that kind of stress in her life."

The intensity dropped from her face. "I'm so sorry you went through that." She hugged him properly, laying her head on his chest. "It breaks my heart that you had to put on a brave face through all of that."

A few weeks ago, thoughts of Madeline would have sliced through his chest like a poisoned blade. Now, they felt like a dull ache from a past wound. One he wouldn't forget, but something that no longer crippled him.

Chloe pulled back and looked at him. "Why the shrine in the nursery? I would think you wouldn't want to see her stuff."

"Madeline moved into that room when I found out about the affair. Even though I was trying to work things out, I wasn't ready to sleep in the same bed as her. Her things around the house—books, decorations—were easy to pack into boxes. When it came to her bedroom, all the personal things and baby clothes… I couldn't bring myself to touch them. Couldn't even walk in there. So I closed it up until Mya came to stay." Thoughts of Mya did hurt— like lemon juice on a paper cut. He hated the way things had ended with her. He was the biggest jerk for hurting her.

"I'm sorry for pushing you earlier to move on," Chloe said, stepping away. "If I'd known what you were going through, I would have been more understanding."

"Would you?" Aiden raised an eyebrow.

"Yes, but—"

"Of course there's a *but*." Aiden grinned. It was amazing how much lighter he felt after opening up to his sister about Madeline and the baby. The secret he'd kept didn't weigh him down as much.

"You deserve to be happy. These past few weeks, I've seen a change in you. You're laughing and smiling again. That loveable old brother of mine was showing himself again, and I know who to thank for that." She stepped closer, concern once again coloring her features. "But something's changed. Right now you've got a sad look in your eyes that I hoped was gone for good."

Mya had pulled him from the dark, but he still couldn't risk opening his heart. "She's better off without me."

"Why?" she pressed.

"She told me she loved me."

Chloe's eyes widened. "Oh, Aiden, that's wonderful! I knew something more than a fling was going on between you two." Her eyes narrowed. "Why do you look like you want to run and hide?"

Because that's exactly what Aiden wanted to do. He rubbed the back of his neck and blew out a long breath. "She deserves someone who can love her back and love her son like the boy was his own."

"And you can't do that?"

"No." He didn't bother to explain.

But he should have known that Chloe wasn't going to let it go. "Why not? I've seen the way you look at her. I can't recall you ever looking at Madeline the way you do Mya. I'm sorry, I know you loved her, but those last few years, I didn't see the spark."

If he were being honest with himself, the spark had gone, even before the affair. Yes, there had been affection, and he'd loved her, but that deep love had drifted away. Some of it was his fault, a lot of it was hers. Maybe they could have gotten the spark back, but death and despair had robbed them of that opportunity. Or really, he'd let the opportunity slip away just like he'd done with Mya.

"Do you love Mya?" Chloe asked while she watched him closely.

He stared out the window again. Mya had gone back home only a few hours ago, but it felt like a lifetime. He missed her smile, her laugh, and the way she blasted his arse when he stepped out of line.

Did he love her? Every cell in his body shouted the answer, but saying it out loud made it real, and then he'd have to deal with it, so he kept his mouth shut. "It doesn't matter. It would never work." He wasn't good for her.

"If you love each other, you can make it work."

He shook his head. "After what Madeline did… I can't." Can't open up again. Can't tell someone he loved them. Can't take care of another man's child. Can't lose someone else. Yes, he'd let the opportunity to love again slip away, but he couldn't handle another heartbreak. That's why he had his rules. His rules protected him.

"What if this could be something amazing? Don't you want to at least try? You deserve to be happy."

"Mya needs someone she can rely on. Someone better than me, who can give all of himself to her."

"What the hell are you talking about?" Chloe blurted. "After Dad died, you and Ethan were the two men in my life I could rely on. So, you've had a couple of screwed-up years—big deal! But you and Ethan are my rock. The people who will always have my back. Ethan's got Holly; any woman would be lucky to have you."

"You can say that all you like, but I know I wasn't enough for Madeline," Aiden said.

Chloe exhaled slowly. "I don't know what went on with Madeline. You loved each other once, but you were both so young; things can change. Love is never guaranteed. But you can either run and hide from everything great you could have with Mya because you're scared, or you can take the risk and tell her how you feel. Just because things ended badly once before doesn't mean it will happen again."

Chloe was right; she often was. He had been afraid to start something with Mya because of what had happened with Madeline. He'd made all of these rules to protect his heart.

Aiden kissed Chloe's forehead. "Thanks for the chat." He turned to leave.

"What are you going to do?" she asked.

Before he answered, his phone rang.

Mya's name filled the screen.

He wanted to ignore it. The sound of her voice would make him want to run to her. But after he hadn't defended her to Lionel, he doubted she'd be calling just to chat, so it had to be important.

"Hello?" he answered as his heart pounded.

"Aiden?" A small voice, childish, definitely not Mya's. "I don't know where I am."

Chapter 34

"*H*ey kid, where's your mum?" Aiden asked, trying to control his rapidly beating heart.

Noah sniffled. "I don't know."

Fear pierced Aiden's chest. Had something happened to Mya? "Where are you?"

"I don't know!" Noah wailed.

He needed to keep the kid calm; clearly that line of questioning wasn't going to work. He changed tactics. "Why do you have your mum's phone?"

"I took it while she was sleeping and Aunty Amelia was washing dishes."

Relief that Mya was okay washed over him, but Noah taking her phone didn't explain what was going on. "Then what did you do?" He needed to keep the kid focused.

The sniffles grew louder. "I wanted to come back to your house. But… but… I don't know the way, and now I'm lost." The sniffles turned into sobs.

Fuck! He could be anywhere and anyone could easily toss him into the back of a car and drive away. Icy tendrils of fear wrapped around his heart. He had to keep calm. He had to—for Noah's sake. "Tell me what you can see." Hopefully Noah hadn't gone too far.

"Umm…" There was silence for a beat before he said, "Cars and trees and houses."

"Are there any signs you can read?"

"I can't read."

Aiden wasn't sure that was true; he'd seen the kid flipping through those books of his time and time again. It was more likely that Noah's fear and stress had paralyzed him. Again, time to redirect. "How did you know who to call?" Aiden wanted to know.

"I called the first name in Mummy's phone."

Aiden came before *Amelia*, but still: smart kid to get that far. "Okay, do you know your letters?" There was silence, and Aiden wondered if he was thinking or if he had nodded his answer so he asked again, "Tell me yes or no if you know your letters."

"Yes."

Okay, progress. "Can you see any signs?"

More silence, then Noah said, "Yes."

"Awesome."

Catching Chloe's wide, questioning eyes, he clicked his fingers and made a *get pen and paper* gesture. She hurried to a small desk in the corner of the room and pulled out a pad and pen and handed them to him.

"Okay, spell the closest sign you can see for me."

"S-T-O-P."

Well, now he knew the kid was at an intersection on a city street and not walking down the side of a highway. "That's really great, kid. Do you see any other signs above that one? Maybe on a telephone pole or a light post? It should look like a rectangle." He hoped Noah knew what a rectangle was.

"I think so. It's pretty high up."

"Can you spell it?"

"M-U-R-P-H-Y-S-T."

"You're on Murphy Street," Aiden said as he parsed what he'd written.

Chloe was already on her phone, Googling the name. "There's one in Fleming Ridge and another in Marsh Bay."

Fleming Ridge was the closest to Mya's house. It had to be that one. "Listen to me. I'm coming to get you, but you need to stay where you are. If you walk around, I might not find you, okay?"

"Okay," he said in a small voice.

"And do not go anywhere with anyone. Don't get in anyone's car unless it's your Mum or Aunt. Understand?"

"Yes." Noah's voice was small.

Aiden wanted to reach through the phone and give the kid a hug, but he couldn't. So he did the next best thing. "Hey, don't worry, kid, I'm not going to hang up on you. I'm on my way. I won't be long. I'm going to mute myself for a moment, okay?"

"Okay."

He turned to his sister. "I need a favor."

"Hit me."

While talking with Noah, Aiden realized he hadn't gotten Amelia's phone number and calling Mya's phone was useless. He gave Chloe Mya's address. "Go there now and tell her what's happened and that I've gone to get him." Without waiting for a response, he ran out of the house, unmuting the phone as he went. "You still with me, kid?"

"Yeah."

"Good. Good. So talk to me. Tell me about the cars that you see."

Aiden didn't really need that information, but he didn't want Noah panicking. Driving to find the kid was the longest trip of his life. What if something happened? What if some sicko found his next victim? He couldn't stop a kidnapper from over the phone. Mya would be devastated, and he'd never forgive himself for not getting to him faster.

He pressed the accelerator harder and ran a red light. Horns blared at him, but he didn't care. He had to get to Noah. He heard the kid talking to someone, and his worry increased. Was the person good or bad? He didn't know, and the uncertainty terrified him.

His tires squealed as he swung onto Murphy Street and slowed down to scan the area. He should have asked the kid if he could see the cross street. But he hadn't. Why hadn't he? He berated himself for not thinking things through. But it was too late now.

One intersection passed.

Then another.

His worry increased tenfold. Maybe he had the wrong Murphy Street. Maybe the kid wasn't on Murphy Street at all, but the sign he'd read was pointing toward Murphy Street. Scenario after scenario flitted through his mind as he continued his search.

One more street.

Two.

Success!

He spotted the kid sitting on a brick fence in front of an old clapboard house. An elderly Asian woman sat next to him. That must have been the person Noah had been talking to. Not a kidnapper, but a concerned citizen. A relieved gush of air escaped his lungs.

The car had barely come to a stop when Aiden vaulted out of his seat. "Noah," he called and rushed to him. The kid's name bounced around in his heart, sealing the cracks. Before, the kid's name couldn't pass Aiden's lips, but now it sounded like a beautiful song to his ears.

"Aiden!" Noah's face lit up, and he ran to Aiden, throwing his skinny little arms around his waist. Aiden held on tight, not wanting to let go.

Noah squirmed in his arms. "I told the lady you were coming to get me and I couldn't go anywhere with her." His head tilted so far back to look at him.

"Good boy." Aiden bent and kissed the top of Noah's head.

"I'm so happy you found your son," the old woman said. "I was about to call the police, but he told me you were on your way."

Aiden didn't correct the woman when she called Noah his son. Instead, the word fanned through his body with warmth and protectiveness. This kid had burrowed into his heart just like his mother, and there was no way of shaking them loose.

"Thank you for sitting with him." Aiden smiled at the woman.

"It was my pleasure. You've raised a lovely boy." She waved and shuffled into her house.

"Time to get you home. Your mum will be worried." Aiden's body still trembled with adrenaline.

"Will she be mad at me?" Noah's lip dropped and trembled.

"Probably, but she'll also be happy to see you and know you're safe. But"—Aiden squatted down so they were eye to eye—"promise me you'll never do that again. It's dangerous."

Noah nodded, and tears spilled down his cheeks. "I just wanted to see you again!"

"I know. I know," Aiden soothed, pulling him into a hug and breathing in his little boy smell. In that moment, he realized it wasn't just Mya he loved.

Chapter 35

*M*ya woke up from her short nap still feeling out of sorts. She'd hoped some sleep would ease the pounding in her head and the ache in her heart, but she didn't get lucky on either count. She could take a couple of Panadol for her head. But there was nothing she could take for her heart. That was going to need time to heal, assuming it ever did.

Making her way downstairs, she stumbled through the living room, stepping over Noah's discarded toys, to discover Amelia in the kitchen finishing the dishes. Amelia turned to her as she wiped her hands on a tea towel. "Feel better after your nap?"

She shook her head and slumped onto a dining table chair. "No, I feel like I've been hit by a truck."

"I wish I could do something for you." Amelia slid onto a chair next to her.

Mya gave her a weak smile. "Thanks, but no one can do anything."

"You should talk to him—"

"No point. He's made it clear he doesn't want me the

way I want him. I won't be someone's fuck toy, and I won't beg." She had opinions on this. She deserved to be more than just a convenient lay.

Amelia nodded and patted her on the shoulder. "Fair enough."

Not wanting to discuss Aiden Doyle further, Mya scanned the room. "Where's Noah?"

"He's in the living room playing with his toy cars."

"He wasn't there when I walked past." Mya frowned, starting to become concerned.

"Maybe he's in his room," Amelia suggested.

"I'll go check." Mya started to rise.

But Amelia stopped her. "No, stay here. I'll go." She left the kitchen.

Mya debated getting up and grabbing the Panadol now, but she couldn't force herself to move. Exhausted to her core, she rested her head on the table.

After a couple of minutes, Amelia came back into the room, looking worried. "He's not in his room or anywhere upstairs."

The concern morphed into full-on worry. "He should have told you he was going to play outside." Mya walked from the kitchen to the backyard. Noah was not in the yard. With her heart in her throat, she ran to the front yard —the empty front yard. Terror filled her.

"Amelia," she yelled, "Noah isn't outside!"

"What? He's probably hiding somewhere." But Amelia's face mirrored Mya's fear.

They combed through all the rooms, checked in all the closets, looked behind furniture, and peered under the beds.

No Noah.

In desperation, Amelia checked the backyard again

while Mya ran up and down the street, calling out Noah's name.

No response.

Fear gripped her heart. Where could her baby be? She went from door to door, asking if any of the neighbors had seen him.

No one had.

Racing back to the house, she found Amelia checking their next-door neighbor's yard. They had an indoor/outdoor cat Noah liked to play with, but he wasn't there.

Noah was missing.

She stumbled back into her house as the realization flooded through her. "Where did he go? Has someone taken him?" Mya's voice cracked as she raked trembling fingers through her hair.

"Don't think like that. He's probably gone for a walk." Amelia was trying to be reassuring, but the crack in her voice showed how worried she was.

"He knows he's not allowed to leave the house!" Mya's voice rose with hysteria.

Could Bob and Julie have come back? Could they have taken him? She'd thought she'd dealt with them—with Julie—but maybe it wasn't enough. Would Julie kidnap Noah in a misguided attempt to protect him? Mya couldn't say with one-hundred-percent certainty what Noah's grandparents would do. All she knew was that her son was missing.

"I need to call the police." Mya snatched her bag from the table and dug around for her phone. She couldn't find it. Frustration and fear warred within her, so she tipped the contents onto the floor, dropped to her knees, and dug through the pile, scattering her things around.

Her phone was missing!

Had it fallen out in the car? Had she left it on the bedside table? She didn't remember seeing it there. Could Noah have taken it? She didn't know.

She turned to her sister. "Can I borrow your pho—"

Someone pounded on the door.

She leaped to her feet, shouting, "Noah!" As she swung it open, her face fell at seeing Chloe Doyle and not her son on the other side.

"Chloe...I don't have time...Noah is miss—" A sob racked her body, cutting her off.

"He's with Aiden!" Chloe blurted as Amelia wrapped her arms around Mya. "He's safe!"

Relief and confusion joined the other emotions swirling through her. Noah was with Aiden? How? Why? How? She had so many questions that needed answers. Mya tore away from Amelia. "What? Aiden came and took him?"

"No! No. Noah got lost and called Aiden. We figured out where he was, and Aiden went to pick him up. Your son's okay; I promise."

"I don't understand." But she didn't ask anything more. The important thing was that Chloe had said Noah was safe.

"Why did Noah call Aiden? How did Noah call Aiden?" Amelia asked, picking up the questioning while Mya sagged onto the couch.

Chloe shot her a sympathetic look before saying, "Noah took your phone and went for a walk, and when he didn't know where he was, he called Aiden—I guess he was the first contact in your phone."

Mya nodded.

"I thought so," Chloe said, pleased. "Anyway, Aiden worked out where Noah was and went to get him. He didn't have Amelia's number, so he sent me here to tell you what happened. I just got a text as I pulled in that he's got

Noah and they're on their way back." She held out her phone, where Mya could make out the words: got him.

"Aiden has Noah?" Tears slid down her cheeks as she placed trembling fingers to her mouth. She barely registered Amelia's comforting presence beside her. "Oh, thank God." The stress drained from her, and she began to sob.

"We were just about to call the police," Amelia said.

"I can't imagine how scared you must have been," Chloe said as she gave Mya's arm an affectionate pat.

A car pulled into the driveway. Mya swiped at her tears and ran outside. "Noah!"

She tore open the car door, and Noah slid from the back seat. Mya picked him up and squeezed him tightly. Her little boy was safe. She never wanted to let him go.

"Mummy, you're squishing me," Noah complained.

She put him on the ground and kneeled in front of him, cupping his face in her hands. "Noah, you scared me! You know you're not supposed to leave the yard."

"I'm sorry." He dropped his head, contrition written all over his face.

She glanced around, noting the neighbors watching from their porches. This wasn't the time for her to lecture or even determine the cause of Noah's disappearance. She pulled her son into another hug. "Promise me you'll never do that again." She tried to sound stern, but it came out more like a plea.

"I promise," he mumbled into her shoulder.

A shadow fell over her, and she glanced up to find Aiden watching them. Getting off her knees, she said, "Thank you for bringing him home. If something happened to—" Her voice cracked, and she couldn't finish her sentence.

"Noah's safe," he whispered.

Mya gasped, staring at him in shock. "You said his name."

Aiden gave a ghost of a smile, then nudged Noah toward the house. "Why don't you go see Aunty Amelia?" He trotted to Amelia and Chloe, who were standing in the doorway, and they went inside.

Mya led Aiden to the backyard away from prying eyes and nosy siblings. When they were alone, she said, "Thank you for bringing him back to me."

"It's no problem."

"I can't believe he ran off like that." she said, shaking her head. "He's normally such a good kid. I'm sorry he bothered you."

"He didn't bother me. I'm glad he called me when he got in a jam." Aiden's voice was soft with what sounded like a hint of guilt. But what did he have to be guilty for? He'd found Noah, brought him back to her safely.

"I suppose it's a good thing that your number was at the top of my contacts. Did Noah say where he was headed?"

"Yeah..." Aiden dug his hands in the pockets of his jeans. "My house."

The answer wasn't a surprise considering the tantrum Noah had thrown earlier. "Did he say why?" But she already knew. He desperately wanted a father figure in his life, had his heart set on Aiden, and was upset about leaving. Mya was angry that Noah had left the house without telling anyone, but she couldn't blame him for his heart wanting something he couldn't have. He took after her, after all.

"No. Maybe he left something behind?" he offered as an explanation.

They stood in the yard, staring at each other, until Mya broke the silence. "Thank you so much for your help. I don't know what I would have done if—" A sob escaped from her mouth.

Aiden pulled her to him and wrapped his arms around her. The action only made her cry harder. She still felt the residual fear over something happening to Noah, mixed with relief at his safe return with the added sadness at the knowledge that Aiden's comforting embrace was temporary. He'd done what he needed to do, and he'd soon drive away and go back to his old life. A life without her.

She broke away and wiped her face with her hands. "I should go inside and make sure Noah is okay."

"Mya…" Aiden reached for her again but stopped, letting his arms drop to his sides when she stepped farther away.

"Goodbye, Aiden," she whispered and turned her back to him. Her heart shattered into a thousand pieces as she walked away from the man she loved.

Chapter 36

Five days later, tears still filled Mya's eyes when she thought of Aiden. Time away from him had done nothing to ease the pain. The ache in her chest only grew stronger each day. When would she stop hurting? Not soon, that was for certain. Maybe not ever.

On top of her misery, she had to deal with Noah's dark mood. Her happy little boy had been replaced with a sulky one who spent most of his time in his room. The first two days home, he'd pleaded with her many times to visit Aiden, but Mya always had an excuse for why they couldn't. He'd eventually stopped asking. She hated how she couldn't give Noah what he wanted—what she wanted too, if she was honest.

While waiting for the kettle to boil, Mya stared out of the kitchen window. Her future plans of having a happy family were scattered in the wind. Having Noah was all she needed. They were happy. Or at least, they would be once they forgot about Aiden.

A text message buzzed her phone.

Pulling it from her pocket, Aiden's name flashed on the

screen. Her trembling finger hovered over his message. If she wanted to forget about him, she couldn't let him back in her life, even if it was only a message.

"It might be important," she said to justify opening the text.

Mya.

I need to show you something. It's important. Please come to my house today.

I'll be waiting.

Aiden.

Oh God, what was she going to do? Should she text and tell him to leave her alone? Or should she risk injuring her heart further by going to his house? She didn't have any answers.

Amelia swept into the room. Seeing the stricken expression on Mya's face, her brow furrowed and she asked, "Hey, what's wrong?"

Mya passed her sister the phone. What did Aiden need to show her? And why couldn't he say it on the phone? The impersonal nature of the message told her everything she needed to know: he didn't ache for her like she ached for him, and he didn't love her, not even a little.

After Amelia read the text, she handed the phone back. "Are you going?"

Mya pulled two mugs from the cupboard, dropped in tea bags, and filled them with boiling water. "I don't think so… No… Maybe?" God, she was so confused. Her heart screamed for her to get in the car and race over to him. She didn't care that seeing him would be torture. But her brain was trying to tell her to think rationally. Being in the same room with him would not help her heal. She needed time and space to do that.

Watching her closely, Amelia sipped her tea, then said, "You should go."

"I can't face him again." Her heart was too battered, too bruised.

"He says it's important," Amelia pointed out. "If you go, this could be the closure you need to move on. I know it's only been five days, but it might help."

Or make things worse. Taking a deep breath, she dumped the remainder of her tea in the sink. "I won't know unless I go. And I won't be able to think with this hanging over my head. I better get this over with."

Amelia pulled her in for a hug. "Whatever happens, you know I'm always here for you."

Tears pricked Mya's eyes. She had the greatest family in the world in Amelia, Noah, and Gran. She didn't need anyone else.

Mya stood on Aiden's veranda, feeling awkward knocking on the door of a house she'd lived in for weeks. A house that had once felt like home.

The door swung open, and her heart skidded to a stop. Aiden stood in front of her, looking sexy like he always did. Her first instinct was to fling herself into his strong arms, and it took all her willpower to hold herself back.

He wore faded denim jeans and a black T-shirt that fit snug around his muscular body. Gone was his unkempt dark hair; it had been cut in a short, neat style that enhanced his square jaw.

God, he's beautiful. And he didn't appear to have been struggling with their time apart. By the looks of him, he was doing great. Not missing her at all. Her stomach twisted into a knot.

A smile split his face. "Mya, I'm happy you came." He gestured for her to follow him inside.

"You said you needed to show me something?" She wanted to get straight to the point so she could leave. Spending another minute with him looking like he didn't have a care in the world while her heart shattered into a million tiny pieces was torture.

He ran a hand through his newly short hair. "Can I get you something? A drink? Coffee?"

Did she detect a slightly nervous tone to his voice? "No, thanks. I can't stay long."

A flicker of emotion passed over his features so quickly that she didn't have time to identify it. "Okay, come upstairs and I'll show you why I've called you over." Without waiting to see if she followed, he made his way up the stairs.

As they passed rooms which held so many memories, she wanted to turn back and run from the house. The kitchen. The library. Oh God, the library.

When he stopped in front of the nursery, he opened the door and let her go in first.

She gasped.

All the baby furniture, bed, side tables, and dressing table were gone. She twirled in the middle of the room, taking in the empty space. Then she opened the wardrobe. It was bare. So was the bathroom.

"Where did everything go?" she asked in wonder as she surveyed the now empty room.

"I donated it all to charity," Aiden said, his expression far more peaceful than she'd ever seen it in the nursery before.

There was something in his tone that made her examine him sharply. "Why?"

"I've been living with Madeline's ghost for too long. Clinging to our mistakes and using them as a shield. Stopping anyone from getting close." He skimmed the windowsill, staring out into the distance like he had the first time he'd shown her this room. "I blamed her for what went wrong in our marriage, and having her things here reminded me what could happen if I let anyone into my life again." Aiden met her eyes. "But it wasn't all her fault. I was so busy getting my career started that I forgot I had a wife at home who needed me. Somewhere over the years, we grew apart, but I still loved her."

Somewhere in Mya's chest, hope began to flicker.

Aiden ran his fingers through his hair and blew out a long breath. "When I found out about the other man and the baby, the betrayal cut deep. I didn't think I could ever hurt as much as I did. Until I let you walk out of my life." He paused as if waiting for a response, but when none came, he continued, "You told me you loved me. I *felt* your love. Not having you by my side these last few days has been the worst time of my life."

Mya's body trembled. She stared at him, unable to speak.

"I've donated all her things and have even put the house on the market." He reached for her but dropped his hand before they could touch. "I need you to know that I never kept her stuff because I still loved her. I kept it because I needed a reminder of what she did to me so I wouldn't let it happen again. Then you came into my life with your rules and those sexy-as-hell glasses, and you helped me see differently." He took a few steps closer to Mya, their chests almost touching. "I thought I didn't need anyone. I was wrong." He ran a tentative finger down her cheek. "You are the best thing that has ever happened to me, and I was an idiot for not realizing it sooner. You opened up my heart again and filled it with so much love and happiness. I want you, Mya. I want to spend the rest of my life with you. I love you."

The emotion pouring from his eyes made her knees buckle, and he grasped her around the waist to support her. God, she'd dreamed of him saying those words to her, but there was still a problem. One he'd made clear from the beginning.

"What about Noah?" As much as she loved him, her son had to come first. If Aiden couldn't commit to being Noah's father, then she couldn't commit to him.

Aiden's face softened. "I don't know how he did it, but he burrowed into my heart right along with you. When he called me panicked because he didn't know where he was, I swear I lost ten years off my life. All I wanted to do was get to him as fast as possible because if anything happened to him, I'd never forgive myself. I love Noah too. I want to be a father to him and to the kids we'll have together." An uncertain expression crossed his features. "That is, if you still want me."

Did she want him? Hell, yes. There was nothing she wanted more than to have Aiden in her life.

"Yes, Aiden, I want you." Her voice hitched with emotion. "I think I've wanted you from the moment I saw you."

He picked her up and spun her around. "I love you, Mya."

Mya laughed and placed a soft kiss on his lips. "I love you too. Always and forever."

Epilogue

"Can you believe the turnout?" Amelia gushed as she helped Mya stack the few unsold copies of *Wally the Lost Whale* on the counter. The book's reception amazed Mya and Amelia. She still couldn't get over that other people liked and wanted to read her writing.

"I can believe it," Chloe said as she stood beside them. They watched the last of the parents and their children leave the bookshop. "This signing has been so successful! Great job, ladies." The sisters' chests puffed with pride as they looked at each other.

Chloe's literary agent, a friend of a friend, had secured a publishing deal for Mya and Amelia, and their books were doing better than they'd ever imagined. Kids loved the adventures of the playful and adventurous whale, and they and their parents were clamoring for more.

Nancy sidled up to Mya and kissed her cheek. "I'm so proud of you both."

"I've already started reading them to Lily, and she adores them," Holly said as she looked lovingly at her baby daughter in Ethan's arms.

Mya laughed. "She's one month old, she has no idea what you're reading to her."

"Oh, yes she does, because the books are amazing!" Holly smiled.

Two strong hands circled Mya's swollen belly. "My *wife* is amazing." Aiden caressed her stomach; as if their baby could feel her father's presence, she gave a small kick.

"Hey, I'm the illustrator!" Amelia said, pretending to complain.

"You're pretty awesome too." Aiden winked at his sister-in-law.

"We should go out for dinner and celebrate," Chloe suggested.

Mya searched for Noah and found him cuddled next to Gran, reading her a book. She hadn't wanted to miss Mya and Amelia's big day.

"I need to get Gran back to the nursing home," Mya said. She'd agreed to let Gran stay at the facility she was comfortable in, even though she and Amelia could now afford a more modern one.

"I'll take her," Amelia offered.

"And Noah can spend the night with me," Nancy said. She wasn't his biological grandmother, but Nancy loved him as if he were her own.

"Thanks, that would be great." Mya had been on her feet for hours, and with the extra weight, her ankles had swelled to the size of tree trunks. It would be nice not having to worry about running around after Noah.

"Where would you like to eat?" Chloe asked.

"I'm going to pass. I'm so tired."

"Everything okay?" Aiden looked at her with concern.

She smiled at her husband. Ever since she'd told him she was pregnant, he'd watched her like a hawk. So protective. She loved it. She loved *him*. "I'm fine."

"I need to talk with Aiden about a movie," Chloe said.

Aiden had given up acting for directing. It had taken him some time to convince the producers to trust him. Because of his past, he'd had a few rejections, but he was now regularly directing a TV series, and *The Conrads* was breathing down *Family First's* neck to be number one in the time slot.

"It's gonna have to wait. My wife needs me." He nuzzled Mya's neck and whispered, "I hope you're not too tired for what I've planned for us when we get home."

"Oh God, get a room," Chloe groaned.

"If you leave us alone, we will."

Mya gave Aiden a playful slap on the arm, but secretly, she couldn't wait to be alone with him.

"Okay, okay. I'll see you later." Chloe waved as she headed for the door.

Mya and Aiden said goodbye to the family as they left the bookshop.

She turned and faced him. He wrapped his arms around her and she snuggled in as close as she could with her bulging belly.

"What do you have planned for us?" Mya quirked an eyebrow.

His smile was slow, crooked, and oh so sexy. Would she ever get used to the impact it had on her heart? She doubted it. He leaned forward and whispered in her ear in detail what he wanted, where he was going to start, and how long it was going to take.

Her body turned to jelly and she kissed him slow and deep. "The doctor did say I shouldn't spend so much time on my feet."

With a sultry shrug, Aiden replied, "And I know how you like to follow the rules."

Acknowledgments

Firstly, I want to thank my loving family, Tom, Jaime, Ryan and Leah. They're always so encouraging and supportive and my number one fans! A huge thanks to TL Swan and her Facebook groups, Cygnet Inkers and S S Cygnets. The ladies in those groups are so encouraging and supportive. Without them I wouldn't be doing this. To my wonder beta readers, Becky, Michelle and Kirstie. Thank you for your time and wonderful feedback. A massive thank you to Vicki. She has helped me in my time of need. Without her I'd be lost.

Finally, to my amazing readers. I can't tell you how much I appreciate you reading my books. It makes my day! Thank you, thank you, thank you.

About the Author

Sonia Stanizzo is a contemporary romance writer living in the beautiful south coast of New South Wales, Australia with her husband and three children. When she's not dreaming up stories about couples and their road to finding love, sometimes bumpy but always a lot of fun, she can be found taking pole dancing lessons, reading and writing.

Thank you so much for reading Rule Breaker. I hope you enjoyed meeting Aiden and Mya and loved them as much as I do.

Say Hello

Say Hello
Visit my website to join my reader newsletter for free
books, new releases and giveaways. Come and say hello on
social media:

www.soniastanizzo.com
soniastanizzo@gmail.com
Facebook.com/soniastanizzowriter
Instagram.com/soniastanizzowriter
TikTok

More titles by Sonia Stanizzo